THE DARK

INTERLAND SERIES BOOK #3

GARY CLARK

For Ash

PART I

1

The faded-blue front cover of the hardback depicted a diagram of a female human body, but instead of being labelled with body parts, it was illustrated with flowing lines of white light around the girl's head. Jay rubbed her hand across the title. *The Physiology of Power.* She crouched in the bookshop's narrow aisle and slotted the text back into its space. Sunlight streamed through the south-facing windows, catching the steel edging along the rows of shelves. The sight of the once banned collection of books sparkling in the sunlight brought a smile to Jay's lips. Those gifted with power - the *Given* - were no longer consigned to the underground. Her feeling of pride sent a tingle of energy rippling through her body.

A handful of customers browsed. The top floor was Jay's domain, *her* responsibility. When Alf, the shop owner, had offered Jay the chance to curate the growing collection of literature on the Given and their powers, she'd jumped at the chance. The top floor now stretched across three town houses. It doubled as a library, and it thrived.

Returning to her desk, she pulled the master index from the filing cabinet, a thick, loose-bound stack of pages she used for recording everything related to the Given that came into the shop. She flicked through and changed one of the entries, then returned it to the cabinet.

'Excuse me,' said a girl. Jay turned to see a child of only nine or ten years stood at the desk. Her skin was a russet reddish brown, and she had big hair that reminded Jay of her best friend, Cassie. Jay smiled, and the girl averted her eyes, then said, 'Can you help me?'

'Of course,' said Jay, sensing a flutter of energy from the girl. Power was rare, and for it to be detectable in someone so young was almost unheard of, but she sensed something. 'What are you looking for?'

'I don't know.'

Jay waited, allowing the girl some space to gather her thoughts. 'I want to read about the Given,' she said, eventually.

'Come with me.' Jay led the girl through the aisles to a section dedicated to books on the Given for young readers. She was used to children coming into the shop to see the collection and ask questions. She encouraged it, although very few of them had power. She'd been to all the local schools to talk about the powers and sell books into the school libraries. Jay was determined to see truth outweigh the speculation and fear-mongering. 'How much do you know about the Given?'

'Not much. My mum thinks it's silly.'

'Do *you* think it's silly?' The girl looked up, and a smile slipped out before she turned away again. 'What's your name?'

The girl paused and turned to look at Jay, as if deciding whether to reveal her name. 'Angie,' she said.

'I'm Jay.'

'I know,' said Angie.

Jay caught a definite wisp of power then. She rocked back in her seat. Her colours were neutral, reserved, naïve. 'And do you feel a connection with the power?'

Angie shrugged. Jay ran her finger along the shelves. She pulled out a book: *The Powers and Me* – something by a writer who Jay once met when she came to the shop, a woman with a remarkable inner clarity and understanding of the power. She had written three books, but this one was specifically for kids trying to understand their own powers, their origins, and how they present before the marking appears.

Jay led Angie to a table. 'You want me to tell you about it, or shall I leave you to read for a while?'

'Can I ask you something?' Angie said, looking out of the window towards the hills of the Downs.

'Anything.' Jay sat and followed her gaze. The afternoon sun cast a glow over Highdown Hill, from which energy flowed freely. The combined energy of the three local hill forts was something that never failed to humble her.

She smiled, ready to impart her wisdom on an enquiring mind.

'Can I see your wrist?'

Jay smiled. It was common knowledge that the marking of the Given appeared naturally on the inside of the wrist like a tattoo - branding those with power as something different. She leaned closer and pulled back her sleeve to reveal the dark figure 8 and its accompanying letter "C". Angie pulled her own sleeve back and rubbed at the skin, searching for signs of a marking. 'Be patient,' said Jay. 'It'll come.'

Angie let her sleeve roll back down and turned her attention to the book. 'How will I know what level I am?'

'Only when the number appears. But you might have a sense of it before then.'

'Did you know, before?'

Jay remembered knowing she had power, but she had no idea she'd be a level eight, let alone 8C. 'I knew I'd be strong. I felt strong. Tell me what *you* feel.'

Angie looked away, as if still unsure whether to speak freely. Eventually, she said, 'I see colours, and sometimes words, too.'

'Wow, that's good at your age. You'll have strength for sure. Can you open up to the energy?'

'What do you mean?'

Jay thought for a moment. For her, to open up to the power, she had to trust in it, allow herself to be moved by the energy so that it became part of her. 'It's hard to explain. Have you ever jumped off a really high diving board into a pool? Or from a rock into the sea?'

Angie nodded. 'At Lulworth Cove I jumped off the big arch into the sea.'

Jay laughed. 'You know that feeling when you've just let go of the safety of the ledge, or the rock, but before you start falling, and you have to go with it, take a leap of faith?'

Angie frowned. Jay scratched her head. 'Well, it's a bit like that. You kind of have to let yourself go.'

Angie looked confused. She motioned to ask more, but then seemed to change her mind. 'Tell me about the different levels, what they mean, what power comes with what level?'

'It's not as straightforward as that,' said Jay. 'Not all people of the same level have exactly the same power. It depends on other things, like how you connect with it, and how you use it. And there are some unusual levels.'

'Like what?'

'Level five is special. Level 5 Given have the power of telekinesis. Do you know what that is?'

Angie nodded. 'Just level five? Not six or seven? You don't have telekinesis then?'

Jay shook her head. 'Not strictly. But with my 8C, I have something a little special too, especially when I have my partner with me.'

'Stitch?'

Jay laughed. Perhaps it shouldn't surprise her that those with an interest in the power knew of Stitch. He was her best friend, and he was her *connection*. His marking was unique. He had no number, just the letter "C". In each of the centres of the power of the Given, the most powerful was the 8C, like Jay. But each 8C was paired with someone who brought their power to its full strength, the "C", and for Jay, this was Stitch. 'You seem to know a lot already?' Jay said.

Angie let leak a sly smile. 'Tell me all the levels.'

'So,' said Jay, 'people at level *one* or *two* have not much more than a strong sense of intuition. Most at that level just seem to know things, like what someone had for dinner, or what music they like, but without really understanding how they know it.'

'Might be handy,' Angie said.

'My dad is a level two, and he can receive my thoughts sometimes, or used to, when we were better connected. It does vary between different people.'

'I don't think I'd want my dad to read me,' Angie said. 'What about level three?'

'Three and four are mostly just extensions of the telepathy you get at levels one and two. Stronger. At level four, you get a deeper connection with people.' Jay paused for a moment. Angie frowned. 'I know a level four who can focus his power into his hands and create heat. He can even make sparks,' said Jay. Angie opened and closed her hands before her.

Jay opened the book on the table between them and flicked through to the centre pages, pointing to a colourfully annotated scale that illustrated the power levels from one to eight. At the top was a picture of a woman in a superhero cape.

'Is that you?' asked Angie.

Jay laughed. 'Kind of. I don't have a cape though. You think it looks like me?'

Angie nodded and grinned. 'Do you know what everyone is thinking? All the time?'

Jay shook her head. 'No. I have to open up to the energy. It's an active process. It's not like I'm hearing everyone's thoughts all the time. That would be a living chaos. And people can shield too.'

'Shield?'

'With practice, the Given can shield their thoughts from other Given.'

'And from Readers?'

Jay nodded. Hearing someone so young even mention the *Readers* made her wince. The collective name for those who drew their energy from a darker source was enough to make Jay feel uneasy. She pushed the dark feelings away. 'And some people are better at shielding than others. My friend Alf...' She looked up as if to point him out. 'He is the best at shielding. If he doesn't want me to know what he's thinking, then I've got no chance, and he's only a level four.'

Angie reminded Jay of herself as a kid. She could read that Angie was impatient for her own powers to come, but scared at the same time. At her age, Jay's powers had felt like a curse. There was so much danger associated with revealing yourself in those days. She saw Angie's confusion too about the mechanism of deploying power. 'Don't over-think it,' said Jay. 'Try to be open to it; let it come to you.'

Angie frowned. 'How?'

'The strength in the energy comes from inside you. The power flows from the environment around us - the earth, the sea, and all living things. If you open to it, let it connect and become like it's part of you. That's how its true strength will come out.'

Angie's frown deepened, and Jay feared she was doing a poor job of explaining. 'Have a read,' she said, motioning to the book. 'And come back and talk to me whenever you like. Remember, there's no rush with this stuff.'

'As long as the Readers don't come,' Angie said, holding eye contact with Jay.

Jay pressed back into her seat, deflected by another mention of Readers from someone who shouldn't have to worry about the darkness. 'They're not coming back,' Jay said. Angie raised her eyebrows with a look that challenged her certainty. 'I won't let them. They have no home here, no means to channel their power. We made sure of that back in the Interland.'

Jay looked up and out the window as thoughts of those they'd lost came into her mind: Reuben, Davey, and even Zadie Lawrence. Their absence weighed heavily on her chest, and their sacrifice was one she vowed to honour.

'I won't let it happen again,' said Jay.

* * *

ON HER WAY back to her desk, Jay caught sight of Alf emerging from the stairwell. He nodded a greeting from across the room, holding up a couple of books for her. He was light on his feet, almost skipping the final stride as he reached Jay's desk, paying no respect to the fact he was well past retirement age.

She loved his enthusiasm. He'd rediscovered his youth since their emergence from the Interland and re-integration with society. Without the threat of Readers, and with the growing prosperity of the country, people had developed a new optimism. They looked after themselves. Alf still took a run every day on the beach with his dog, Buster, and was up and down the three flights of stairs in the shop a dozen times a day. He was as fit as Jay, for sure. But, like all the Given who lived through the battle for the Interland, Alf was wary of the powers of darkness. When he extended the shop, he included a safe-room connected to his apartment, constructed in the basement. It was his protection should the Readers ever rise again. He vowed they would never again take him from his own bookshop, his own home.

Buster scampered up the stairs behind Alf, almost knocking him over as he slid through his legs and bounded across the shop towards Jay. She crouched to greet him, leaning away as he lapped at her face. 'That dog will be the death of me,' Alf grumbled.

'Hey, old man,' Jay said.

Alf scowled at her, handing over the books. Buster explored the top floor, tail wagging. 'These are for you. Where's Cassie? I thought she was coming in to work with you today?'

'She didn't turn up again.' Jay took the books and linked her arm with Alf's, turning him around. 'Come, I want to show you something.' She led him to a new arrangement of the shelves and cabinets on the back wall, presenting them with pride.

Alf said nothing but opened the cabinets one at a time and flicked through the papers. He looked at the picture Jay had hung on the wall, the picture of Sasha Colden that used to hang in the main hall of the Interland. This arrangement of material was the culmination of weeks of work by Jay, cataloguing and filing the historical documents on the Given, the powers and the myths. There were maps, old notebooks, and other documents that had come in to the shop from all over the country.

'These are from the Interland,' Jay said, motioning to the shelves packed with literature previously stored at the Interland, as well as the old notebooks and maps from the Gateway that survived. She'd systematically worked through them, ordering and referencing. In front of the cabinets was a long desk with chairs where people could study the materials.

'This must have taken you weeks. You kept this a secret?'

Jay nodded, trying to suppress a beaming grin. 'I wanted to surprise you.'

'This is amazing,' he said, looking across the cabinets, the desk and the wealth of organised material that Jay had obviously worked so hard to get in order. 'I should promote you to head librarian,' he said.

'Pay rise?' asked Jay. 'Look, there's a gold mine of information here.' She'd read a lot of it over the weeks and months of collecting and cataloguing. Not all of it was in English, and even some that was in her native language was unreadable, or in a dialect that took some interpretation. She opened the last of the cabinets and pulled out an old hard-backed notebook and carefully opened it on the desk.

'I recognise this from back at the Interland,' said Alf. 'It was originally in the British Library before they flagged it for early references to the power.'

'I've read some of it,' said Jay. 'It's hard going.'

Jay had picked up bits of information from what she'd read in the ageing pages. The old English language was hard to interpret. The notebook spoke of a darkness coming to the land in the seventeenth century, long before Sasha Colden, Jay's grandmother, who Jay had previously thought was one of the first of those with power.

'It's not clear, if I remember correctly,' said Alf. 'But I can see in your thoughts that you've found something interesting?'

Jay nodded for Alf to continue.

'It talks of a dark power, if I recall,' he said, 'before the power of the Given. But it reads like a fairy tale.'

Jay pulled the book towards her and flicked to a particular page. 'See here,' she said, pointing to a line with the name *Atta*.

Alf nodded. 'I remember reading this.' His tone was solemn.

Jay reached and opened another cabinet, rifling through loose-leaf papers until she found what she was looking for, a single sheet of paper, A2 size. She unfolded it and placed it on the table next to the book. 'Here,' she said. 'Read that.'

Alf strained his eyes, then pulled his glasses down off his head and onto his nose. Jay reached for the magnifying glass attached to a piece of string next to the desk and handed it to Alf. '*Blindnes néahlæcaþ*... I've seen these words before. I think *néahlæcaþ* means *approaches*, or something like that. It's talking of a blindness coming, or a darkness.'

'Keep reading,' said Jay.

Alf scanned across the page, running his fingers over the words as if trying to find some that he recognised. He stopped in the place that Jay had wanted him to. '*Atta*,' he said, the letters sticking on his tongue as if he were reluctant to let them out. '*Atta... becíeseþ... Maram*.' He sat back as if worn out. 'I've read the name *Atta* many times, in association with the power of the darkness. *Becíeseþ* is old English for *fight*. This passage is about a battle between the dark and the light, between Atta and Maram. Now, where have I heard Maram before?'

Jay turned to the shelves behind them and picked out a book – the Sasha Colden biography that she'd read countless times and still returned to as a kind of therapy. She flicked through to a page near the back and handed it to Alf.

He read from where Jay pointed. 'Sasha *Maram* Colden...' He looked up. '*Maram* was Sasha's middle name?'

Jay nodded. 'But this document,' she pointed to the notes on the desk, 'is way older than Sasha Colden. So it can't be referring to my Sasha, my grandmother. It's referring to something older, after which they then named my grandmother.'

'We'd need to get a proper translation, but the implication is that there was power back in the sixteen hundreds, way before Sasha, and before the Given were formally identified.'

'Except everyone believes powers didn't exist before the twentieth century.'

'You'll be writing an academic paper on all this at some stage.' He stood and his knees creaked. 'I need to cash up.'

* * *

BUSTER FOLLOWED Alf back down the stairs. The only remaining customer was the little girl, Angie, still reading. She was a good third of the way through the book. She jumped when she sensed Jay, then snapped the book closed.

'Hey,' said Jay. 'It's OK.'

'Sorry,' the girl said, standing. 'I have to go.'

'Look,' said Jay, picking up the book from the desk. 'Do you want to take this on loan? Bring it back when you've read it and I'll exchange it for another one?'

'No,' Angie snapped. She sighed. 'I can't take it home.'

'That's OK,' said Jay, tapping the front of the book. She considered pressing a little more about what was going on with Angie at home, but she sensed it wasn't the right time. 'Come back whenever you want. Just help yourself. After school. Whenever you like.'

'Thanks,' she said, turning to leave.

'And, Angie...'

'What?'

'You're safe here. You don't need to be afraid of Readers, not anymore. I promise.'

Angie opened her mouth, but then closed it before disappearing around the corner. Jay returned the book, but left it poking out a little from the other books, easier for Angie to find on her own if she came back.

Something moved. She looked towards the stairs. 'Angie?' she said, although she knew Angie was already out of the shop and likely into the street. A minor adrenaline spike sent her powers into readiness. The shop was quiet.

She scanned the rest of the room, down each aisle, before looking back towards the stairs. A feeling bubbled in her stomach, the feeling she knew so well from when the Readers were in control, and it was the Given doing the hiding. The first time she'd seen a Reader, she'd been standing much like she was now, on the top floor of Alf's bookshop, locking eyes for that split second with Marcus.

The Head Reader's scar had glinted in the light, evil laced his face, an evil that Jay eventually destroyed in battle. The memory ran a shiver up her spine as she recalled the oppression, the fear, and the lack of basic freedoms. She scanned the room once more, opening her senses and allowing her power to expand and fill every corner of the room.

Nothing.

She made for the stairs, switching the light off as she left.

* * *

Downstairs, Alf finished with the cash register and waited for Jay. 'Come on, get yourself home. Your dad will curse me for keeping you so late.'

Jay stepped down from the last stair and flung her rucksack over her shoulder. It was too light. She'd forgotten The Sasha Colden biography, her comfort blanket. 'Forgot something.'

'Go on, I can wait.'

'You go, I'll let myself out.' She jangled her set of keys.

'As you like. I'm heading out back.'

Alf sighed, and the light from above cast a shadow over his face that made him look old and vulnerable for a moment. Jay never thought of Alf as anything but invincible. 'Have a lie-in tomorrow if you like,' she said. 'I'll come and open up in the morning.'

Alf smirked, knowing Jay would never get to the shop early enough to open up before him. He turned to leave, ducking under the low doorway and out to the back door that led to his apartment.

The Colden book was still on the table where she'd left it. The warm glow of the streetlights bathed the room.

Outside, a figure in a shop doorway on the other side of the street caught her eye. He stood facing the bookshop, but the shadows hid his features. She stepped back from the window, out of view, then leaned to turn off the light in the stairwell. She opened up to see if she could sense him, read his intentions, but when she turned back to the window, he was gone. The street was empty. *It's nothing*, she told herself. *Someone sheltering for a minute before heading home. Nothing.* Sometimes, what felt like her powers tingling was just left-over memories.

Outside, darkness settled in and a salty breeze blew off the sea. She slung her bag over her shoulder and headed for home.

Turning off the main high street towards the Beach Lane estate, the noise of Saturday night entertainment dissolved into the background, replaced by the sounds of crashing waves over stones. The tide must be in, she thought. Five minutes more and she turned into Beach Lane.

In the quiet, away from the beach and the town, her lonely footsteps echoed off the houses. Shadows danced between the streetlamps. She stepped up the pace a little, looking over her shoulder. The pulsing heartbeat in her ears muted the sound of her footsteps.

A noise?

Nothing.

She ran.

The bag on her back slammed into her with every stride as she powered home, not daring to look back, her eyes focused only on the pavement ahead. She hit her front door and gulped in air. This wasn't paranoia. Someone was behind her, someone who must have kept pace, someone about to drag her back into the alleyway.

A hand on her shoulder.

She screamed.

'Jay, it's me, Sammy.'

Jay's younger brother stared back at her and she screamed again before he gave her a gentle shake, a hand on each shoulder. 'Sis. It's me. What is it?'

Jay grabbed Sammy and hugged him tight, looking past him into the street beyond. Nothing but darkness. Streetlamps. Front gates and low hedges.

The sea turned dark under a dusk sky. Waves raced towards the girl sitting on the stones under the pier, reaching for her outstretched feet as if to take her away, only to swirl around and then retreat. The girl waited for dark. Then it would be time.

The last she remembered being by the sea, the proper sea, not the inter-dimensional shores of the *Islands*, was way back. Before her life became one long conflict. She had craved a moment like this, time alone, with just the sounds and smells of the seaside and her memories.

She ran a finger along the outline of the figure 7 on the inside of her wrist. Sometimes it still startled her. She still expected to see the number 3, the number she was born to display, before she became a Reader and her power increased. With that power came the protection of the Dark. It was like joining the most established and powerful club in the world where nothing and no-one could touch you. She had simply done what her parents would not do, a choice for which they made the ultimate sacrifice. She would never take their path. They were gone, but she wasn't alone. The *Dark* was her protector.

The girl picked up a handful of stones, throwing one at a time into the water as it rushed up the beach. Whispers came from the sea, and she thought she must be imagining it, confusing the mark of a Given energy with the sound of sea on sand and stone. Her transformation to a Reader should have silenced them. But still they came. She dropped the stones and put her hands to her ears. Still they came, circling the inside of her head as if scolding her. Whispers turned to screams - like the cries of pain of the Given, those with power who had fallen at the hands of the darkness.

The tide retreated and the screams abated. The breeze dropped. She was alone once more. She looked down at the figure 7 on her wrist and clenched her fist. On the post in front of her, two names were carved in the grain: *JAY* and *STITCH*. Her fingers filtered through the stones, looking for one with a sharp edge to it, discarding three. The fourth, a piece of flint as yet unsmoothed by the ebb and flow of the tide, had the edge she needed.

Under the name of *JAY*, she carefully scraped her own name into the wood.

FLICK.

* * *

FLICK MOVED with purpose along the promenade. She imagined the echoes of the day's seaside tourists rising from the black surface as she walked, mixing with a lingering smell of hotdogs and sweet roasted nuts. An image of her parents. A pang of nostalgia quickly brushed away.

A salty breeze buffeted her as she walked. Despite having

no desperate need to hide herself, it was in the pools of darkness between the streetlamps where she breathed easier. Under each light, she pulled her hood tight against her head and sped up a little as she moved through the glare.

She crossed the wide seafront road and hopped onto the opposite pavement, ducking into an alcove. She crouched in the darkness next to a discarded bag of rubbish, pulled her hood back down over her eyes and watched the bookshop.

It was nearly half an hour before the lights went out. Another five minutes and the shop door opened with the clang of a bell. Jay had her back to the high street as she turned the key in the lock and pulled the door to make sure it was secure. Flick stepped back into the darkness and Jay turned. Flick sensed her glance in her direction before she made off up the high street.

Spooked that Jay had clocked her, Flick waited a minute in the shop doorway before daring to emerge onto the high street. She needed to confront Jay on her own terms, and not in the middle of the high street. When she finally stepped out, Jay was already out of sight.

Tomorrow will be OK, she thought. But she could feel her strength of power was weakening. She was too far from the source of Reader energy on Island 7, and she would have to make a move soon, before it was too late.

Sammy slid a pawn forward one square. Jay was enjoying watching her brother squirm. His streak was down; his mum had beaten him twice in the last few days. She leaned over the chessboard and sucked in air through her teeth as Sammy stared in silence at the pieces. 'The pupil becomes the master,' Jay said.

Ben called Jay from the kitchen, and Jay jumped up from the sofa. 'What's up, Dad?'

'Don't wind your brother up,' he said, continuing to stir the pan - the smell of onion and garlic filling the room. Jay pulled herself up to sit on the worktop. Ben added chicken to the pan. He stirred and lowered the heat. 'How's work? Alf behaving himself?'

'I finished the archiving yesterday. Alf was impressed. There's a lot of information there. You should come and have a look. When's the last time...'

'Slow down,' Ben said as he stirred the food. 'I just meant in general, how is it?'

Jay sighed inwardly at her dad cutting her off when she got enthusiastic about the shop. 'I enjoy working there.'

'Long term?'

Jay ignored her dad's baiting question. In his mind, she should think about university. Her attention was elsewhere.

She was thinking about the names Atta and Maram, wanting to ask her dad about them. He gave mixed messages on the world of the powers. One minute he'd be heading out to his old group to talk about the resistance to the Readers, and the next it was as if to talk of the power was to invite trouble.

'There's something in the older literature on the Given that has me confused,' she said. Ben said nothing, apparently distracted by the challenge of measuring the correct amount of rice for four people.

'What?' he said, eventually.

She paused, thinking of the Legend. The power of the Given was centred at the confluence of three rivers - the Interland. Legend said that this location became a big sink-hole, disappearing underground and taking one of three sisters with it. 'You know the Legend we talked about before, of the sink-hole lake and the three sisters and all that...'

'Yes.'

'Was there another story? An older Legend that spoke of the powers in terms of the *Darkness,* or the *Dark*?'

'You mean the Readers? Not really, because the Readers came later and...'

'No,' Jay interrupted. 'Not the Readers. Before them, before all that. Something else. A darkness of some form that allowed the Readers to exist. Something that came before the Given.'

'The Given came first. The Readers are a twisted version of the Given. You taught *me* that.' Ben placed a lid over the pan and turned to face Jay.

She scratched her head, trying to connect the dots in her

mind. While the power of the Given came from the source at the Interland, the power of the Readers emanated from a different place, somewhere deep below the surface. 'Readers get their power from the core, right?'

'Right.'

'And the *sink-room*, the place we destroyed at the prison, was their means of channelling that power.' She paused, recalling the combined efforts of her and her friends in taking apart what the Readers left behind - the building where they imprisoned the Given. It housed their sink-room, their means of routing the dark power from the earth's core. 'But before the sink-rooms, the power was still there, it was just that it was chaotic.'

'I guess...' Ben mused.

'There's a reference to someone called *Atta*, but it's like he's a mythical being, or something. He's a physical manifestation of the darkness that comes from the core.'

'*Atta*?' Ben repeated the name. 'I've heard that before somewhere.'

'What about *Maram*?' asked Jay, watching her dad for his reaction.

'That was my mother's middle name. Sasha *Maram* Colden.'

'I thought so,' said Jay. She jumped down off the kitchen top. 'But the weird thing is, in the older literature, from the seventeenth century, there's mention of Maram as the power who opposed Atta. But this *Maram* was decades before Sasha.'

Ben thought for a moment. 'Sasha could have been named after this myth?'

'Do you remember anyone talking about it?'

'I hardly knew her, remember?' Ben's mother, Jay's grandmother, left without a trace when Ben was just three years old. It wasn't until the past year, in the discovery of the Interland, and long after her death, it came clear that Sasha Colden was Ben's estranged mother.

'I know, but did anyone in the family talk about it?'

Ben stirred the rice and checked the bubbling curry. 'I think you're getting too deep with this stuff. The Readers have gone. Look out there,' he nodded to the window. The sun had dipped in the sky and the clouds reflected a deep orange colour. Houses in Jay's street previously abandoned and boarded up were once again occupied. The lawns were cut, flowers emerging.

Jay sighed. She knew her dad wanted her to stop obsessing about Readers and get on with life, but she couldn't let it go. She needed him to engage, to help her like he used to. There was no puzzle that she and her dad together couldn't solve. She leaned to look out the window. 'Maybe I'll head to the Island. Talk to the other 8C. He might know something.'

Jay and Stitch had been to the Island, the inter-dimensional space between lands, twice since they first left the Interland. 'Last time we went, there was no sign of the other 8C. His island looked OK, but we didn't cross to it.'

'Why do you need to go there?'

'Research,' said Jay, thinking of the bookshop. 'I might be able to transport there without Stitch. My power is strong enough. With the source, I could probably...'

'Don't be stupid,' said Ben. 'Stitch is your connection. That connection keeps you safe.'

Jay didn't answer. She knew her dad didn't want her to be at risk. But she had others to think about, a responsibility to protect more than just herself. She contemplated how her powers had failed to prevent the damage by the Readers before, and the lives they took. She thought of Davey and

Reuben and her heart ached. Nothing she could do would ever bring them back.

'If you like, I can ask my group tonight about the history of those names: Atta, and Maram.'

It was a Tuesday, and Ben would head to the pub basement for his regular meeting with his friends - the *resistance*. It was more of a social club than anything else, but people there knew about the powers, not as much as Alf, but it could be useful. Ben used to ask Jay to join him. He joked that she'd be like a celebrity making a special guest appearance. Anyone with interest in the powers knew about Jay, what she and her friends had accomplished, and the strength in her abilities. But she'd never accompanied him, and eventually he gave up asking.

She surprised them both when she asked, 'Can I come with you?'

ON THE WAY to The Smugglers, Ben filled Jay in on the activities of the *New Resistance*. Jay had to conceal a smirk behind her hand on hearing the group's updated name. There was very little that was *new* about the well-meaning bunch she was about to meet. The pub basement had been the venue for their meetings for as long as the group had existed, back from when the Readers posed a genuine threat, and the group's numbers swelled to nearly twenty.

'Evening, Ben,' the landlord greeted them, his eyes on Jay. Ben nodded hello and Jay gave a wave of her hand. 'Usual?' he said to Ben. 'And for the lady?' Jay resisted a roll of her eyes and asked the landlord for a Coke. 'I'll send 'em down.'

They squeezed through a narrow door and onto a cast

iron spiral staircase. The basement was dimly lit, with a scent of competing aftershaves and the sound of hushed conversation. Plastic chairs with rusty steel legs were arranged around a central table. The six men in the room, all standing, talking with pints of beer in their hands, stopped their conversations and turned to look as Ben and Jay stepped off the foot of the staircase. Matchstick, Ben's closest friend and fellow ex-inmate of the prison for the Given, held out his arms to Jay for a hug. 'The old man drag you down here at last?'

'Something like that,' said Jay.

'Samir is here too,' Matchstick said, turning just as Stitch's dad, Samir, approached. She'd not seen him for a few weeks. He occasionally came into the bookshop. She used to see him when Jay and Stitch would hang out at Stitch's house, but that was rare these days.

'As-Salam-u-Alaikum,' Jay said, remembering Samir's greeting and nodding respectfully.

'Wa-Alaikumussalam wa-Rahmatulla,' said Samir. 'Where is that boy of mine? Never home helping his old father like he should be.'

'I'm sure he's studying hard, looking to make you proud,' Jay said with a smirk.

Samir laughed and turned to show off Jay to the others. 'Here she is,' he said, and the other four men greeted Jay enthusiastically, reaching to shake hands and saying how much they'd heard about her.

A chime rang out, like the single strike of a grandfather clock. Ben opened a hatch in the wall, revealing an old service shaft. A pint of beer and a Coke sat on a tray. Ben took the drinks and rang the bell. The tray disappeared once more, ascending smoothly on a hoist. Ben handed Jay her drink. 'You can't beat old-school service,' he said. 'Let's sit.'

Matchstick and Samir took seats on either side of Jay. The group descended into individual conversations for a while until a man raised his hand as if in a school classroom. It was the man who had introduced himself to Jay as Colson. He had rich black skin, and an unassuming demeanour, a warm smile. As the others quietened, Colson asked Jay from across the table, 'What brings you here tonight?'

Colson had a level of power – the only other one in the room with power but for her dad and Matchstick. Colson had something greater than Ben's level two, and she could read that he was a kind man, his colours warm and open. 'In your work,' said Jay, 'have you come across the names *Atta* and *Maram*?'

Murmurs rippled through the basement room with no-one voicing any recognition of the names. Jay kept her eyes on Colson, whom she was sure had immediately recognised the names. 'Atta and Maram represent the very essence of the fight between the dark and the light.' Colson's voice was soft, paced slow and measured. Despite his outward calm, his colours changed when he spoke of Atta and Maram. Those words meant something profound to Colson, and they clearly raised his levels of anxiety.

'Who were they?' asked Jay.

Colson reached for his tobacco in the inside pocket of his jacket on the back of his chair. He pulled a cigarette-rolling contraption from the other pocket and thumbed tobacco into it, on top of a Rizla. 'The legends are vague. The stories have been written, translated, re-written and re-interpreted to the point where the truth is indistinguishable from a fairytale. The principles of good and evil are presented as physical entities.' He licked his cigarette paper and completed rolling, lighting it with a match. 'Whether any higher power ever existed in a physical form is doubtful.' He exhaled a puff of smoke that rose in the cool air of the basement and hung like a cloud above the table.

Matchstick spoke up, 'Well, this is news to me. I've read nothing about these older powers. I always thought that the power of the Given only came into existence in the last century.'

'Not true,' said Colson. 'We've talked about it before.' He looked at Ben.

Ben nodded. 'Before your time here with the group.' Then back to Colson, 'But it was just speculation. We had no hard evidence, nothing unequivocal.'

Jay straightened in her seat. 'We do now,' she said. 'The work that Alf has done...' Two men snorted at the mention of Alf. Like her dad, others in the group continued to distrust Alf, despite it being clear that his allegiance was to the Given. 'He's probably the most knowledgeable living person on the powers,' Jay said defensively, her back stiffening with anger.

'Why doesn't he join us then?' said one of the men.

'Hey,' said Ben, raising a hand. 'Let's not go there.'

Jay continued, 'The work Alf has done, with others at the Interland, has helped us pull together a load of information on the powers. There's a lot of contemporary writing, but also some of the older literature, from as far back as the seventeenth century.'

'And what does it tell us?' asked Colson, puffing on his cigarette.

'Talk of the *darkness*. Atta. Maram. But, we also know that Maram was Sasha Colden's middle name.'

Colson shook his head and looked at Ben for confirmation. 'Are you sure? If that's true, then...'

Ben nodded.

'Then what?' said Jay.

'I don't know,' said Colson, scratching the grey stubble on his chin that stretched up into his sideburns to join with the hair on his head. 'Sasha Colden was your family, your blood, right?' Ben nodded and Jay confirmed. 'I'm afraid I can't shed any light, but I'd like to come and see what you have at the bookshop.'

* * *

THE FOLLOWING SATURDAY, Colson trawled through the literature. He was like a kid in a sweet shop, hungrily devouring the information Jay had curated. 'It's ambiguous,' Colson said. 'Open to interpretation.' He placed the old notebook back on the shelf.

Jay sighed. 'There's something in it though, right? Maram is more than a myth. She's the original who drew power from nature. And Atta is the original who drew the power of the Dark?'

'I may need to consult the London branch,' said Colson. 'There are people in the London office of the resistance who have other material. They have their own research agenda, but we compare notes from time to time. They may be interested.'

Alf appeared at the end of the aisle, heading towards them, Buster at his feet. Colson looked up, pushed his glasses to the top of his head, and leaned back in his chair. It took a moment for Alf to recognise Colson, but when he did, his pace slowed and he looked like he might turn around and head back the other way.

'Alfred,' Colson said, a coolness to his tone.

'Colson,' Alf returned the greeting. 'I didn't expect to see you in here. Find anything useful to inform the *New Resistance*?' A mocking tone.

'Sit down,' Jay said with a sigh.

'I've got work to do...'

'Please,' she interrupted. Alf relented, taking a seat at the end of the desk, the seat furthest from Colson. Jay sat between them, bridging the gap. Colson reached out a hand to stroke Buster but pulled it back as Buster's top lip curled and he released a low rumbling growl.

'Look, Alfred,' Colson began, 'Jay's dad is a friend of mine, and you two here seem to be getting on just fine, so we must have some common ground we can work on?'

'It wasn't me who started this whole thing if I remember right.'

'Alf,' snapped Jay. 'Let's be grownups, shall we?'

Alf rolled his eyes and crossed his arms, leaning back in his chair. He said, 'Tell Jay what you did. She deserves to know.'

Jay waited patiently as Colson shook his head. 'What Alf is referring to was a misunderstanding, a mistake.'

'He sold me out to the Readers,' Alf said. 'Back when this place was taken, and I was cast aside. If it wasn't for a bit of luck, and contact from the Runners, I'd have been in that place, the prison, and reduced to nothing. All thanks to Colson here.' Alf sat back in his chair.

'Why?' asked Jay, attempting to delve into Colson's mind. She saw his sorrow. He had screwed up. He'd misunderstood Alf's position. Alf was probably the best shielder Jay had ever met. He led the Readers to thinking that he was helping them, informing on the Given who used the bookshop to learn about the powers, so that the State could keep records of persons of interest. The reality was that Alf used his position to gather intelligence on the Readers, and feed information through to the Interland for the benefit of the Given – work he progressed further when he made it to the Interland himself. Colson had misinterpreted this as Alf working against the Given.

'I didn't know,' said Colson. 'I thought... we *all* thought, including your father, Jay. We thought Alf was on the side of the Readers. After all, that's the front he presented. For God's sake, you can't blame us for thinking that.'

'My dad didn't think that,' said Jay. 'Or he'd never have let me come here.'

'He had his suspicions. He didn't like you talking to Alfred.'

'Well, you were all wrong,' said Jay.

Colson nodded. 'I know, and I've apologised for the part I may have played in revealing your allegiance to the Given. Truly, I didn't know.'

Alf turned to Jay. 'It didn't take the Readers long to hit the shop. I've never felt such pain.' He paused, staring at Colson.

Colson refused to meet his gaze. Under his breath, he said, 'We got it wrong. I'm sorry.'

4

As Jay walked home, the high street seemed darker and quieter than usual. The pub on the corner had just one man outside smoking a cigarette. Thoughts of being followed drifted into her mind, and she brushed them away.

As she turned into Beach Lane estate, she couldn't shake the sense that she wasn't alone. She altered her route, heading into the alleyways around the side of the housing estate that she knew like the back of her hand. She picked up speed and turned onto a path lit at the entrance by an orange glow from a streetlight half buried in the trees. Ahead, the alley was dark. The next streetlight was beyond the corner. With a quick glance over her shoulder, Jay ran to the corner and ducked into a hedge. She waited. From the shadows she could see back to the entrance, and in the other direction she could see the streetlights stretching to the next corner. Her heart pounded in her chest, pulsing through to her eardrums. The twigs and leaves of the bush dug into her side.

A hooded figure appeared at the entrance to the alleyway. Jay's stomach clenched. If she ran now, she could probably outrun them. She hesitated. Seconds passed. The figure stepped into the alleyway. As they passed, she sensed power, dark power, not the power of the Given. This was a Reader, Jay was certain, but Readers had no means of drawing power with no source, and the source, sink-room, had been destroyed. Who was this person?

The Reader stopped and Jay sensed that their power, although of great potential, was weak. She climbed out of the hedge and stood in the alleyway. Slowly the person turned, head down, face in shadow.

'Who are you?' Jay said, stepping forward.

The Reader pulled aside the hood. Jay stepped back in surprise from the woman standing before her. Of all the Readers she'd fought, not one had been a woman, all were men. Instinctively, she attacked.

Power of the Given raised through fear and anger was often the most deadly, and the least controlled. As Jay channelled the power of the earth beneath her feet, the energy of the sea to the south and the hills to the north, and directed them into the Reader, she felt her power grow. The ease with which Jay could raise the power of the environment spurred her on. Energy pumped through her veins, attacking the Reader like a powerful scatter-gun. The girl had no defence against this show of strength.

'Stop!' the Reader shouted, as she fell to her knees, her hands to the sides of her head. 'I just want to talk.' She looked up at Jay, her eyes pleading. Messages came through to Jay, begging.

Jay was confused, both at how this Reader had got to her, and how she seemed different to other Readers. She felt little threat from this woman.

She stopped, but just for a moment, poised to resume.

The Reader flopped to the floor, then slowly raised herself to her knees, then to her feet, holding out both of her hands as if in a truce. 'I came here to warn you. Don't kill me.'

'Who are you? What do you want?' asked Jay.

'My name is Flick,' she said.

'Why are you here?' Jay saw a faint scar on the side of the woman's face.

Flick raised her hand to the scar, the characteristic marking that came after an attack with power. 'This is old. It wasn't you. Look, can we talk somewhere? I think I need to sit before I fall.'

'Why don't I just take you in? You know what the State will do to you, right?'

'You could,' Flick said. 'I can't say in your position that I wouldn't, but I think you'll want to hear what I have to say.'

Flick wobbled again, and Jay held out a hand to stop her from falling. As their hands touched, a stream of information passed to Jay. She saw Readers, scores of them, working at the construction of a complex of buildings... darkness, swirls of darkness... the Islands blackened. Jay dragged away her hand. 'What was that?'

'The reason I'm here,' said Flick. 'Where can we talk?'

JAY PUSHED OPEN the door of the bookshop, careful not to let the bell above the door ring for fear of alerting Alf. She let Flick in and locked the door behind and, without turning on the light, she led Flick up the stairs to the top floor. She switched on a lamp at a reading table and motioned for Flick to sit. She headed to the kitchen out the back and returned with two mugs of tea.

'Thanks,' Flick said as Jay sat opposite her.

'You're a Reader. How are you able to keep your power? There is no source, no connection to the core.'

'There *is* a source. You might have destroyed the sink-room, but the connection to the core remains. I came here from Island 7. Readers can move through Islands in the same way as the Given, you know that.'

Jay nodded.

'But I can't keep power here for long. I'm risking everything to come here, and you nearly killed me.'

Jay tapped her finger against the rim of her mug, waiting for Flick to continue.

'I've been looking for you,' said Flick, taking a sip of tea. 'Yes, I'm a Reader. I transformed a few months ago. Not that I had much choice. I was one of the first from the new facility.'

'Facility?' Jay said.

'The one I just showed you when you touched my hand. It's on Island 7.'

Jay saw the images in her mind again, the buildings, a room with dozens of Readers at work.

'A sink-room,' said Flick. 'A big one. Much bigger than the ones on the other islands, and much bigger than the one you destroyed on this island. That's why I can retain power here, from a source on Island 7. But not for long. My power is weaker here, and with time it will diminish, until I go back.'

Jay's mind raced with questions. If Island 7 had a new sink-room facility, what had happened to the 8C, their companion? Flick seemed to read Jay's thoughts and shook her head. 'You need to forget about Island 7 and start thinking about your own homeland.'

'Why are you telling me this?'

'I was never a willing subject for transformation. I was forced. I did it to stay alive.'

'What's changed? They'll kill you for reaching out to the Given.'

'They'll never know. I shield well.'

'Why should I believe...'

Flick sighed. 'I risked my life, don't you get it? They messed with my mind and body without my consent. If you can't believe me, then I don't know what to tell you, believe whatever you want. Just be ready for a darkness you couldn't even imagine.' She looked out of the window.

Jay studied the scar on the side of Flick's face. 'You've been reduced in the past? But you still have the power of a Reader?'

'It's a long story.'

'What level are you?'

Flick turned over her arm to show the black number 7. Jay wasn't surprised that she had a high level of power. She'd felt her potential - the sharp nip of her energy searching and exploring. 'What were you before the transformation?'

'Level three,' said Flick. 'That shows the strength of these new facilities, these mega sink-rooms.'

'There's more than one?'

Flick nodded.

'What's in this for you?'

Flick sighed. 'If it carries on the way it's going, there won't be anything left. The Readers are coming here next, to this place, *your* land.' She looked around her. 'None of this will survive. The Given cannot exist in a world controlled by Readers. The very existence of Readers depends on the conversion of the Given.'

'They can't come here,' Jay said.

'They can, and they will. Unless you act.' Flick leaned back in her chair and spoke slowly, 'You know what happens when the Readers reach a certain number?'

Jay had read in the literature about the theory of the balance of power. If the Readers' numbers reached a certain level, then legend said that a darker power would emerge, one that assured their ascendency. She nodded. 'I know the myths.'

'Not myths,' said Flick. 'It's happened before, way back.'

'If that's true, then how are the Given still here?'

'The presence of the deeper darkness does not stop more of the Given being born, but it enables the Readers to control them, convert them to their own cause before they can become a threat. The balance must have tipped back between now and the last reign of the Dark. But now it's tipping again. The Dark is working its way through the islands.'

'I won't let Readers come here,' Jay said, looking Flick in the eye.

Flick shook her head. 'You're not hearing me. Not just Readers. The *Dark*. It's more than just Readers. It's the balance, like I said. They're creating a connection, a channel for the power that will enable the Dark to move between Island 7 and here. It's just a matter of time. The power of the Given won't be enough to stop it. You need to do more.'

'What do you mean by more?'

Flick leaned towards Jay again. 'Connect with The Dark. Use it before they can.'

5

Otis used a stick to lift the lid of the pan and check his soup. Steam billowed. The broth made a pleasant simmer, the smell wafted over him and his stomach rumbled.

One thing about living outside was food was more satisfying, but took forever to prepare. With a different stick, he flattened the embers a little to lower the heat. He looked up into the trees on the south side of Highdown. This was his favourite time of day, when the light had faded to grey, but he could still see enough to go about his business - food nearly ready, tiredness creeping in, no people to mess with him.

Otis startled, the skin on the back of his neck tingling. He sensed a presence. For one with significant power at level 5, Otis's key skills weren't in sensing others - the energy of his abilities was concentrated almost entirely on his telekinesis. So when he sensed someone, it usually meant that they were close.

He stood, scanning the slopes of the hill up towards the ring of trees at the summit. He held his breath, his eardrums throbbing in the silence. A flutter of birds took flight. Something in the bushes moved and his eyes stretched wide to take in as much of the remaining light as he could.

Nothing.

A rustle in the bush up on Highdown was not something to be afraid of. He'd lived with the scurrying sounds of the animals, the wind in the trees, and the groaning of the woods for years. He must be overreacting. He sat back on his log and collected his stick, rubbing his thumb against the rough bark.

He scraped the last of the soup from the bottom of the pan. He didn't mind the burnt taste, liked it even.

Footsteps. Clear this time, not his imagination. Closer. Too dark to see.

He picked up a thick branch as a weapon and readied himself.

'Cassie?'

'Hey,' Cassie said as she came into view, eying the branch in Otis's hand. 'Ready for a fight?'

'You scared me. You could've told me you were coming tonight.' It was unusual for Cassie to turn up on the Hill unannounced. She'd normally get a message to Otis using her powers, something to let him know to expect her. He didn't always hear the message clearly, but he always knew.

'I tried to. You've not been receptive today. Something on your mind?' Cassie took a seat near the fire.

'I thought I felt something just now. It spooked me. Probably a deer.' Otis rubbed at his mop of curly hair.

'Hey.' Cassie reached over and touched his arm, her tone soft. He opened his arms for a hug and Cassie pulled him close.

'Don't know what's wrong with me today,' said Otis as they pulled apart.

Cassie stared into the fire and Otis sensed that she too was not feeling right. She'd been withdrawn more often than usual in the past few weeks. As things had settled in their post-Reader world, the pain and hurt of what had happened to Cassie seemed to bubble to the surface, pushing down on her energy, stifling her passion for life. She hardly spoke of Reuben's death, her childhood friend, or the time she spent incarcerated by the Readers, but Otis knew it wasn't something that she'd easily forget.

'Tell me what you felt. The deer, or whatever it was?' said Cassie.

'Why?'

'Just tell me. What did it feel like?' Her voice was intense.

'I don't know...' He stumbled, thinking. 'Like I said, probably an animal, but...'

'Different?' Cassie prompted. 'Darker?'

Otis nodded. 'It wouldn't normally spook me like that. You know what I'm like. My senses are rubbish at the best of times, but my anxiety levels are sky high lately.'

Cassie stood and scanned the side of the hill. Nothing visible for as far as they could see. 'I felt something on the way up here.' She paused for a moment. 'Actually, it was weird. I sensed nothing, but I saw something. I thought it was you at first, except it was taller than you. And quicker.'

'That doesn't narrow it down by much,' Otis said.

'We need to get away from this place.' Cassie sighed, sitting back down by the fire.

We, thought Otis. He allowed himself to feel warmth before it was taken over again by his and Cassie's unease. 'Are you having those nightmares again?'

She shrugged. 'It's claustrophobic, don't you feel it? I feel like we're just waiting around for something.'

'We need to stick together,' said Otis.

'Me and you?'

'Yes, but… all of us,' he said.

Cassie huffed and turned away from him. 'I don't want this anymore.' She stepped towards the trees.

'Wait. Stay up here with me tonight. We can talk.' Otis hated it when Cassie was like this. What did she mean by not wanting *this* anymore?

'I can't,' Cassie said, striding into the trees and disappearing into the darkness.

Otis called after her, but she was gone.

6

J ay leaned back on the roof tiles and looked up from her book to the hills on the horizon. Turning her eyes back to her book, she re-read the first paragraph of the chapter entitled *The Origins of Power*, then closed her eyes and opened her mind to the energy of the hills and of the sea. Her home on Beach Lane, positioned as it was between the great sources of energy in the land mass and the vast seas, brought comfort.

Within seconds, whispers flowed from the sea, bouncing excitedly around her head like a child eager to play. Her skin tingled, and with her eyes firmly shut, the colours of the whispers swirled and connected with her own colours, and with those sweeping down from the hills. Her chest filled with the warmth from the environment. Her ears bubbled with the pressure of the pulsing energy and her cheeks flushed hot.

A noise distracted her from the connection. Someone approaching from the alleyway around the back. The colours swirled away into the distance as Jay's vision returned and she squinted in the light to see a figure approaching from the other side of the roof.

'Stitch?' she said as his big, round, smiling face came into view.

'The one and only,' he said, sliding down the roof tiles to take a seat next to Jay. He took out his tobacco. 'You mind?' he asked, holding it up.

Jay looked away, back up to the hills. 'You want to kill yourself, be my guest.' He sighed and returned the tobacco to his inside pocket and leaned back on the tiles, the sun on his face.

He'd matured over the past year, since the Interland. He looked older, his features sharper, his face weathered. The experience at the Interland had taken its toll on all of them. But Stitch, more than anyone, seemed to feel the effects of the power of the Readers. It was like their darkness infiltrated his core, messed with his mind.

'I saw your dad the other night, at the group,' Jay said

'The *New Resistance*?' Stitch laughed. 'Why were you there?'

'Has your dad ever mentioned a bloke called *Colson*?'

Stitch shook his head. 'Who's he?'

Jay shrugged. 'I think there's a history to the power that goes back further than everyone thinks. Like, way back. Seventeenth century.'

Stitch turned on to his side and rested his head on his hand. 'We always said the powers probably went back further. There are many stories in the folklore, the myths and legends and all that. We've talked about this before.'

'There was a central force of darkness back then called *Atta*. Have you heard of it... him?'

Stitch shook his head again, then lay back on the tiles, closing his eyes. They heard someone climbing up the back wall from the alleyway and Jay guessed it was Cassie before her head popped up above the roof tiles.

She stepped over Stitch and settled next to Jay. 'Where's Sammy?'

'With Toyah somewhere,' said Jay. Toyah and Sammy had been spending a lot of time together since the Interland.

'How are his powers progressing?' Cassie asked.

Sammy's marking had come through a few months ago, Level 3, but his powers were unusual. He couldn't read minds like most low-level powers, not even a little, not even when the person whose mind he was reading actively opened to him. But he had something different.

'He took another flight this week,' Jay replied. 'With a flock of seagulls. He saw half the coastline. It sounded magnificent, he said it felt like he was really flying.'

'Amazing,' said Cassie. 'And now he's off with Toyah, huh? That one's odd.'

Stitch laughed. 'No more odd than the rest of us. I think we forget what it's like talking to people without power. *That's* normal.' He looked up at the horizon, towards Highdown. 'How's Otis? Has he come in from the wilderness yet?'

Cassie ignored Stitch, not taking the bait.

'When are you coming to help me in the shop?' Jay had been asking her for a while, figured it might give her a little focus.

'I will,' Cassie said with a shrug. 'Soon.'

'Anyone seen Pinto recently?' Jay asked. 'He used to come around. Not seen him for a few weeks.' Toyah's little brother Pinto was not yet a teenager, but he and Jay had a connection. She sensed his developing level 5 power. The only other level 5 she'd ever sensed after Otis.

Stitch said, 'Last time I saw Toyah, she told me that Pinto

was struggling to settle in at school. The kids know he has power, and everyone wants a piece of him.'

Jay felt a pang of sadness and anger at the thought of Pinto having trouble at school. She knew that feeling of isolation, but she was lucky. She had Stitch. She looked up towards Highdown and for a moment thought she saw a wisp of darkness flow around its peak. She stood, moving as close to the hills as the short section of the roof allowed.

'What?' said Cassie. She and Stitch stood to join Jay at the edge of the roof.

'Probably nothing,' said Jay, staring at the crest of the hill for a moment. She screwed up her eyes, blinking. 'I've had a weird couple of days. My mind is playing tricks.'

TOYAH CLIMBED out of Jay's window - past Jay, Stitch, and Cassie - her orange hair tied back but spilling over her face, and made for the route down to the alleyway without a word. 'Hey,' called Jay, exchanging glances with Stitch and Cassie. 'What's up? Where's Sammy?'

'I need to get home,' Toyah called over her shoulder as she slipped down onto the wall and landed with a thump on the pathway below and out of sight.

Sammy appeared at the window. 'Toyah!' he called after her, but she was gone.

'What is it?' Jay asked as Sammy climbed out and took a seat next to Stitch on the roof.

Sammy shrugged and said nothing, leaning back against the tiles. Stitch said, 'We hear she's been struggling with her little brother recently.'

'It's not Pinto,' said Sammy. 'It's the situation. With their parents out of the picture, I think Toyah takes on the role.'

'But they're in the unit. There's support there?' said Jay.

'Of a kind,' Sammy said. 'But she still feels a responsibility. And she's not even supposed to be there. The unit is for kids. They let Toyah stay there because Pinto is there, but she doesn't really belong. She doesn't really belong anywhere. That's the problem.'

'She belongs with us,' said Jay.

'I think she's pissed with me too, but she won't admit it,' said Sammy. 'I can't get in her head.'

'They've been through a lot,' Jay said, thinking of the journey that Toyah and Pinto made together to reach the Interland after their parents had been killed. The day they lost their parents was the day Toyah's life changed - from kid to parent. She had to be strong for Pinto.

'Like I don't know that,' Sammy snapped at his sister. 'Whatever I do makes no difference. She's just pissed off with the world and everything in it, including me.'

* * *

CASSIE LEANED FORWARD and looked at Jay, scrunching up her eyes. 'Spill the beans,' she said.

'What?' said Jay.

'There's something on your mind. I can see it, we all can.'

Stitch nodded his agreement.

Jay sighed. She'd not been shielding. Perhaps she needed her friends to know. It was muddled. 'A Reader tracked me down yesterday,' she said.

Stitch and Cassie both stared. 'Why didn't you turn him in?' said Stitch.

'I needed to hear what she had to say.'

'She?' said Cassie. Jay nodded and Cassie balked. 'There's a first.'

'She said she came to warn me,' said Jay. 'There's something happening on Island 7.'

'Warn you about what?' said Stitch. 'How do you know we can trust her? She's a *Reader*.'

Jay shrugged. 'I saw her thoughts for myself. She told me that the Dark will come here.'

'The *Dark*? You mean the Readers?'

'No, more like their source. A tip in the energy's balance towards the Dark. She told me I need to connect not just with the power of the Given, but with the darkness too, if we are to protect our homeland.'

'Connect with The Dark? That's not possible,' said Stitch.

'We don't know that. The powers come from a different source, but they are of the same essence. They manifest in similar ways. Like two sides to the same coin. There's a logic there. If I can tap into it, then perhaps I can reach a greater power.'

'If there is such a thing,' said Stitch. He stood, pacing the roof. 'Anything else? Any more revelations? Why would you even *think* about connecting with the darkness? We used to be a team. We used to work this stuff out together.' Stitch's voice was getting louder. Cassie sank further into the roof tiles.

'Stitch?' Jay tried to catch his eye, but he wouldn't look at her.

'Why are you even listening to a Reader over us?' Stitch said, continuing to pace.

'Leave me out of this,' said Cassie, standing and pushing past Stitch to head back down to the alleyway and away.

Jay recalled how scared she'd been, back when she first came across the Readers. When faced with Marcus, she had no idea how they would get away, or if the Interland even existed. The feeling she had now was different. She was scared, yes, but not for her own safety. She could handle the Readers. She was fearful for the safety of her friends and her family. Cassie was at the end of her rope. She clearly wanted no more of this fight, a fight they all thought was over. And Stitch. She looked over at him, his head down, inspecting his hands. She loved Stitch, probably more than anyone. He was like family. And more.

Sammy nudged into her. 'What are you going to do?'

Jay shrugged. 'I can't risk the darkness coming here, not again. I need to know that Island 7 is OK. I don't have a choice.'

7

The next day, Jay reached the bookshop just before closing. She pushed through the door to the sound of the bell. No sign of Alf or Buster. She took the stairs to the top floor and saw Alf hanging out of the window with a cigarette in his mouth.

'Hey,' said Jay. 'You said you gave that up years ago?'

Alf jumped, like a kid rumbled by his parents. 'You scared me. I *have* given up. This is an illusion.' He took a final drag and flicked the cigarette away, then pulled the window shut. 'What are you doing here on your day off?'

'I wanted to ask you something.'

'Your little friend was in earlier, reading that book again.' 'Angie?'

Alf nodded. 'She asked for you. I said you'd be in tomorrow. Is Cassie ever going to take you up on your request for some help in the shop?'

'Doesn't look like it.'

Alf motioned for Jay to follow him to sit at the table. 'What's up then?'

'Someone came to see me.'

'Who?' Alf remained calm.

'Her name is Flick. She's a Reader, and she came with a warning.' Jay explained to Alf how she'd faced up to Flick, and how they'd talked there at the bookshop. 'She took a big risk to come here and meet me,' Jay said.

'Do you think it could be a trap?' Alf asked.

'No,' Jay said, no room for doubt in her tone. 'When I touched her I saw it, the new sink-room, the hundreds of Readers. It's all true.'

'We need to be careful,' said Alf, his voice low and controlled. 'Why are you so sure that Flick is for real?'

'Why else would she risk her life? What has she to gain?'

'There is still so much we don't know about the powers. What we read the other day raises more questions than it answers, and if this *Flick* is genuine, then something's happening and we need to be on our guard. And if she's not...' He stood, turning to head over to Jay's display section on the old literature on the powers. Jay followed. He pulled one of his old prized books from the humidity-controlled cabinet, a heavy tome. He carefully flicked through the pages. He said, 'There's something in here I read before...'

Jay leaned around to watch as the pages drifted by under Alf's gentle touch. There were no pictures, chapters, or even breaks in the text. It seemed to be just page after page of small text cramming all the available space. 'How old is it?'

'Early seventeen hundreds. I studied it on and off for years. It's essentially a book of old stories. It's stories like these that fuel a lot of the folklore. If my memory serves me, there are sections in here that talk of the superstition and witchery of the seventeenth century. Something you said just now jogged a memory.' He continued to leaf through the book, his noises of frustration growing louder as he failed to find what he was looking for. He stroked the book shut. 'It'll have to wait. Come on, we need to lock up the shop.'

'What's the rush?'

'I have something I need to do,' said Alf.

'I'm intrigued,' Jay said with a smile. 'Who is she?'

Alf sighed, frustrated in his inability to keep anything from Jay. 'Her name's Judith. And it's not like that.'

'Where did she spring from?'

'Say nothing to your dad. He knows her. She does some work with the resistance team based up in London. We're just catching up. Don't say anything. Promise?'

Jay smiled and looked at Alf's book on the table in front of them. 'Can I stay a while?' she asked, reaching to re-open the book. 'I'll be careful with it, and I'll return it to the cabinet. And it will help me not to talk to Dad about the London resistance.'

Alf rolled his eyes. He agreed and turned to head for the stairs. 'Do you have your keys?' he asked. Jay nodded. 'I'll lock you in. You can see yourself out. Don't stay too late, you're on shift tomorrow.'

'I know,' Jay said. 'Where's Buster?'

'He's in the flat.'

'OK. Have fun.'

Alf grunted something in reply, but her attention was already on the pages in front of her.

* * *

JAY WOKE with a gentle hand on her shoulder. 'Jay.' Alf's voice. She prised her eyes open, closing them again to keep the light from penetrating her brain. She groaned. Alf encouraged her head off the desk so that he could extract the book. He closed it and pushed it aside.

'Sorry,' said Jay. 'I fell asleep.'

'I gathered,' said Alf as he tidied the papers on the desk and collected his book to return it to the cabinet.

He returned with coffee and sat next to Jay as she stretched and yawned. 'What time is it?' she asked.

'Half hour until opening. Drink that and then get yourself home. I can manage this morning.'

'No,' insisted Jay. 'I'm fine.' She cradled her mug. Her hair stuck up at the side where she'd been laying her head on the desk. There was a line on her cheek where she'd rested her face on the edge of the book. 'How was your evening?'

'Judith never made it, caught up in London.'

'Sorry about that,' Jay yawned again.

Alf frowned at her dishevelled look. 'Come back tomorrow when you've had some sleep. You're no good to me in this state.'

'Sorry,' Jay said again, taking a longer drink from her mug.

Alf forced a smile. 'I need to open up the shop. Go home and clear your head.'

Jay headed home and went straight to bed. Later that afternoon, she woke to the sound of Sammy coming into her room. He sat on the edge of her bed and started talking as if continuing a previous conversation with no preamble. She pulled her head under her cover to muffle the noise.

'Jay? It's three o'clock in the afternoon.'

'Go away,' said Jay, her voice croaky. Sammy stood to open the window, allowing the blind to roll itself up and the remains of the day to pour into the room. Then he put on a James Taylor record and sat back down on the edge of the bed. Jay groaned. 'What do you want?'

He pulled back the cover so he could see his sister. 'I was

just saying that I don't know what's up with Toyah at the moment and wondered if she'd said anything to you?'

Jay sat up in bed. 'You could at least have brought me a cup of tea.'

'Has she said anything?' Jay rolled her eyes, then shook her head.

'She's been cold,' Sammy said.

'Talk to her. See her.'

'She told me she's busy today.'

'Give her a bit of space, then. She'll come around.'

'Space? You mean like a break?'

Jay sighed inwardly. 'No, I just mean...'

'You think she needs space from me.'

'Sammy!' Jay snapped. 'Relax. Don't blow this up.'

'I think I'll see if she's down at the pier. She goes there sometimes.'

'If she needs a bit of breathing space, then...'

'I'll go find her,' Sammy interrupted. He stood. Jay slumped back against the wall, watching her brother as the thoughts whirled around in his head. 'Yes, I'll see if she's there and we can talk about it. Thanks,' he said, flashing Jay a smile as he left the room. Jay lay back and pulled the covers over her head.

'I THOUGHT YOU WERE AT WORK?' Ben said as Jay walked into the kitchen. Sonia glanced up briefly from the washing up.

'Day off,' she said as she opened the fridge and pulled out a carton of milk.

'What happened to you last night? I didn't hear you come in?'

'It was late. I got engrossed in some papers Alf had for me.'

'Sammy was looking for you earlier,' her mum said.

'He found me. Woke me up. Talked *at* me for a bit, then disappeared again.'

Ben put the kettle on and said, 'Colson was asking after you at the club last night.'

Jay poured milk onto her cereal. 'What did he want? He came into the shop earlier in the week. He and Alf finally made up.'

'I heard,' said Ben. 'He asked me to give you this.' Ben passed Jay a book from the kitchen counter. 'He didn't say what for, just said you'd need it back.'

Jay spooned cereal into her mouth, then placed her bowl down so she could take the book from her dad. It was the Sasha Colden biography, the copy from the bookshop, Jay could tell by the condition, and the turned down pages and her own bookmark. 'He took it from the shop? Cheeky...'

'He told me to say that it proves the point. Whatever point that is?'

'The point about the old power,' Jay said absently, then looked up at Sonia and Ben, who both stared back at her. 'What?'

'What's going on?' asked Sonia.

'Nothing, Mum. It's just research.' Jay contemplated opening the discussion with her mum and dad about Flick and the fear that Alf had voiced about something changing. But decided against it. 'You making tea, Dad?'

* * *

BACK IN HER LOFT ROOM, the sight of Toyah climbing in through her window made Jay jump, spilling her tea. 'For ff...' Jay said.

'Sorry,' Toyah said as she slipped in through the window and sat down on Jay's desk chair.

'Sammy's not in,' said Jay, wiping spilled tea from her hand and sitting on her bed. 'He's out looking for you.'

Toyah swung from left to right in Jay's desk chair for a moment and then said, 'I know. I wanted to have a quick word with you, if that's OK?'

Jay's heart sank a little at the thought of having to be the go-between for Toyah and her little brother. 'Sure, I guess.'

'Don't worry, I just want to know if Sammy has said anything?'

'About what?'

'He's been closing in a bit recently. Stifling, you know? I mean, he's great, but things have been hard recently and he's...' She trailed off.

'*Talk* to him. Tell him things are tough and you need a bit of space.'

Toyah nodded. She looked around Jay's room. 'Sorry for just dropping in.'

'It's fine.' Jay smiled. 'What's going on?'

'I just need a bit of breathing space.'

Jay waited.

'Everything seems like hard work, you know? Pinto's struggling, which is hard on me.'

'How?'

'He's only just moved up to secondary school, and he's already having a hard time. It's not full-on bullying, it's more insidious than that. Bullying by stealth. Little things. He gets left out, ostracised, and things get said. His powers are growing, so sometimes they don't even have to speak to bully him. He can see what's in their heads.'

'Poor Pinto,' Jay said, a lump in her throat. She had a genuine fondness for Toyah's little brother. He was like a little version of her own brother, and he played a large part in their victory over the Readers at the Interland. 'Anyone we need to rough up a bit?' she said, a semi-serious expression on her face.

'Maybe,' said Toyah. 'I'm kinda hoping he'll be able to sort it out himself. We can't be there every day for him. And what happened to you last night?' Toyah asked. 'You were supposed to meet us at the pub.'

Jay recalled promising Stitch she'd meet them in the Beach Arms. 'I lost track of time at the shop. Then I fell asleep with my head on the desk.'

Toyah laughed. 'What? All night?' Jay nodded and joined in Toyah's laughter.

JAY STOOD outside Pinto's school and checked her watch. The students were due out any minute. She just wanted to see him, see that he was OK.

Pinto appeared in a crowd of kids who all seemed to be a good foot taller than him. He was on his own, head down. She read him and she saw immediately that he was avoiding making eye contact with a group of boys just to his left and a little behind him. All his focus was on trying to make himself invisible to them.

One boy threw a stick over the heads of other kids, which then hit Pinto on the back. He was jolted from his concentration, stopping to look at the boys in an instinctive reflex. The boys reached Pinto and laughed, jostling him.

One of them put his arm around Pinto's shoulder and, for a moment, Jay thought she saw a smile on Pinto's face, like they were all mucking around. But his inner thoughts betrayed him to Jay. He was scared. He was losing sight of where he fit into this world.

Around twenty feet behind Pinto, Jay sensed someone else with power. She scanned the faces until she pin-pointed the energy in a girl, much the same age as Pinto, and taking a similar approach of keeping herself out of the limelight – head down, shields up.

At the main gate, Jay called Pinto's name. He looked up and, seeing Jay, his colours brightened, his oranges and greens flowed like a dam had burst.

The boys looked over at Jay and then moved on, heading away from the school in the opposite direction. Jay and Pinto embraced. 'It's been ages,' he said.

'Too long, my friend. I've missed you.'

'What are you doing here?'

'Let's walk.' Jay nodded toward Pinto's foster home.

'You going this way?'

'Who's that?' Jay asked, nodding towards the girl she'd seen walking behind Pinto.

Pinto looked up at Jay and smiled. 'You can sense her power? I can too. Her name's Sasha.'

'Sasha?' repeated Jay. 'As in Sasha Colden?'

Pinto laughed, 'Yes. But her name is Sasha Jenkins, not Colden. I can tell she has something, some level of power developing.'

'You should talk to her.'

'She's not exactly inviting people in,' Pinto said, his expression a little sad.

'Bit like you then?' said Jay.

Pinto shrugged, and they stopped at the crossroads

where Sasha's route diverged from their own. They watched as she walked alone into the distance. After a minute, they continued into Pinto's street. 'Thanks,' Pinto said, turning to head up the pathway to the front door of what looked like a big manor house set back from the road in the trees. 'You want to come in?'

'No,' Jay said, smiling. 'I need to go, but next time I see you, you can tell me what Sasha's like?'

'I don't know what she's like,' Pinto called from his front door.

'Find out,' Jay shouted as she turned to head home.

8

I n her room that evening, Jay was distracted from her book by the sounds of the wind whipping over the rooftops, rattling her window. For almost an hour, it was as if the world outside had been trying to get her attention. She looked up, then back to her book, trying her best to shut out the noise. Dusk crept up on her. She leaned over to switch on her bedside lamp, its orange glow warming the room. She heard the front door slam and figured Sammy was heading out to see Toyah, or her dad, heading to the pub.

Speaking as if directly to the wind and rain battering her window, she said, 'What do you want?' Persistent gusts squealed and swirled, shaking the roof tiles. She pulled on her hoodie and opened the Velux, the wind immediately rushing through her room as if searching for something. She climbed out onto the tiles and closed the window behind her. The wind pushed at her hood and she had to hold it to keep it from exposing her ears to the pounding cold. She crouched and sat back against the tiles, the wet seeping through her jeans. 'What am I doing?' she said, breathing the words into the wind so that they disappeared before they could reach her ears.

With a final gust from the south, a parting reminder of its power, the petulant wind died suddenly, and the silence was deafening. Jay looked around her. The sense of sudden calm was unnatural. A gentle breeze caught her hair, brushing it from her eyes.

The sun had dipped behind the crest of Highdown Hill in the distance so that the only light remaining cast a monochrome greyness over the Beach Lane estate. With the parting of the wind, the twilight felt warm. Jay pulled down her hood and leaned back against the tiles. She closed her eyes, reaching out to the power, the energy of the land.

The whispers came first. It was always the whispers first, and always urgent, like there was something desperate they needed from Jay.

Before the Given emerged from the Interland, the dominance of the Readers and their darkness had impacted the land, the environment, and the very existence of the Given. Cities were run down, the natural environment degraded. Even without their ill-fated plan to destroy the source, the Readers had been edging further into power, and the natural world retreating all the time. Now, Jay's world, Island 8, thrived. The eco-systems had re-balanced, and humans, both with and without power, lived in a more free, reciprocal relationship with nature. If Flick was right, then the threat to the new stability was unimaginable.

The whispers turned to white noise, and a smile crept across Jay's face as the messages came. Warm colours flowed through Jay's mind, from the hills, the ground beneath the Beach Lane Estate, and from the sea. The colours seeped into Jay's skin, into her veins and the marrow of her bone. She tingled with energy; fizzed with power.

Tentatively, she thought of the Dark, and Flick's ambiguous challenge. If she could connect with the Dark core, as well as with the source of the Given, she might be able to see into the Dark energy, to see its truth, and the reality of any threat that it might cause. She hesitated to open up to it, searching her mind for the consequences but unable to shake the feeling this was the right thing - a chance for a deeper power, greater control, and a more permanent means to protect her homeland. She focused on the darkness – on her memories of Hinton, the myth of Atta, the power of the Readers. She breathed deeply of the energy that flowed through her chest.

An unusual taste nagged at the back of Jay's throat. It had a bitter metallic tinge. She swallowed and a cool liquid re-emerged at the roof of her mouth, bringing more of the bitterness. She tried to open her eyes, but she couldn't move. She swallowed again, and the bitterness intensified. Fear bubbled under her skin. Her heart raced as she lay frozen against the tiles, heavy like lead.

As frequently as she could swallow the bitterness, it would return, forcing her to swallow once more to keep from choking. She struggled for breath, nauseous with the vile taste. She forced her eyes open. As she did, she sank harder into the tiles, as if in a centrifuge. She was sure the roof would give way beneath her.

She looked to the hills. Black tentacles reached over the crest of Highdown and down into the valley towards Beach Lane, like an infection radiating from a wound. A black mist circled the air, creeping towards her. Jay gasped, and the blackness entered her body through her open mouth. Her head tipped back, opening to the Dark which poured into her body, pushing her own colours out through her skin.

The bitter taste spread.

It was cold. It froze her from the inside out, spreading further to her limbs as if searching her for a place to reside. Her breathing became shallow, and she slumped to her side, her body so cold she had no energy or will. The Dark seeped through her, down into her legs, her arms.

'Jay,' a shout from Stitch, coming from Jay's room. A spark of electricity ran through Jay's head and the Dark retreated a little. 'Jay?' Stitch again, close this time, leaning out of the window. 'Jay!' His voice urgent now. The sound as he clambered out of the window. His touch. He rocked back as if he'd touched a live electric cable, but he returned. He reached for Jay once more. The energy in his touch was so powerful it forced air into Jay's lungs, warmth to her skin and energy back into her bones. She gasped for air and sat up straight, her eyes snapping open. Stitch crouched in front of her, his hands holding hers, his eyes full of fear. The energy flowed through Jay like warm water. She reached for Stitch and he held her as she thawed and slowly returned to herself.

Stitch held her hands for a moment longer before disappearing back into the house, returning a few minutes later, drink in hand.

'What *was* that?' asked Stitch, climbing back out onto the roof and handing Jay the drink.

'I opened to The Dark.'

'You did what?' he said, his tone accusing.

She nodded. 'I've done it before, but not like this.'

Stitch lit a cigarette. 'I thought that was just a feeling, like a sense of the presence of Readers, not *connecting* with it as such?'

'Same thing, really. It's just a sliding scale. This time I got a bit close to the end of the scale, that's all.'

'So, what did you see?'

'It felt like when I was reduced, in the sink-room. But...'

'What?'

'I don't know. It was more like a dream. I don't feel any effects now. I feel fine.' She decided not to reveal to Stitch that she felt weirdly euphoric. With the euphoria came a nagging guilt, like she'd been unfaithful. The feelings were confusing.

'I wish you wouldn't mess with it,' said Stitch.

'What if he's trying to *use* me...' Jay's words trailed off.

'Who's *he*?'

Jay snapped out of her thoughts. 'I don't know.'

Stitch flicked his cigarette over the hedge at the end of the roof and stood. 'I need to get back to Dad. Are you going to be OK?'

Jay nodded, but her smile was forced.

'I need you to promise me not to do that again, OK?' Stitch leaned down and kissed Jay on the top of her head. She smiled up at him, but he'd already turned to leave.

9

S titch lay back on his bed, his thoughts bashing around on the inside of his skull like a swarm of bees. He turned onto his side and forced his eyes closed. 'Empty your mind,' he said to himself, breathing steadily. 'Count sheep.' Every time he got close to settling and calming himself, the bees returned and his head filled with questions.

He couldn't shake it. He harboured a dark, nagging thought that today was the end of the world. He stomped over to his bedroom window, unlatched it and threw it open in one swift move, leaning out over the threshold and taking a deep breath of cool night air. Breathing out some of the tension, he looked up towards the hills of the Downs, mostly concealed behind the trees at the bottom of his garden, but the peak of Highdown just visible. The hills brought energy and calm. He could just about hear the sounds of the sea in the distance - more of a continuous hiss than any distinctive breaking of waves. He shivered in the cold, his bare torso goose-pimpled. He brushed his fringe from his eyes and was about to turn back to his bed when something caught his eye.

He stopped, looking down the length of his back garden. Nothing but darkness. He recalled the vision of the figure he'd seen before in his garden, the white glow that had helped them get away from the Readers many months ago, and he looked towards that spot in the garden, straining his eyes to see.

The darkness at the foot of the trees at the end of his garden spread. Stitch rubbed his eyes. It spread across the grass towards the house, like an oil slick. He blinked and leaned further out of his window. It approached the house like a wave of thick tar, steady, relentless. His heart rate increased by the second. Darkness engulfed the whole of the back garden and reached the foot of the wall beneath Stitch's window.

He needed to move, to run, to find his father, Samir, and get out. His feet stuck to his bedroom carpet as the black wave climbed the wall of the house towards his window. Wisps of black smoke seemed to drift off the surface of the wave and fizzle away into the night.

As the black wave of darkness reached his windowsill, a pungent smell hit Stitch's nose, and a bitter taste filled his mouth. His head spun so fast that his legs could not hold him. He slipped to the floor and his world plunged into the blackness.

HE WOKE WITH A JOLT, lying face down on his bed, his covers on the floor.

Light poured through his bedroom window; sunlight streaked across his carpet. He shot out of bed and to his window, which was open and swinging gently in the breeze. The lawn shone in the sunlight. The trees at the foot of the garden bristled in the wind, the smell of pollen in the air.

He turned back into his room, scratched his head, and looked over at his clock. It was past ten o'clock in the morning. He'd been asleep for hours. 'A dream?' he said aloud to himself, then shook his head and looked back out over the garden. Deep down, something told him it was no dream. Something was coming.

He closed his window and pulled on some clothes. He needed to get to the bookshop, to Jay.

JAY HANDED Angie another pile of books to return to the shelves. 'See the number printed inside?' she explained. 'Match that with the shelf reference and there should be a gap. Easy, eh?'

Angie staggered off with her arms full of books. She had been waiting at the shop doors when Jay arrived to open up. Her guarded nature had evaporated, and she insisted on helping Jay with the books, following her around the shop like a sheep until Jay gave her something to do. Her thirst for knowledge was growing. Every opportunity she quizzed Jay on the powers, the Readers, and how she should expect her own abilities to surface. Angie's power was evolving and growing almost by the minute.

Jay took the weight off her feet and slumped down on a chair by the windows, allowing the early sun to warm her face. She looked towards the cabinets of literature on the powers, then beyond the window to the sea in the distance. Clouds spread across the sky like chalk on blue canvas. She opened the window an inch and breathed the salty air.

A gust of wind blew the window open further. The handle slipped from her hand and the frame slammed against the wall. Book covers blew open and pages rustled on the shelves. Angie looked back over her shoulder at Jay in surprise as she battled with the window to secure it on its latch.

As Jay scanned the horizon, white clouds darkened and cast a shadow over the seafront. Jay walked to the back of the shop, and the door that led to the top of the fire escape. She leaned on the push-bar and spilled out onto the steel landing from where she could see Highdown.

The sky was black above the hills and it took Jay's breath. She looked back to the hills as a shadow poured down the slopes towards the town. This was not like the tentacles she had experienced the night before, the stretching black roots that had entered her head when she connected with the darkness. This was different. This was a slow, creeping encroachment of darkness over the land. She squinted to see more clearly, to convince herself that this wasn't an illusion.

Angie walked up behind her and Jay said, 'Do you see that?'

'What is it?' Angie replied. 'I feel like I'm hallucinating.'

The approaching black sea brought with it a palpable wave of energy. It buffeted Jay, and dragged on her body as Angie pulled her back towards the door, pleading with her to go back inside.

The weight of the darkness was too much. Jay sank to the floor, crouching on the landing of the fire escape with Angie tugging at her arm.

The wind howled around the buildings. Jay's breathing became shallow. As the darkness reached overhead, and

Angie had all but given up trying to get Jay back inside, Jay heard a familiar voice. 'Jay! Move!'

She looked up to see Stitch in the doorway. He lifted Angie and helped her inside, returning for Jay. He took her hand and dragged her arm over his shoulder so that he could lift her. The door slammed behind them, silencing the screaming wind.

The top floor of the shop was pitch black.

The Dark smothered the building like a blanket. There was a pressure in the air. A blinding pain shot through Jay's head. She slipped again to the floor and looked up at Angie and Stitch, their features melding into the darkness. As she felt she would surely pass out, confused and scared, the darkness intensified and a high pitch scream filled the book-shop. A moment passed before all the windows of the top floor imploded, shattered glass spreading through the room ahead of a wave of blackness so deep it swallowed everything.

Stitch fell. Angie turned towards the Dark and it passed through her, entering her body through her eyes, her mouth, and ears.

It was quiet then. The pain in her head was crippling. She dragged herself onto all fours and squeezed her eyes tight, waiting for the ringing and shooting pain to subside. When she opened her eyes, she saw a thin cloud of dust in the air, shimmering in the sunlight. The darkness had gone. Debris covered the entire top floor. She frantically scanned the chaos for Angie and Stitch.

Angie lay on her back, serene, seemingly untouched by the dust and debris. Her chest rose and fell with shallow breaths. She was alive. She looked more asleep than injured. There was no blood on her. No visible marks. Not a cut, bruise or scratch. Jay took her hand. It was cold. She used her power to delve into Angie, but came up against barriers. She couldn't read her. She turned to see Stitch stumbling in their direction. 'Help her,' she said, pleading with her eyes for Stitch to affect healing. He had done it before.

'I can't,' he said, his face barely concealing his rising panic. He put his hands on Angie's head and closed his eyes.

'Please,' said Jay. 'Try again.' She placed a hand on Stitch to reinforce his power of healing, the power that seemed to have slipped away from him in recent weeks.

Stitch looked at Jay in despair. 'I've got nothing,' he said.

10

J ay pulled the old Ford into the overflow car park at the back of the Black Rabbit pub, where she knew it would sit unnoticed. She switched off the engine, her eyes fixed on the rear-view mirror. The car park was empty. She was alone.

Since the incident in the bookshop, Jay could think of nothing but to get to Island 7 to see for herself what was happening. There was a threat coming, and she needed to understand it. Angie felt like Jay's responsibility, and she had let her down.

Angie hadn't yet regained consciousness. In the hospital they said that she was stable, but that they'd keep her under for a few days as a precautionary measure while they investigated the extent of any brain damage. Jay had to sneak in to see her outside of visiting hours. Angie's parents had refused to allow anyone else permission to see her. They blamed the powers.

The sight of Angie shocked her. She was pale and cold. She wanted to take her out of there, take her up to one of the hill forts to allow the Given energy to flow through her again. The medical profession was still learning about the effects of the powers. They would not understand how to deal with someone like Angie, suffering the effects of an attack from the Dark. Their standard response was a medically induced coma to reduce stress on the brain and allow the body to stabilise.

First, Jay had reached out through the powers to see if she could sense Flick, but she couldn't locate her. She figured Flick would be able to help her understand what was happening. But she seemed to have vanished as suddenly as she had appeared.

Jay hadn't wanted to tell Stitch about her plan to head to Island 7 because she knew he'd try to persuade her against it. But he read her intentions without her saying a word. 'What good can come of it?' he'd said. 'We'd be better to work out a defence from here. Plan for it. If it's coming, then you heading to Island 7 won't stop it.'

'I need to know,' Jay said. 'I need to be sure that there's nothing coming. That Island 7 is OK, and we won't be under attack.'

In the pub car park, the only sound was of the gush and flow of the water around the wooden posts of the river wall. Jay opened her car door. She'd travelled this route to the Interland three times in the past year. Each time she'd taken the route via the Arun, the quickest and easiest way in. She pulled her small rucksack onto her back and stepped into the trees.

As she walked, the usual sense of calm and safety she got from her connection with the environment was tainted by the darkness from the bookshop, leaving her with a nagging anxiety. She pushed through the bushes, cursing the brambles that cut into her skin.

When she stepped out into the clearing on the riverside,

the river level was high, the water stretching out towards her at the tree line. She dropped her rucksack to the floor and rested on a log. She pulled out her orange lifejacket and blew through the valve to inflate it. She had no intention of making a raft; she would drift with the currents through to the gateway. Tugging off her shoes, she deposited them in her rucksack before sealing everything inside a plastic bag. She placed her lifejacket over her head and fastened the straps.

At the edge of the shallow section, Jay leaned into the water and allowed herself to sink up to her chest. She kicked her legs, and after a minute calmed her breathing and relaxed into the flow, allowing herself to drift.

As she turned the first corner, a piercing scream rose from the riverside, back where she'd entered the water. She twisted to look in the direction of the scream, then was shaken by a second call, louder this time and more desperate. Scrambling to reach for the reeds at the side of the river to slow her progress, she got a hold and twisted her hand so that she swung into the bank.

From the riverbank, she looked back towards the tree line. There was someone in the water. A girl had fallen, or been dragged in, and was struggling for air. She ran back along the bank, closing the distance between her and the girl in just a few seconds.

It was Toyah, bobbing in the water as she floated downstream, struggling to keep her head above the surface.

Jay stood on the bank, closed her eyes and opened to the power of the environment. She saw Toyah in her mind's eye, tugged and pulled at by the streams and currents. Reeds and wisps of the dark pulled at her legs, her torso, her neck. Jay squeezed her eyes tighter and connected with the energy of the river, an energy that seemed to Jay more subdued than normal, stifled. She prised the dark tendrils from Toyah's body, freeing her legs just as she was about to give up and sink to the riverbed. Jay continued to guide and support the energy of the river to push Toyah to the surface, where she gasped for air.

Toyah drifted, coughing. Jay ran along the bank to keep up, then get ahead of her. She slid down to the water's edge and grasped for her outstretched hand, finally making contact and clamping her fingers around her wrist. She immediately felt Toyah's fear flash through her body through the connection.

Laid out on the riverbank, Toyah trembled. Jay held her hand to reassure her. 'What are you doing here?' she said, at the same time reading her intentions. She'd wanted to join Jay at the Interland. 'Why didn't you just ask?' said Jay.

'You'd have told me not to come,' said Toyah, still panting. She was right.

'We need to move,' said Jay. 'We can rest and dry out when we get to the Interland. We'll need to drift. It's not much further. Can you do this?'

Toyah stood and nodded. Jay pushed her lifejacket over Toyah's head and led her down to the water's edge. They re-entered the river and held on to each other as they continued downstream, using Jay's bag and Toyah's life-jacket for buoyancy.

* * *

JAY BUILT a fire and fed it with scraps of wood as she and Toyah dried themselves.

There was a space on the wall where the picture of Sasha Colden once hung. Jay had taken it on their last visit. Toyah pulled her top back on over her head, now dry from hanging by the fire. She sat with a blanket around her shoulders and stared into the dancing flames. Jay found a few tins of food that had survived in the side cave that used to be the storeroom of the Interland. She pulled out her penknife and used the can-opener to start work on the tins.

'That was pretty stupid,' Jay said to Toyah. 'You could have drowned in there. What happened?'

'Sorry,' Toyah said, running her fingers through her wet hair. 'I meant to catch you up before you got to the river, but it was harder going than I thought.'

Jay looked at Toyah. She was athletically built, more than capable of trekking through that terrain. Sammy had said how fit she was, stronger than him. 'When I got to the river, you'd already gone.'

'Did you follow my car on your moped?' asked Jay.

Toyah nodded.

'I thought I saw you,' Jay said.

'Then in the trees, it was so dark. The clouds seemed to close in. I couldn't see three feet in front of me.'

'The *Dark*,' said Jay. Toyah looked at her for more. 'Something I've been feeling for a few days now. Then the thing at the bookshop. Something's going on.'

'Is she OK? The little girl?'

Jay shrugged. 'We don't know yet. I told her I'd keep her safe...'

'You're not responsible for her.'

Jay's throat clenched. She felt entirely responsible. 'I'm not sure that's true. I didn't intend to, but I might have opened a channel for The Dark.'

'What?' said Toyah with a deep frown.

'You're a level 6, have you felt it?'

Toyah shook her head, but her eyes and her thoughts

told Jay otherwise. Toyah turned back to the fire. She pulled the blanket tighter around her shoulders.

Jay continued: 'Since I connected, there's been this taste in the air and a presence of Readers. Then the Dark hit, yesterday at the shop.'

Toyah stood, looking up into the roof of the cavern where the last of the day's light leaked through the opening. 'Is that what you're doing here?'

'Yes. I need to make sure everything's OK on Island 7, and see for myself if what Flick said is coming true.'

'You're heading through the source?'

Jay nodded. 'Yes. Alone. You can pick up a taxi to your moped.'

'There's nothing back there for me right now.' She looked away from Jay once more.

'What do you mean?' Jay threw another branch onto the fire. Sparks rose with the hot smoke and fizzled into the darkness.

'I just need some space for myself for a while. I need some air, you know?'

Jay shook her head. 'You can't come with me.'

Toyah snorted a laugh. 'Stitch travelled with you.'

'He's my connection. With you, I don't even know if it's possible. It's too risky.'

They were quiet for a minute.

'Has something happened with Sammy?' asked Jay.

Toyah shook her head. 'It's not him.'

'What is it then?'

Toyah sighed and threw a stone across the room, a piece of rock that had crumbled from the wall. 'I just need to do something useful. More than sitting around waiting for stuff to happen: for Pinto to do something stupid, or for me to get moved on from the foster home. They won't keep letting me stay there.'

'They love you there,' said Jay. 'Why wouldn't they let you stay?'

They were quiet as the fire died down. Jay decided that she'd sleep, then slip off to the source before Toyah woke. That way, she wouldn't have to continue this debate. If she was to move quickly through Island 7, she had to be alone, with no-one to slow her down.

Jay woke at first light, Toyah still asleep by the fire's remains. She stepped fully clothed from her sleeping bag and rolled it tight to squeeze it into its bag. She packed her rucksack in silence, pausing only to drag her fingers across the well-thumbed Sasha Colden book in her bag. She opened it at random, somewhere near the middle. In the light grey dawn light, she absorbed the words. Almost immediately, her mind settled as she connected with the energy of her ancestors, drew strength from the weight of the past.

She returned the book to her bag and glanced at Toyah, her nose poking out the top of her sleeping bag. She sighed, wishing for a moment that Stitch was with her. He injected a strength in Jay that no-one else came close to. But she had to do this alone. She wasn't about to put any of her friends at risk.

She pulled her hoodie over her head and crept towards the exit from the main cavern to the passageway that led to the source. The steps down to the depths of the Interland seemed narrower than Jay remembered, the walls and roof closer. Cool air washed over her face, a light breeze drifting up from the deep. The only sound was the trickling of water. She pulled a box of matches from her pocket and lit the candles in each of the alcoves in the rock.

The three streams of water from the rivers on the surface were as strong as ever, purposefully combining and generating the energy of the Given - a natural turbine. Jay took a deep breath of the moist, fresh air. She dipped her fingers into the pool where the three flows combined and light flashed behind her eyes.

She opened to the energy. The whispers in the power were confused. She focused on filtering the noise. The light faltered and dimmed. Jay stepped back from the water, rubbed her hands together and then wiped the fresh water over her face, blinking away the remains of sleep from her eyes.

The source felt strong. She took a deep breath and plunged her hands back into the pool. The power of the connection nearly knocked her off her feet. She strained to keep her hands in the water, drawing the energy. The white light behind her eyes intensified.

She sensed a presence. Someone with her. Toyah was there, her hands in the water, connected. Jay kept focus, channelling the power until the blinding white light filled her head and there was nothing.

11

J ay prised her face from the floor and spat grit from her mouth. She wiped away the sand and dust and blinked in the white light pouring from the sky. Toyah groaned nearby.

She stood, brushing down her clothes, white dust billowing. The act of transporting through the source was never elegant. Her eyes slowly adjusted and the blinding light receded. But what she then saw made her wish the blindness would return.

Island 7 was black from the shores to the top of the withered oak at its centre. The entire island was charred, dead. Between the islands, the water flowed black. The dark had closed in so that the wisps and swirls of black that Jay and Stitch had seen before had thickened to a homogenous darkness.

Toyah appeared at Jay's side, looking but saying nothing. Her eyes darted between the blackened features of the island and the water that separated them. 'What the...' Toyah studied her own hands as if she were not real, then looked around at the island on which they'd landed. A smile flickered across her face, only to fade when she saw Jay's pained expression. She put a hand on Jay's arm. 'What is it?'

Jay turned on Toyah. 'I told you not to come. We don't know what's over there. Look at this place!'

'What?' Toyah said, but she wouldn't know what it looked like before. Jay peered into the light to see if the other islands were visible. Gradually, the mist-like white light dissipated. The islands in the distance, from Island one, all the way through to Island 6, there was nothing but blackness. Jay's heart filled with dread.

Toyah followed her gaze, taking in the sight of each island. 'What does it mean?'

Jay gathered herself, thinking of how to explain the little she understood. She should take Toyah back to the Interland and leave her there, continue alone on the journey she'd intended. 'As I understand it, this place,' she said, eventually, 'is here because of the Given power, the energy of the land. Each Island represents one of the eight sources of power in eight different locations around the world.'

'What's happening to them?' asked Toyah, looking over at Island 7.

'The Dark.'

'It looks dead.'

'I don't know,' said Jay. 'This is a representation, but someone brought me a warning and it's beginning to look like the truth.'

'So what can we do?' asked Toyah.

Jay strode towards the shore and shivered at the sight of the black gloopy sea of danger between her and her destination on Island 7. She recalled Stitch writhing in agony when he'd touched just a thin wisp of the darkness in the water.

In the streams were intermittent patches of clear water and soon a pattern revealed itself.

'Look,' Jay said, pointing into the water. 'We can't walk through this darkness. It burns. But these clear sections come around with every cycle of the flow.' Toyah moved to the edge, poised to step through. 'Not yet,' said Jay, pulling her back. 'We need more space.'

A moment passed. 'Now!' Jay pushed herself into the water, wading deep into the section of clear water in the channel between the islands and then walking with it as it moved. She scanned for the connecting patch of safety that she hoped would materialise before she became enclosed by darkness. Toyah stepped into the next wave of clear water behind Jay, pushing through the waist-deep water as she looked over her shoulder at the approaching dark.

The black shore-line of Island 7 shone in the light like freshly cleaved seams of coal. Toyah should have been close behind, instead she was hesitating to step through to the next clear zone. 'Toyah!' Jay yelled, then looked to the water. The dark swirls encroached on the gaps. The route through the channel, Toyah's window of opportunity, narrowed.

Jay stepped back into the water, beckoning Toyah to hurry, reaching out a hand although she was still ten feet away. Toyah lunged for Jay, but the tendrils of blackness had marked a line between them. She stepped to the side and lifted a leg out of the water so that she could step over the dark swirls and closer to Jay. She held Jay's hand as she teetered and stumbled safely to the blackened shore. Jay followed Toyah, but something caught her foot.

A piercing pain shot through Jay's foot, and she stumbled. She went down, swirls of black around her foot. The water hissed. Her left foot burned, and she screamed as Toyah dragged her from the water. The pain was intense. Jay held her ankle, watching as the skin on her foot purged steam and smoke as if on fire. Her head swam and just as she thought she'd pass out, Toyah's action of cupping and pouring cold, clear water onto her foot eased the pain. She returned to the water, finding clear sections and depositing the cool, soothing liquid onto Jay's foot, over and over, until the pain subsided. She lay back on the black sand and dirt, breathing heavily. Her foot throbbed from the ankle downwards. She couldn't feel her toes.

'It's OK now,' Jay said in response to Toyah's expression of concern.

'What now?' said Toyah, looking around the blackened island.

'Is the source there?' said Jay, motioning for Toyah to look at the base of the tree, then returning her attention to her throbbing foot.

'You can't go anywhere on that foot,' Toyah said as she stepped towards the tree.

'I'm not sure,' Jay said. 'When this happened to Stitch, passing back through the source seemed to neutralise the injury, like the injury is only real when we're here.'

'The source is here,' said Toyah, surprised. 'There are three streams, weak, but they are here.'

'Let's do it,' Jay said, dragging herself off the floor and limping towards the base of the tree. 'Come,' she said with more urgency to Toyah. She dug her hand into the area at the base of the tree and reached for Toyah's hand. Toyah placed her other hand into the source and connected the ring.

The white light came like a slowly descending mist, intensifying as it drifted to ground level and becoming blinding. Then there was nothing.

* * *

IT WAS DINGY, but light enough to see. They were lying in a
basement somewhere. The floor on one side was under an
inch of water, three of the walls wet with streams of water
leaking from above. The air was warm. Jay pushed herself to
sit as Toyah stirred and cleared her throat, her voice croaky.
'How's the foot?'

'Still there,' said Jay. 'I mean, the pain is still there. It's
weird. This water soothes it a little.'

'What is this place?' Toyah said, standing and looking
around the room. 'It's hot,' she added, wafting her hand to
cool her face. The room was only ten feet across in both
directions. The ceiling had fallen in, leaving exposed wires,
ducts, and concrete beams to hold up the debris from above.
Chunks of concrete lay around them on the floor, and the
only exit appeared to be a single door in the far wall. There
were no windows, but natural light sneaked through from
somewhere above their heads. The warm air was thick with
dust.

Toyah was already at the door, pulling at it, to no avail.
'Locked,' she said, turning and looking up into the ceiling.

On the only remaining shelves on the near wall, Jay
sifted through some old papers, water damaged and barely
decipherable. 'Maps?' asked Toyah.

Jay shook her head. 'Building information. I think we're
in this building.' She pointed to a drawing of a high-rise
tower. 'Or at least what's left of it.'

'So this is the source. The building must have protected
it. You think they levelled the building to destroy the
source?' asked Toyah.

Jay put her hand up against the wall where water flowed
from above. She looked at her hand to see the sparkling

within the water, a blue tinge to it. The feel on her hands was immediately energising. Toyah reached to touch the water. 'Like the unnamed river. You think this water is formed from the three streams?'

'There's one way to find out,' said Jay. She scanned the room for the point at which the water from above converged to a single body. 'There,' she said, pointing. She strode over to the part of the basement floor that was under water and crouched down. 'The three streams converge here.' She pushed her hand into the water and immediately there came a white light behind her eyes, and the urgent whispers of the environment. The noise was confused; the whispers were pained.

'They've destroyed the building, but the energy is here. We at least have a route back.'

'We're not going back,' said Toyah. 'We're here now. Let's do it.' She looked up into the roof, searching for the source of the light that filtered through the floors. 'There must be a way through.' She climbed up the only dry wall in the room, using lumps of concrete and fallen sections of the roof as a ladder to the top of the wall. 'Here,' she called. 'There's a route through here.'

Jay looked up to where Toyah waited. The route up to the hole in the ceiling was no accident. It had been used before. She shuffled her weight onto her good foot. 'Can you walk?' Toyah called. Jay nodded and climbed up the wall to where Toyah had disappeared into a hole through to the floor above.

They crawled through layer after layer of debris, heading towards the light. They emerged in the middle of a vast crater, full of bits of the demolished building. Jay could sense no power – either Reader or Given, nothing. The sounds of the City emanated from the ridge at the top of the crater. Car horns, a jack-hammer. The sun pounded its energy down onto their skin through a gap in the clouds.

They picked their way across the bomb-site and out to the periphery where they stopped to catch a breath. Jay looked back over the expanse of demolished building, probably three hundred feet across. Concrete slabs with protruding steel bars scattered the area like the remnants of an earthquake. Furniture littered the surface, much of it smashed into pieces, stripped, scavenged, and pilfered for anything useful. A thick layer of white concrete dust covered everything so that they were both caked by the time they reached the edge.

'Up there,' Toyah said, pointing up to the rim of the crater. 'We can see from there.'

They climbed the dirt bank, reaching a fence-line with barbed wire. Toyah held up the wire fence for Jay to crawl under.

Signs attached to the fence line at intervals around the perimeter read "Radioactive". Toyah stared. 'Surely not?'

'I don't think so. It's a deterrent,' Jay said. In all directions, a thin smog hung over the City. They stood at the edge of a main street with cars passing nose to tail. Energy from the environment was weak and intermittent. A scent of the sea comforted her, brought a little of home to this unfamiliar land.

Toyah crossed the road between two yellow taxis. A derelict-looking building on the other side of the street with a collapsed front wall exposed its kitchen. She stopped at the remains of a kitchen sink and turned on one of the taps. Nothing. She tried the other, and it spluttered into life, spraying cold water all over the floor. She rubbed her hands together and splashed water over her face. She drank from the tap. 'Water's good.'

Jay looked up at the façade of the building, which must once have been a block of apartments. It stretched higher than most of its neighbours. She followed Toyah's lead and went to the tap. As soon as the cool liquid touched her lips, she realised how thirsty she was and drank greedily. She cupped her hands and poured water over her head, rubbing away the dust and heat that had penetrated her skin.

'Let's get to the roof,' said Toyah. 'We might see through this mist, so we can see what we're dealing with.' She led the way, pushing through the line of orange tape that cordoned off the main staircase. Jay followed, limping on her injured foot.

Every one of the six floors was long-deserted and littered with debris. On the roof, the smog was thinner and they could see over the top of the nearby buildings and into the distance across the City.

Toyah gasped. The City fell away into a bowl in front of them, stretching far into the distance and bounded by the sea – a grey-blue expanse of water as far as they could see. The collapsed building over the source marked the northern edge of the City. A layer of dust and smog hung over the buildings, which looked to be in a poor state – a collapsed wall, missing roof, smoke rising from its depths. Other high-rise buildings looked abandoned. People filled the streets, baking in the heat of the sun.

'What now?' said Toyah. Jay thought about the Island's 8C. Her feeling was that he was alive, despite the obvious absence of any sense of Given power. In hiding, perhaps.

'Look,' Toyah said, pointing to the east. Outside the eastern boundary of the City stood a series of smaller, low-rise dwellings. Smoke rose from discrete locations from within the settlement. A road protruded from the edge, heading out east, through to the mountains barely visible in the mist. There was a checkpoint on the road. Men with guns checked vehicles coming in and out of the City.

'Readers,' said Jay, a little fear prickling her skin.

Toyah looked to the hills in the east. 'What's out there that they need to control access to?'

'That's what we need to find out if we are to know one way or the other.'

'Know what? It's obvious this place is owned by Readers.'

'Atta,' said Jay. 'We need to know if what Flick said is true. If he exists. We need to know what we're up against.'

DESPITE THE DRAW that Jay felt to head into the City, they chose instead to head north-east into woodland and navigate their way around to the eastern hills while all the time remaining outside the City boundary, avoiding the checkpoint they'd seen from the top of the building.

They travelled for nearly two hours before reaching the foothills of the mountains. The pain in Jay's foot seemed to ease a little and a numbness set in. The eastern pathway meandered through the hills, and the further they got, the stronger Jay's sense of dark energy, and the greater her concern for Island Seven's 8C. 'We're close,' she said, looking up at a steep slope blocking their path, filled with a sense of foreboding. Whatever was beyond this ridge, she had to see with her own eyes. Toyah staggered a little on her feet. She exchanged a look with Jay and she knew that Toyah too felt the energy of the Readers and their darkness.

The climb – an hour of hard graft - took them to a ledge overlooking what appeared to be an old, disused and long since drained reservoir. Jay was the first to reach the lip of the depression and the scale of the operation knocked her back. The reservoir crater must have been over a kilometre in diameter. Down in the vast cavern, a depth of almost half its width, was a hive of activity. Mechanical excavators moved across the northern section, expanding what appeared to be an already vast warehouse-like structure. Groups of people moved between the buildings.

'They're building a City down there.'

'Sink-room. A big one.' Jay thought back again to what Flick had told her. She'd spoken of a *mega sink-room*, but Jay never pictured something as vast as this. 'We need to see what's in those buildings.'

'That's an entire community of darkness,' said Toyah. 'You sure about this?'

'They're not all Readers,' said Jay. Those with power had a certain aura that was visible to Jay. 'Look at them. Regular people under the control of the Readers.'

'Atta?' said Toyah.

'Maybe,' Jay said. 'There's Given power down there too. I can feel it.'

'The 8C?'

Jay pointed into the depths of the crater to a small, single-storey building at the south end. 'That one is guarded.'

'Readers,' said Toyah.

Jay agreed. 'If there are Given down there, that must be where they're holding them. But why here? And why keep them alive?'

'Transformation?' said Toyah.

Toyah was right. What they were looking at was a production line for the creation of Readers, which needed a supply of those with power, the Given. 'Stay here,' Jay said.

'I'll head down and see what's going on. I just need to know for sure, then I'll come back and we can leave.'

'If you go, then I go,' said Toyah, standing.

'No!' Jay said, pulling Toyah to crouch again. 'I can't protect you down there. I won't let anyone else be hurt.'

Toyah simply rolled her eyes and stood, leading the way down the slope towards the buildings.

12

A scuttle of stones knocked into the metal structure and made a noise that raised Jay's heartbeat. They froze, and Jay put a finger to her lips. Toyah continued down the slope and stood with her back up against the grey corrugated façade. She waved Jay to join her, then held up a hand for her to wait as she pressed her face against the building and peered through a crack. From the building came a deep humming sound.

'What is it?' asked Jay, edging to get a look through the crack.

Toyah moved out of her way so they could both look. 'I think it's a power plant?'

Around the edge, on the inside of the warehouse, was a concrete walkway about three feet wide. Beyond that, a hole opened up in the earth, stretching down as far as Jay could see. The hum they could hear was coming from the hole. 'I can't see anyone,' Jay said.

'There,' Toyah said, nodding towards the other side of the building. Several people worked on a piece of equipment, while two more with guns patrolled. 'And there.'

Toyah pointed up at a platform constructed above the hole. Two guards paced the length of the walkway, both carrying guns.

'Just two,' said Jay. She stepped away from the crack to see that Toyah had already wandered off. She was looking up at a metal staircase that led to a door halfway up the side of the building. She waved for Jay to join her as she began climbing the steps.

At the top, the door led to the walkway that the two guards were using to watch over the facility. 'Guards,' said Toyah. 'They're not Readers.'

Jay nodded. 'Are we ready?'

Toyah flung open the door and strode directly towards the two guards. Jay had no choice; she followed. The guards turned and raised their guns, but Toyah's energy was already powering towards them. Jay put a hand on Toyah's shoulder, the touch helping her to amplify Toyah's attack. Together, they entered the minds of the two guards. Jay read their fear and confusion as they fought to raise their guns.

The guns clattered to the floor, and both guards put their hands to the sides of their heads. Jay broke off her energy, leaving Toyah to manage the guards, who offered no resistance.

Jay looked down over the elevated platform. So far, they were undetected. The deep humming sound pulsed in waves, creating vibrations in the air. The hole was black, as if the light itself was being pulled in and swallowed up. The strength of power in the building was palpable. This was the sink-room, far more powerful than the sink-room the Readers had used in her homeland.

Her head pounding and heart racing, Jay looked back at Toyah, transfixed on the two men writhing on the floor at her feet. She was in a trance, focused on digging into the minds of the guards as their life force seeped away.

'Toyah!' Jay shouted, while sending a disruption to Toyah's energy flow, enough to break her concentration. She turned to Jay, allowing her to pull her away from the two guards.

'They're not Readers!' Jay said. 'And look. Something's moving down there.' Beneath them, a machine rotated like a fairground ride, sending waves of power and glimmers of light with each rotation.

'Is that a control panel?' Toyah pointed to a panel on the wall of the building at the other end of the walkway. Behind the panel door, a switchboard stared back at her with a series of buttons and levers. Toyah skimmed a finger over the labels on each control and then pulled down a lever with a clunk. Lights powered on around the crater below them. The rotating machine came into view. It was like a giant waltzer. Three arms with grey chunks of metal at the end rotated at speed. With each rotation, a spark emitted from its centre and a wave of vibrations expanded through the air.

Jay's skin turned cold. A bitter, metallic taste seeped into the back of her mouth. With each pulse of energy, her eyes lost focus, as if the whole of the earth vibrated for a moment. *This is their mega sink-room or whatever they call it*, she thought to herself. 'This is their source,' she said aloud.

Toyah came back to her side.

'It's like a tap into the core. Like the one we destroyed back home, but bigger.' Jay was no longer sure that they'd destroyed the source of dark power in her homeland. Yes, they destroyed the buildings that housed the sink-room, but if the power came from a connection to the core, then it was possible that the connection remained. The strength of the dark power that emanated from the hole below them was undeniable. This was a force of power they'd not encountered before.

The pulsing energy churned Jay's stomach. Her legs wobbled. 'We need to get out of here,' she said, staggering back towards the door at the end of the walkway. She felt Readers. The darkness closed around her from all sides. Readers whispering inside her head. The pulsing energy from the core made the walls of the building quiver like a hologram, an illusion. She dropped to her knees, no longer able to hold herself up against the weight of the darkness, and slid to the floor, the cold metal grating hard against her face.

Toyah's touch energised her. She opened her eyes and dragged herself to a sitting position. 'I'm OK.'

'What happened?' asked Toyah.

'Just keep a hold on my hands for a minute,' Jay said, looking into Toyah's eyes and trying to understand what was happening to her. She returned her gaze and took both of her hands, squeezing tight and allowing their energy to combine.

Jay opened to the energy and allowed Toyah to help her to stand. She rubbed her eyes and shook her head to clear the fog in her mind.

'I can feel Readers,' she said. 'Not like just a few, but hundreds, thousands.'

'That's not possible,' said Toyah.

'I know.' Jay looked down at the machine, the channel to the darkness. 'Atta,' Jay said, locking eyes with Toyah. 'This power of the Dark. It must be Atta.'

Before her eyes, Toyah seemed to quiver in the energy from below. A dark stream of mist swirled around Toyah's head and the walkway beneath their feet shifted. They stumbled, breaking their grip on each other and reaching for the handrail. The sound in the warehouse changed, as if they'd been submerged in a thick liquid. As Toyah reached for the railing, it moved away from her, down into the depths below, Toyah following it, a muffled scream escaping her lips as she went.

Jay remained standing on the edge of a broken walkway, reaching out as her friend slipped further away and into free fall. The section of walkway that had held Toyah plummeted towards the hole in the ground. She watched helplessly as Toyah faded into the darkness at the edge of the hole. She landed heavily in the dirt, unmoving. Jay's heart pounded in her ears. She screamed Toyah's name and stepped towards the edge of the broken walkway.

'Not sensible,' said a deep, smooth voice. A man stood a few feet away, a vision in black clothing with pale features and white hair, like a ghost. Jay was paralysed in his presence. He exuded immense power, an aura that flowed with the energy of the darkness, as if Readers floated from him, surrounded him, were part of him.

'Help her,' Jay said, looking over the railing into the hole below, the only words she could formulate. The man glanced over the edge as if he didn't know what Jay was talking about.

'I'd like to thank you,' he said, his voice authoritative, tone silky. Jay kept her eyes on him but her senses reached for Toyah. She found her. She was still alive.

The man stepped closer, peering into Jay.

'Who are you?' asked Jay.

'You know who I am. I can see that you know. I knew you'd come. We are connected now. Thank you for that.'

'Atta...' Jay said under her breath. 'What do you mean?'

She edged away from him, feeling his energy, her heels edging over the end of the broken walkway.

'You opened the channel. I knew you would. You are so very predictable. We connected, and now it is just a matter of time.'

'You have no power over my homeland.'

Atta laughed. 'We will see.' He motioned towards the hole beneath them. 'We have the means to open the earth to the core. *This* brings power in a way you wouldn't understand.'

Jay turned to look into the abyss, scanning for signs of Toyah.

'There's someone I want you to meet,' Atta said, and without another word, turned back to the door.

Jay followed without conscious thought. She was drawn to him as if connected with a length of rope. He passed through the door and down the steps to the outside of the building. The sound of the rotating power machine and its pulsating waves of energy at last dampened behind the closed door as Jay reached the ground.

He led her to the building on the periphery of the abandoned reservoir crater – the building guarded by Readers who parted like curtains as Atta approached, allowing him a wide berth as he flowed into the building, Jay close behind.

Atta's presence dominated as he entered the room, the power of the darkness pushing others back against the walls.

There was a woman, her face drawn, smooth brown skin scratched and bruised, her eyes with a look of someone lost. She felt no power flow from her, only a life-force weakened to the point of extinction. As she looked up at Jay, she saw the red, angry scar on the side of her face, the characteristic marking, like a tick mark from beneath the chin up to the temple – a confirmation of her reduction.

As their eyes met, the woman seemed to deflate further, as if her only hope had finally been extinguished. 'You shouldn't be here,' she said, struggling to release the words. She lowered her eyes.

Jay looked at Atta, a smile on his face. 'Here we are,' he said to the woman. 'This is the best of the best,' he motioned at Jay. 'The ultimate power of the Given, right here in this room.' He laughed. Jay's fear turned to anger, and she took a deep breath, searching for her inner power to deflect the control of Atta. She felt a momentary release, like she'd shaken herself from his grip. She searched for life in the ground to connect and strengthen her power. She scanned for Toyah to reinforce her strength. Then a wave of darkness slammed her into the wall and she slumped to the floor, Atta's energy gripping her around the throat and squeezing life from her.

He stood above her, a few feet away, his eyes flitting between her and the woman behind the bars of the cell. Jay's lungs emptied and she gasped for breath. The woman shrank to the floor as Atta turned his attention to her from Jay.

'Leave her,' pleaded Jay. The woman's arm flopped to her side and Jay saw the inside of her wrist. She was the Island's level "C".

The woman grew smaller by the second. Jay tried to scream, to push out at Atta's control over her body. The more she tried, the heavier her limbs became. The C made no sound as she disintegrated into the soil, her body becoming nothing but a pile of ashes, blackened by the energy flowing from Atta.

Jay felt Atta's grip loosen, and she flopped further to the

floor, as if his power had been physically holding her up. She tried to open her eyes but couldn't prise open her eyelids.

Nearby, the woman was dead.

She felt Atta's presence as he approached and crouched next to her. She felt his breath on her face, warm with bitterness. He whispered in her ear. 'Who do you think you are, Jay?'

A sound distracted Atta for a moment. Readers entered the room, only to rock back on their heels when faced with Atta's energy. Atta stood. 'What is it?'

'The electro source has stopped turning. We're investigating.'

Atta marched towards the door. 'Watch her. If she stirs, kill her.'

Toyah, thought Jay, desperately hoping that Toyah was already safely away. She turned to look at her guards, considering whether she'd be able to draw enough power to get away from them.

TOYAH WATCHED the rotating machine slow and grind to a halt. The third boulder she'd pushed from the lip of the crater had wedged in the central core, breaking in two and settling to jam the mechanism.

She turned and scanned the inside of the vast warehouse for signs of movement. Nothing yet, but she guessed there'd be Readers all over her soon enough. Moving towards the back wall, she ducked behind a spoil heap, out of the line of sight from the remains of the walkways above.

She could feel the power of Atta, but had no sense of where Jay had gone. Atta's energy was everywhere, as if he were part of everything around her – the walls of the warehouse, the sink-room machine, the earth, and the very air that she breathed. She had to concentrate on shielding from him. He was looking for her.

Toyah was not easily shaken by Readers. She'd seen worse. Since her epic journey to the Interland with her little brother, Pinto, back when she was just a kid, she'd developed a resilience to the paralysing effects of fear. The responsibility for someone else, someone more vulnerable than yourself, has some kind of transformational effect on your ability to shrug off a threat to your own safety. She looked around the vast building, the roof hundreds of feet above her. The place nipped at the ankles of her confidence like nothing had since before the Interland. The pull of the darkness was draining.

She leaned up against the wall of the warehouse. People, only some of them Readers, moved above her head on the walkway, entering the building from the staircases at either end and then exiting once more when they saw that the route was blocked – the walkway collapsed over its central section. Over the far side of the building, more people entered at ground level, edging towards the sink machine, guns raised. A flash of an image passed inside her head and she knew Atta was coming for her. *I need to get out*, she thought to herself. *Jay will find me.*

Readers pored over the sink-machine. A loud clunk vibrated the ground. Another, and the machine kicked into life, the three arms spinning once again. Toyah immediately felt the strengthening waves of darkness.

She turned to the wall of the warehouse and dug her fingers behind a loose piece of corrugated metalwork. She prised open the metal panel, grunting as she gave a final push, creating a gap big enough to squeeze through.

Outside, the southern slope rose at a steep gradient. She took a last look along the side of the warehouse. No one in sight. She began the climb.

* * *

ATTA HAD LEFT THE ROOM, but his presence remained. He was a source of energy for the rest of them. The two Readers left to guard her seemed more powerful than others. They guarded knowing that Atta was there with power to draw upon.

A pain shot through Jay's temples like a stab of a knife, then withdrew. 'Don't even think it,' the nearest Reader said, his eyes piercing.

Jay put up her shield, the version that appeared invisible to others who might attempt to read her. She gave herself a little space to think.

Angie came into her head, her smiling face a vision of light amongst the darkness of her captivity. *What are you doing here?* Jay said without speaking. Angie's smile broadened. *I don't know*, she replied. With her presence came a confidence and energy. Angie seemed to be able to enter her mind and work with her, provide avenues of thought and energy that weren't available to her alone.

'Together,' Jay muttered under her breath. The Readers turned to her, but she had already launched her energy at them. She attacked with all her power, plus Angie's support. The Readers went down, both of them working hard to raise their inner shields. But Jay was too quick for them. She stood, drew more power from beneath her feet and the weight of the hills. The Readers squirmed. She stepped back towards the door, continuing her attack until they lay unmoving.

She breathed heavily, taking a moment to recharge a little. She focused her energy on Toyah and found her, making her escape to the hills. Jay breathed easier. She put up her shield with all her remaining energy, flung open the door and ran, the adrenaline masking the pain in her foot.

At the crest of the hill, she spotted Toyah, crouched amongst the rocks. 'You're a sight,' Toyah said as Jay approached. 'What happened?'

'Later,' Jay said. 'Let's get some distance between us and this place.' She pointed to the south, not to the pathway on which they'd come, but to the hills. 'That way.'

Toyah nodded.

'Shield,' said Jay, looking back down towards the buildings, immediately sensing Atta. 'As much as you can. We need to get a clean break.'

PART II

13

On the edge of a barren slope, worn out from what felt like hours walking through the difficult terrain of the southern hills, Jay flopped to the floor in exhaustion, her foot aching. Toyah sank down next to her. 'There,' she said, pointing towards a string of farm buildings in the valley before them. 'We can rest there.'

'What about the people who live there?' Jay pulled off her shoe and peeled back her sock to inspect her bad foot.

Toyah scanned the valley. 'No Readers,' she said.

Jay couldn't scan. The energy from Atta's lair, although weakened with distance, confused the signals she felt from her own energy, and shook her confidence in reading the signs.

'No people either, by the looks of it,' said Toyah, 'and we have to rest somewhere.'

There was a nip in the air. The sun had dipped in the sky. The alternative to risking the farmhouse was camping in the hills. They'd be up higher and able to see all the incoming routes.

Toyah stood, stretching out her shoulders. 'You OK?'

'Fine,' Jay said. 'Let's do it.' Her desperate thirst clinched the deal. She pulled her shoe back on and stood, tentatively putting weight back on her foot. Toyah steadied her, but Jay refused the hand. Toyah seemed older suddenly. In control. Jay turned to the pathway.

At the foot of the slope, Jay led Toyah around the back of the farmhouse, along the fence line, careful to remain out of sight of the windows of the building. The bushes and shrubs in the yard had taken over every available space. Dust clung to the glass in the windows. The house had been empty for weeks, but not months. The back door was ajar, hanging from a single hinge. Jay looked up at the old building and felt for its owners, driven out of their beautiful home nestled in the valley between the hills, now stuck between the City and the rats' nest of the Readers' lair.

Inside, the house was tidy, as if someone had been careful to leave it ready for their return. The ground floor was open-plan, criss-crossed wooden beams holding up an imperfect ceiling, sagging from years of structural effort. In the kitchen, a layer of dust covered the surfaces. Jay held her breath and turned on the tap. Cold water flowed immediately, and she breathed again before leaning down to drink until she had to gasp for breath, then took some more. She wiped her mouth and moved aside for Toyah to fill a glass from the tap.

She opened each of the kitchen cupboards. 'Well stocked,' she said. There were tins, pasta, rice. She checked a loaf of bread on the worktop, knocking it against the side to show how stale it was. A turn of the dial on the hob proved that they had gas. She pushed the ignitor switch and smiled at the sound of the rush, hiss and whoosh as the gas caught and the girls knew they'd be able to eat well that evening.

* * *

THEY SETTLED IN THE LOUNGE, spread across the two sofas with bedding brought from upstairs. With no electricity, their only light came from the few candles that Toyah had retrieved from the drawers in the dining room. The silent television on the wall hung like a blacked-out window.

Full from their meal, Jay sank deep into the sofa, her mind taunted by images of Atta. She couldn't get a hold of what he was, or how they would deal with him.

'I can read that expression,' Toyah said. 'Don't tell me, *we're gonna need a bigger boat...*'

Jay nodded. Toyah was too close to the truth for Jay to laugh. The words of Atta nagged in the back of her head: *Who do you think you are...?* It was as if he couldn't believe that she'd even have the gall to confront him.

'He said something to me,' Jay said. 'He said I'd opened a channel. Like I opened the gate to our land, Island 8.'

'What *gate*?' asked Toyah. 'They can't cross over to Island 8. There's no sink-room.'

Jay rubbed her temples, searching her mind for the snippets she'd read in the bookshop – the history of the powers, and the myth of Atta. She wished Alf was there to help her piece it together. She tried to picture Atta. He had a kind of glow about him, like a dark aura. And he seemed to be fluid, his outline continually changing, like a trick of the light.

'What is he?' asked Toyah, reading Jay's thoughts. 'A Reader?'

'No,' said Jay. 'It's difficult to explain. I think he's a kind of manifestation of the energy of the Readers. But he only comes to being when a critical mass occurs.'

'Critical mass?' Toyah repeated, looking confused.

'When the numbers of Readers gets to a point, the

energy balance tips in the darkness's favour...' Jay trailed off, unsure of her own words. 'My understanding of this is vague in the extreme. This imbalance hasn't happened before as far as we can tell, and for it to happen so quickly is unlikely.'

'We dealt with Hinton, and we can deal with him,' said Toyah.

Toyah's words comforted Jay, but she missed the calming presence of Stitch and the fearless confidence of Cassie. When the three of them were together, it was like they had an impenetrable shield, like they could do anything. The darkness of Atta was deeper, more profound than the anomaly that was Hinton. 'We need to get back to the source so we can head home. We need to regroup and tell the others.'

* * *

JAY TURNED over on the sofa and looked at her watch - nearly an hour since Toyah had dropped off and still she couldn't sleep. Three out of the four candles continued to burn, casting ominous, moving shadows across the walls and ceiling. Electricity fizzed inside her head.

She turned onto her back and stared up at the ceiling. The flowing shadows above her head moved and merged, continually changing shape. The darkness formed waves that flowed between the walls, receding for a moment, then raging as the candles flickered. Her mind played with the shapes, creating images from their outlines, stories from their movement.

She thought of Angie, probably lying just like her, on her back, motionless. She closed her eyes and tried to empty her mind. Her breathing steadied and as soon as she had relaxed, whispers came.

These whispers were of a different tone and feeling to those back home. They whirled around her head, more subdued, less urgent. The sense they brought was one of defeat. Inside the whispers, Angie came back to her. It was her voice that came through, her colours that shimmered behind Jay's eyes. Her oranges and red hues were among the warmest Jay had ever seen. Angie's presence took Jay deeper into the power, further into her subconscious. She was connected.

A flash of white light.

Jay was on the shore of Island 7. Darkness pervaded. The water was thick with swirls of black, the tree charred, the sand mottled with black grains. She looked over to Island 8 , her homeland, to see Angie standing on the shore, her body rigid as she gazed over the water towards Jay.

'I'm here too,' Angie called, excitement in her tone.

Jay staggered towards the shore, her head pounding. She squinted in the light. 'What's happening?'

Angie shrugged. 'This is the place you told me about. You brought me here.'

'I don't know how...'

'It doesn't matter,' said Angie. 'This is amazing.'

'Where are you really?' Jay asked.

'I don't know,' said Angie, thinking. 'In hospital. Still under. They're bringing me around tomorrow, I think. I don't know how I know that.'

'You're OK?' asked Jay.

'I reckon,' Angie smiled. 'Where are *you*?'

Jay looked around her. 'In some farmhouse, on our way back home.'

'Toyah is with you,' Angie said, a statement, not a question.

Jay nodded. The white light intensified and Jay sensed they had no time. Whether it was Jay's subconscious or Angie's, she couldn't tell, but either way, they were about to be thrust back into their physical worlds.

'Hurry home,' said Angie.

'We're coming,' said Jay, her words swallowed as the light pierced the Island world and all turned white.

14

When Jay woke again, it was pitch black, and it took a moment for her to remember where she was. The candles had burned themselves out and the smell of hot wax tickled her nose. Toyah snored lightly.

A noise. A thump from outside, like the closing of a gate on its sprung hinge. Jay's eyes widened; she didn't dare to move in the dark, there wasn't even a glint of light to dilute the madness that comes with pitch black.

As her eyes adjusted, she could just about make out the lighter shade of black that was the blind at the window. She slipped off the sofa, nudging into Toyah's legs as she sloped onto the floor, arresting her snoring for just a moment. She crawled around to the window and pulled herself up to a crouching position. She edged the blind back to see over the yard.

People.

Jay fell back into the room, then lifted herself once more to look through the blind. By the light of the moon, there were six people stalking through the yard towards the house, military-style, dressed in black. Every one of them carrying a rifle.

'Hey!' Jay shook Toyah.

She grunted, unmoving for a moment, before launching into action. Jay turned on a torch and frantically packed her rucksack.

'Readers?' asked Toyah.

'Yes,' Jay whispered. Toyah remained calm, systematically packing her things away and pulling on her shoes like there was no need to hurry. As Jay slung her bag onto her back, Toyah motioned for her to follow as she led the way to the internal door that connected through to the garage.

'How did you know...' Jay started, but Toyah put a finger to her lips and motioned towards the two vehicles – one a Land Rover, the other an open-back truck.

Jay moved towards the Land Rover, jumping into the front seat. Toyah went to the truck. Jay searched for keys but found nothing in the ignition, nothing above the sun visor.

She turned to look for Toyah, but the truck was empty. A moment later, Toyah appeared in the open doorway to the house. She stepped down onto the garage floor and closed the door behind her. A finger to her lips, she flung her bag into the open-back truck and held up a set of keys, then jumped back into the front seat.

Jay stepped out of the Land Rover and unclipped the garage door, opening it a crack and quickly closing it again. She shook her head and climbed into the truck next to Toyah. 'We'll have to make a run for it.'

Jay sensed Readers at the door between the house and the garage. She reached out and held onto Toyah's arm to strengthen her connection with the power, then pushed into the minds of the Readers behind the door to confuse and delay them. Toyah started the engine. It spluttered for a moment and kicked into life. Black smoke belched from the exhaust. The door flung open. Toyah slammed the truck into gear and launched the truck at the garage door, slamming it back on its hinges.

Out front, three vehicles stood in the yard, Readers on guard. Toyah slid the truck past the vehicles and onto the main road that led up into the hills. Jay looked into the eyes of the first Reader through the door of the garage as he ran towards the truck. In the wing mirror, she saw the strength of his power in his eyes, felt it seep into her consciousness as he tried to infiltrate her. He reached for her, but was not quick enough. Toyah accelerated away as the Readers rallied around their vehicles and Jay knew they would catch them up before long.

'You feel that?' Jay said to Toyah, still looking back towards the Reader who chased them. 'He was strong.'

'Evil, I'd say,' said Toyah, sliding the truck around a sharp bend in the dirt roadway.

'I haven't felt a Reader that strong since...'

'Hinton?' said Toyah.

'Hinton wasn't a Reader. Marcus.' Marcus had been the strongest of the Readers, the only level eight Jay had come across.

'Level eight,' said Toyah, a sideways glance at Jay.

JAY LEANED back in the truck's cab, watching in the wing mirror through the dust and the darkness for any signs of Readers. The disappearing road glinted in the moonlight. She rubbed her eyes. They must have had little more than a couple of hours' sleep.

The road narrowed as they stretched deeper into the

hills. Toyah slowed to negotiate the bends and avoid the steepening drop on both sides. Jay looked out over the edge and shuffled closer to the middle of the truck as if to keep the centre of gravity away from the steep drop. They passed over a wooden bridge and Jay felt the supports flex. 'Stop!' She shook Toyah's arm, and she slammed on the brakes. The truck screeched to a halt just past the bridge. Jay jumped out. 'Come!' she shouted.

Toyah followed her back to the wooden bridge where she had already side-stepped down the embankment and was pushing her body weight into one of the wooden bridge piers. 'Help me out here!'

Toyah joined her, and the wooden strut moved under their weight. A few more shoves and the strut moved again, its joint with the bridge slipping. 'It's moving,' said Toyah.

In the distance, headlights approached. Three vehicles. 'Keep going. One more,' said Jay.

With a last shove, the bridge pier creaked and gave way, its base sliding down the slope and into the valley. The bridge deck remained suspended. 'It's not falling,' said Toyah.

'But it won't hold their weight,' said Jay.

They returned to the truck just as the Readers' vehicles came into view around the corner.

Toyah slammed the truck into gear.

'Wait,' said Jay, looking out of her open window as the Readers' Land Rovers approached.

As they watched, the truck engine idling, the front Land Rover stopped just the other side of the bridge. 'Shield,' said Jay. 'Don't let them read you.' A moment later, the convoy continued onto the bridge.

The first vehicle was almost halfway across, with no obvious movement of the deck. Jay and Toyah remained calm. As the second vehicle rolled onto the bridge deck, the road surface twisted violently, then dropped three feet. Both vehicles remained upright on the deck. Both stopped. The front Land Rover then continued, picking up speed, but the bridge deck disappeared from beneath its wheels and it plummeted the short drop to the slope of the valley. Jay craned her neck to see as the Land Rover slid down the bank and onto its side. The second Land Rover had reversed off the bridge. 'One down,' said Jay.

'And the other two are not getting through here,' added Toyah.

Jay looked over at Toyah and they smiled. She put the truck into gear and they pushed on deeper into the hills.

Sunrise crept up through the valleys, the light breaking the darkness and bringing a little optimism after their minor victory.

Through the hills, they skirted the southern edge of the City for a few miles before they dared turn towards the centre. The peace and safety of the hills was difficult to give up for what would surely be a hard journey through the City and back to the source.

As soon as the truck crossed the boundary into the City, Jay felt it. A sense of the power of the Given, not of the source, but of someone with strong Given power. The Island Seven 8C was close.

15

'Take a left here,' Jay said. Toyah frowned, but maybe for the first time since the Interland, did what Jay asked.

'Where are we going? The source is on the north side.'

'Head that way.' Jay pointed in the direction of the energy.

Toyah parked the truck on the side of a street. Across the road, a row of townhouses stretched several storeys above street level. 'Can you feel it?' Jay asked Toyah.

'Nothing,' said Toyah, to Jay's surprise. 'I'm getting no power from this place.'

But Jay needed to know more. They stepped out of the truck and the cool, early morning breeze felt good on her face. They stood shaded from the sun beneath the branches of a chestnut tree, its pink blossom scattered over the ground across the street from the townhouse. The black door with the number 42 had a small window in the top section. A note pinned to the glass on the inside said something in a language Jay couldn't translate. Meanwhile, their presence was already attracting attention from passers-by. 'Let's check it out,' said Jay.

'Wait,' said Toyah, looking uncharacteristically nervous. She looked up into the branches of the tree above their heads and drew a deep breath. 'Are you sure?'

Jay nodded. 'I feel powerful energy here.'

'It's too dangerous. And we don't even know how much power we have, how well the source is functioning here,' said Toyah.

Jay moved around to the rear of the tree, out of the main path of pedestrians, and placed her hand on its trunk. She held out a hand to Toyah. In their connected energy, they travelled into the earth's crust, through the tree and into the parched topsoil and deeper, searching, exploring. They hit groundwater. Within it, life thrived, hundreds of feet below the surface. Jay felt its energy. It fed her power, and she glowed with it. She and Toyah opened their eyes, and the whispers swirled around their heads as they leaned against the tree. The power flowed between her and Jay through their joined hands. Jay's energy reciprocated that of Toyah, combining with the energy from below.

The girls blinked in surprise. 'There *is* power here,' Jay said. 'But it's a long way down and we'll have to dig deep if we are to use its full force.'

Together they turned to face the street and stepped out into the road towards the black door.

* * *

THE CURTAIN in the window twitched, and Jay knocked again.

Without warning, the door swung open, and a gun was

thrust into Jay's face. A hand on her shoulder pulled her into the house. 'Get in here,' the man said, without lowering his gun. He slammed the door shut behind them. Jay recognised him immediately as the man they'd met before - the 8C.

'It's me,' said Jay.

The man lowered his gun, but kept it pointed in their direction as he scrutinised Jay, recognition in his expression. She peered into him but he was closed down tight. 'Jay?' he said.

Jay nodded.

'How did you find me? What are you doing here?' He lowered his gun.

'Through the source.'

The 8C shook his head and moved to the door, peering through the spyhole to check for anyone who might have followed. He muttered to himself - something about sensing her presence but not believing she'd be so stupid as to come here.

'How long's it been like this? Readers in control?' asked Jay.

'Months. What planet you from?'

'You know where we are from,' Jay said, keeping her tone friendly, reassuring.

The 8C continued to hold his gun. Jay sensed his confusion, his fear, and desperation. At last, his defences lowered a little and Jay reached into his mind and saw his name, *Tiago*. 'You're Tiago?'

Tiago nodded. He lowered his gun and clicked on the safety.

'You shouldn't be here,' he said to Jay. Then, with a little reluctance, he ushered them through and into a wide, open-plan ground floor room that formed a kitchen-dining area.

Jay heard a noise and looked towards the stairs, sensing others in the house.

'Come,' he shouted to his family. 'It's safe.' He turned to Jay, 'Sit, here,' motioning towards a chair at the table.

'It's OK...' Jay started, but Tiago cut her off.

'Sit. I bring you water. You need food. You must eat.'

'We just...' Jay tried again, but Tiago interrupted once more.

'Sit!' he blurted, then raised his hands in apology. 'Please.' Jay and Toyah stole a glance and then took a seat. Toyah edged back from the table, looking over her shoulder as if planning her exit.

Two little feet appeared on the stairs, followed by the rest of a little girl, hand in hand with a woman Jay assumed was her mother. The mother held another girl in her arms. All three stared at the travellers, nervous of their intentions. 'Come,' said Tiago, ushering them into the room. 'This is my wife, Thabisa. And my children, Enzo, and Faith. My name is Tiago, but you know that already. We are happy that you are here. Sorry for the gun.' His words were welcoming, but he remained guarded.

Jay looked over at the two little girls. 'I'm Jay, and this is Toyah.' The older of the two girls smiled, the younger turned her head into her mother's shoulder.

'Can I see?' Tiago said as he placed two glasses of water on the table for Jay and Toyah. He looked at Jay's wrist. He turned his arm to show his "8C". Jay drew back her sleeve and smiled. Tiago sighed, as if relieved. To Toyah, 'But you are not the connection, no? The "C"?' Toyah shook her head.

'Stitch is back home,' said Jay.

'I would have liked to meet him. He has some healer in him, no?'

Jay nodded, surprised that Tiago knew this. 'Like my wife, Thabisa here.' Thabisa looked away, embarrassed.

'Where are we?' said Jay. 'I mean, what *country* are we in?'

Tiago reached for Jay's hand and led her to the window. 'See there?' He pointed into the distance where the low-lying mist had cleared and the outline of the mountain range was visible. Jay recognised the distinctive shape. The central section was flat, as if the peak had been sliced away. The wide expanse was flanked by narrower peaks on either side, like sentries watching over her. The slopes were a dark red colour in the sun's glare through the mist. 'This is *Kaap-stown*,' Tiago said. 'You are in South Africa.'

* * *

THEY GATHERED around the table to eat, squeezed up against each other as Tiago and Thabisa prepared the food. Enzo was eight years old, and Faith just three. The two girls sat quietly, nudging each other and occasionally conversing in Afrikaans, giggling.

Jay and Toyah had hardly spoken since they walked through the door of Tiago's family home. Jay was a little shell-shocked at the fact they'd travelled through the source in the South Downs of England, through to the source of Island 7, in South Africa. She needed to focus, to straighten her thoughts.

'Tell me,' said Tiago, placing a bowl of stew in the middle of the table. The smell of the spiced, cooked food filled the room. 'I thought the source was destroyed, so how did you move?'

Jay shook her head. 'The power is still there. As long as the three sources combine, then the power will come.' Jay reached down to rub her foot. She'd pushed the pain to the back of her consciousness, but now they were resting properly, the pain was again intense. 'I caught my foot in the swirls of darkness between the shores. It's still painful.'

'Let me look at it later.' Tiago smiled, dishing out the food. He exchanged a glance with Thabisa.

'Thank you,' said Jay.

'I have not felt safe to visit the destroyed building where the power resided,' said Tiago. 'We dare not leave this house. Atta's people are everywhere, not just his Readers, but his informants. The entire City works for Atta.'

'But you are so close to the source here,' said Toyah.

'It's dangerous. The source is in the City's heart. My level "C" was taken months ago. No-one has seen her. She is probably a Reader by now.'

'They can't force transformation,' said Toyah, more a question than a statement.

'They are strong persuaders,' said Tiago.

'I saw her,' said Jay, lowering her gaze but opening her mind. Tiago stopped eating and turned to glance at his wife.

Tiago put down his knife and fork. 'She is gone?'

Jay nodded.

'Atta?'

Jay nodded again. 'He killed her in front of me. I couldn't help her, I'm so sorry…'

Tiago raised a hand to stop Jay from continuing. 'I knew this. I felt her loss just yesterday. She has grown weaker over the months. Some weeks ago, I thought she had died, as I no longer felt her pain. I was relieved that she was no longer suffering. But she was still alive?'

'Until yesterday,' Jay said.

'I should have done more.'

'What could you do?' Thabisa spat the words. 'What good is it to die for nothing. What help would you be to the Given?'

Tiago stood and walked from the room, returning a moment later with a bottle of something that looked like a dark wine, or port. He filled four shot glasses and raised one to make a toast. 'To my connection. To Annika.'

Tiago swallowed his drink in one. Jay and Toyah followed Tiago's lead. 'To Annika,' said Jay.

'To Annika,' said Thabisa.

* * *

TOYAH AND ENZO made faces at each other across the table. Enzo giggled. 'You look older than eight. You're so tall,' said Toyah.

Enzo smiled coyly. 'I am nearly nine,' she said.

'You speak English well,' said Toyah. Enzo nodded.

'English is the strongest second language here,' said Tiago. 'They learn at school. Enzo is top of her class, right Enzo?' She nodded again, pride brimming over at her dad's words.

Faith had curled in Thabisa's lap, silently observing their guests with a thumb in her mouth. Jay sensed a twinkle of power in the little one. Thabisa's expression was stern, reserved. She was uncomfortable having strangers in her house, especially strangers who might bring trouble. She had been through enough conflict, and had no appetite for more. Her focus was on her daughters and their survival. The Readers would have torn through the City without compassion. After they had eaten, Jay turned to Tiago: 'What happened here?'

Tiago's expression darkened. He caught Thabisa's eye,

and they silently agreed that she'd take the children upstairs.

Tiago began, speaking slowly at first. 'There were always Readers, we knew that. They had a sink-room east of the City, and there were fights. But the Given were strong here. The source was at the centre of the Mother City. The connections between the heart of our great City and the surrounding environment were strong – the strongest. The Readers were small in number and small in power compared to the Given.'

Toyah said, 'Why did the Given not destroy the sink-room?'

'We did,' said Tiago. 'But as we only learned later, you cannot destroy the link to the core. You can take away what is on the surface, but underneath remains.'

Toyah and Jay exchanged a look that flickered with fear.

'We should have been in control, but we made mistakes,' Tiago said. 'You saw the mountains. The energy in these living mountains was unparalleled. Then there is the ocean. Our City is in an epicentre of energy between mountains and ocean. The Given should have been impenetrable here.' He shook his head, his eyes on his shoes, a pair of faded trainers.

Tiago pointed through the window towards the hills. 'Look.' Jay searched the horizon. The mountains, although shaded by dark clouds, seemed to shine. They were a dark red, almost black. Tiago shook his hand at the window, urging his guests to see what he saw. 'The flora is depleted. The trees are wilting. The shrub-land, the fynbos, are grey.'

'But you survived,' Jay said.

Tiago looked up. 'Some of us remain. But only because we know how to evade their scanners. They search for us, but we have become good at hiding. There are materials in these walls that help us to shield.'

Jay looked at the walls and frowned. 'But I was drawn here,' she said.

Tiago nodded. 'I'm hoping that it is because we are the same. A particular connection?' He brushed his hand over the marking on his wrist.

'You can fight back. Connect with the Given who remain?'

'There are too many Readers, and there is Atta.' Tiago shifted in his seat, agitated. 'It's not a fair fight anymore. We've already lost...' His words trailed off. Jay waited. 'We have a resistance. It is small, but it could grow.' He looked again at Jay and she saw a glint in his eye, a determination. 'Give me your hand.'

Jay eyed his outstretched hand, understanding that he intended to impart information, to show Jay what they'd been through. 'You too,' Tiago said, looking at Toyah. Jay reached to hold on to Toyah's hand and the three of them connected in a ring.

Flashes of images embedded in their subconscious. The Readers had come in night purges, taking Given or suspected Given without warning and without confirmation of powers. None had returned.

Jay broke the chain and rocked back in her seat. Toyah slipped off her chair and onto the floor in a daze. Tiago went to her, helping her up. Jay reeled as the information percolated through her conscious mind. The darkness had come over the hills to the mountain peaks and then down into the City. In its wake, the Given were rounded up. Women and children dragged from their houses in the middle of the night and taken to camps to the east. Readers walked freely through the City. Those without power were left alone, unless they resisted or harboured the Given - then they were killed. As the number of Given taken grew, so did the number of Readers.

Toyah stirred. Tiago helped her back on to her seat and poured her some water. She looked at Jay, wide eyed and scared.

'How did Atta come here?' asked Jay.

'We don't know if he came into power once the balance tipped, or if he found a way to move here from Island 6.'

'How many in the resistance?' Jay asked.

Tiago shook his head. 'Not enough. With each purge, we become weaker. Some have left the City to settle in the hills, seeking places away from where the Readers patrol.'

'We saw a checkpoint on the eastern side?'

Tiago nodded. 'Readers control the access into and out of the City from the hills. The eastern road is the only one remaining. It connects the City with the rest of the province. Nothing comes in and out of here except through the eastern checkpoint.' He rested back in his chair and sighed. 'The resistance is on its last legs. The City is no longer safe.'

'We've been to the hills,' croaked Toyah, regaining her composure.

'Atta is there,' added Jay. 'The sink-room is bigger than you can imagine, and the power is immense.'

Tiago lowered his head. 'We thought so. It is now just a matter of time.'

'Come back with us,' said Jay.

Tiago laughed. 'This is my land. These are my people. We are all they have left, the only thing between them and the Readers. We are weakened but not yet defeated. We need help, not asylum.' Tiago shook his head and pulled a packet of cigarettes from his back pocket. He stood, motioning for the others to follow him out back. They stepped out into a small back garden. 'So what's your plan?' he asked Jay.

Jay glanced at Toyah. They had no plan. 'We need to get back home,' she said.

Tiago leaned back against the house. 'Rest here tonight. We will top up your supplies. Get you as strong as we can.'

* * *

TOYAH SLEPT, but Jay was restless, the pain in her foot distracting. Out on the landing, she saw light and heard talking coming from downstairs. She limped down to find Tiago and Thabisa at the dining room table, smoking. Tiago quickly stubbed out his cigarette. 'Ah, I thought you were one of the kids,' he said. 'I need to quit this.'

Thabisa smiled at Jay and nodded to a chair. Jay stumbled and sat, taking the weight off her foot. Tiago looked concerned. 'It's bad?'

'It comes and goes.'

Thabisa turned to Jay. 'You want me to try something?' She showed the figure "3" on her wrist. 'I've had mixed results, but your power might help me.'

Stitch's healing power, too, had been unreliable. Since he helped to release Sammy from the spreading infection in his leg back at the Interland, he'd had little success, although he understood the mechanisms well, and the rest, Jay was sure, was about self-confidence and belief.

'Let me try,' said Thabisa.

Jay lifted her leg and rested her foot on the chair in front of Thabisa. 'That's nasty,' said Tiago. The skin over the toes and up to the ankle was an angry red colour, like a severe burn. 'How can you walk on that?'

'Close your eyes and relax a moment,' said Thabisa as

she placed her cool hands on either side of Jay's foot. The cold brought a little relief, and Jay relaxed. She breathed deeply. Thabisa's hands slowly warmed, as if taking the heat from Jay's foot. She opened her eyes, half expecting to see a glowing light emanating from Thabisa, but there was nothing. Her eyes were closed and head bowed as she focused on Jay's injury. Tiago watched in silence. Thabisa's hands continued to absorb heat so that Jay's foot became cold. She moved her hands to another position and Jay saw that the redness on her skin beneath Thabisa's fingers had faded. Her foot was stiff, as if frozen. She moved her hands once more before finishing and sitting back in her chair, her eyes remaining closed.

Jay leaned forward to inspect her foot. The redness had almost entirely gone. She rolled her foot around, stretching the ankle. Tiago smiled, pride in his eyes. Jay lifted herself carefully from her chair, naturally avoiding putting weight on her foot. Tentatively, she shifted weight to her vulnerable side. It felt strong. No pain. She looked to Thabisa as she opened her eyes, snapping out of her trance. 'That felt like it went well,' Thabisa said. 'The energy was strong. How is it?'

Jay laughed. 'It's good!'

Tiago laughed too. 'This is progress.'

Jay paced the room, testing her foot. 'It's good,' she said, again. 'Thank you.'

* * *

Toyah navigated the truck through the City without urgency, deciding that inconspicuous was preferable to quick. She chose the back roads to stay out of sight of any Readers who might be patrolling. It was early morning, and the streets were already bustling. People hopeful for fresh bread formed long queues through the buildings. There were more mopeds and motorbikes than cars, weaving in and out of each other, their exhausts spewing smoke.

The warmth and humidity already rose from the streets. It wouldn't be long before the hot South African sun burned through the clouds and scorched their skin. She stretched out her foot, testing for signs of any residual pain, and felt nothing. Thabisa had done a good job.

Toyah sped up around a corner and passed by a police Land Rover. Jay instinctively sank down in the passenger seat of the truck as Toyah maintained speed. The police Land Rover turned off into a side street and Jay breathed again. Toyah eased off the accelerator and took a sequence of turns so they were deep in the back streets of the City centre. They were out of sight, and once again edging slowly towards the demolition site that was once the source of power for the Given in this land.

A little under half an hour later, they parked alongside the perimeter fence that marked the edge of the crater. A thin layer of dust hung in the air above the mangled concrete and steel that was once a high rise building. In the heat hung a smell like the construction site near Jay's home, when they doubled the size of the housing estate in less than six months. Scanning the perimeter, Jay noticed something she'd not seen when they had emerged from the source. There were two huts, one on each side of the site. They were small, just big enough for one or two people to shade from the sun.

'Security?' said Toyah. A man emerged from a hut, leaned up against the security fence, then returned to the shade.

'And there,' Jay said, and pointed towards the other hut.

'They weren't there before,' Toyah said.

A Land Rover pulled up by the one on the south side. Half a dozen people spilled out from the vehicle. 'Readers,' said Toyah. 'Can you feel it?'

Jay nodded, not daring to take her eyes off the group of Readers, one of whom approached the security guard. 'That's him,' said Jay. 'That's the one from back at the farm. He's a level 8.'

'We need to continue to shield,' said Toyah, already moving towards the fence. As Toyah manipulated the fence so they could squeeze through, a second Land Rover appeared on the north side, screeching to a halt at the other security hut. A new group of Readers emerged.

'They're looking for us,' said Toyah, before following Jay through the fence. Their strategy would have to be speed. They scampered down the slope and into the concrete labyrinth.

Toyah led the way as Jay concentrated on shielding as best she could, hoping that the tangle of concrete and metal around them would help to at least confuse any signal to the Readers.

They picked their way through the concrete jungle, following the route back that took them past a vending machine, emptied of its chocolate bars, and the row of cabinets spewing files.

Toyah reached the hole that led down to the basement where the three watercourses converged and was about to lower herself through when they heard a bang.

Readers moved across the concrete beams above their heads. Jay made a signal for Toyah to press on, and she disappeared into the hole. A scatter of dust and debris fell on Jay's head and she shielded, but felt the Readers tapping away at her defences. Their leader, the level 8, was directly above her, his heartbeat, his anger beat in Jay's veins.

She draped her feet over the hole, not taking her eyes off the figures silhouetted against the sky above her head. If they looked down, they might not see her, but would sense her. As these thoughts passed through her mind, the level 8 Reader looked straight at her, catching her eye through the gaps in the tangle of rubble between them. He read her immediately, his blue-eyed gaze penetrating her mind. In a moment, he knew where both she and Toyah were – and how close they were to the source.

Jay slipped through the hole and began running. She was moving too fast, her foot slid on a wet surface and she bashed her knee, crying out. She caught up with Toyah just as she manoeuvred herself to hang and then drop to the floor of the basement. 'Get ready,' Jay called.

A shot rang out behind them – the bullet ricocheting off the concrete. A speculative effort by the Readers. Jay landed on the floor of the basement as Toyah rested one hand in the water and held out the other for Jay to connect.

Debris tumbled through the hole in the basement's ceiling.

White light radiated from the middle of the connection between Jay and Toyah.

The black boots of a Reader emerged from above. His legs, then his torso. He dropped to the ground, launched himself at Jay.

White light filled the basement. The Reader fell, and Jay saw his physical form dissolve into the light, his face a picture of agony.

* * *

JAY WOKE WITH A START, recoiling from the image in her mind of the Reader in the basement – his piercing blue eyes dissolving into nothing as the energy of the source overcame him.

She brushed the sand from the side of her face and sat up. The tree to her side was blackened. A coil of darkness stretched up its trunk into the canopy above, where it had already strangled and suffocated the life from its branches. Across the water, Island 8, her home, remained a shining light amongst the darkness of the rest of the Islands.

She took a deep breath and pushed herself to her feet.

Toyah woke.

In the water between the Islands, there was a clear pathway avoiding the swirls of darkness. The two friends exchanged a glance. 'Let's get home,' Jay said, and stepped into the water.

16

The blinding white light that characterised the passage through the source rapidly dissipated as Jay plunged into the water of the Interland pool.

The aftereffects of moving through the source messed with her senses. Disorientated, she struggled in the water, unable to discern which way was up. Her lungs burned. She exhaled forcefully to ease the pressure and pain and saw the surface of the water, an impossible distance away. She kicked her legs and began to rise.

As she neared the light, debris rained down on the pool, the rocks shooting past Jay as she powered toward the surface. As she drew closer, the muffled noises became louder and clearer.

Shouting.

Explosions.

Her head burst through the water and as she gasped for air, a piece of rock glanced off the side of her head, cutting a gash down her cheek. Blood diffused into the water. She cried out, gasping. Her head swam with pain, the water stung her wound. She kicked hard to get back to the surface, her focus on nothing else but getting to the edge of the pool before another rock stopped her for good.

Another explosion.

This time, Jay ducked under the surface as the rocks rained down, dodging the full force of the debris.

She pulled herself into the shallows and finally looked up at the devastation before her. The caves of the Interland had been all but destroyed. There were people, Readers, busying across her field of vision, unaware of her presence. They continued to position explosives. 'Clear!' came a shout from the rock face, then an almighty explosion and a further downpour of rocks.

'Toyah?' Jay whispered under her breath.

A scream rang out from the other side of the pool where Toyah tussled with two Readers. They knocked her to the floor, but she recovered, kicking out as the men approached her once more, this time subduing her. Jay watched, too far away to help. She and Toyah had landed in a completely different world to the one they'd left.

Toyah screamed again. Jay thought about running the perimeter of the pool but knew that too many Readers would see her. She wouldn't be able to fight them all, not injured and alone. Instead, she tucked herself tight to the wall and focused on the two Readers who had Toyah by the arms and were dragging her away. Jay's heart pounded, pumping the anger through her body.

Jay easily entered their minds and began to dig. She closed her eyes, pinpointing her focus. The two men fell to their knees, their hands to the sides of their heads, and Toyah ran, heading for Jay. Jay continued digging into the Readers until she was sure they wouldn't get up again.

The Interland pool was fast becoming a lake as the caves

continued to disintegrate and the ground beneath their feet shook.

Jay felt the power of darkness nipping at her consciousness and turned to see Readers on the side of the lake, facing them. They were joining their power together to infiltrate the minds of Jay and Toyah.

Jay and Toyah stood facing their attackers across the water. They held hands. Jay grit her teeth and together they focused their energy. It was like a torrent through Jay, channelled from the power of the Interland.

The three Readers nearest them took their full force and stumbled back against the rock face. Jay pushed, drawing energy from the ground, and from the water of the lake, the hills, and the source. Vines and tree roots broke free of the rock face and entwined the three Readers, pulling them into the cliff, deeper as Jay opened to the power flowing through her. Their physical forms squeezed into the side of the hill until they were no longer visible.

Jay moved on to the second group of Readers, pushing until they each dropped to their knees in the shallows of the lake. They sank deeper as Jay summoned the full power of the environment. Soon they were up to their chests in the soft bed of the lake. As Jay pushed harder, they fought back. Their combined power strong given their distance from the nearest sink-room and source of dark energy. But Jay's power, with Toyah, was at its peak. She gave one final push and the heads of the three submerged Readers disappeared below the surface of the lake.

With the remaining Readers scattered into the caves, Jay and Toyah picked their way back across the rocks to an alcove in the cliff wall.

Toyah looked around in disbelief. 'The Interland...'

'Gone,' said Jay, feeling a deep sadness.

'Like Island 7,' said Toyah.

The landscape around the lake was unrecognisable. They stood at the base of a pit, like a quarry, the sides steeply rising to woodland above. It was as if the entire area of caves had imploded, bringing the surface into the hole, and disturbing the natural flow of the three rivers. The mass of rock that formed the underground cave network had been levelled, leaving a barren slope of boulders and rubble down to the shore of the lake. What was once a deep pool some hundred feet across at the most was now a wide lake spread over an area that, before, was underground. Jay couldn't tell where the original source would have been - somewhere below the surface of the lake. Three rivers continued to feed the lake. The sparkle of the unnamed river was clear as it meandered through to the eastern side.

Sun warmed Jay's face. A light breeze played with her hair, bringing the scent of the woodland. 'The power is still here,' said Jay. 'Same as on Island 7. The power comes from the convergence of these three watercourses.' Jay dipped her hand in the shallow edge of the lake. The energy flowed into her body as she expected. 'Try it,' she said to Toyah.

Toyah did the same, turning to Jay with a smile to acknowledge that she felt it too. Her expression darkened. 'It's been a long time since I've seen that many Readers here.'

'They weren't strong,' said Jay. 'They offered almost no resistance. Maybe they were using the power of the source on Island 7. Like Flick.'

'How do they come here?' asked Toyah.

'Through their source, the power from the core that exists at the old prison.'

Footsteps sounded on the stones and Jay turned to see a figure approach. Toyah peered into the shadows at the base of the rock slope as the figure emerged and walked towards them.

'Flick?' said Jay.

Toyah looked at Jay, then at Flick. 'The Reader? She's the one. She led them here. She did this?' Toyah reached for Flick as she approached, knocking her to the floor as soon as she was within reach. Before Jay could intervene, Toyah was astride Flick and grappling to hold her down, the anger glowing red in her face. Flick resisted without a word, protecting her face from a glancing blow from Toyah.

Jay grabbed Toyah by the arms, dragging her away. 'It's not her,' she said.

Flick stood and brushed herself down while Toyah seethed. Jay put a hand on Flick's arm and felt that her energy was weak. She'd been away from the source of power on Island 7 for too long. She'd had enough of the battling, the fear of the Given, and the fear of Atta. She was exhausted and had nowhere to go.

'What happened here?' asked Jay.

Flick held Jay's eye. 'I don't know.'

'Why are you here?' Toyah blurted.

Jay answered, 'She came to find us.' Flick's shoulders slumped. Her face was drawn, and she swayed as she struggled to remain upright. Jay pulled Flick's arm around her shoulders. 'Let's get out of here,' she said.

17

J ay dropped Toyah at home, then drove Flick to the bookshop. Alf set up the spare room in his apartment out the back of the shop so that Flick could rest. She was asleep before Jay and Alf even left the room.

'Maybe we should let her know about the panic room, just in case?' Jay said, knowing that Alf would never agree but testing his response.

Alf gave a single, emphatic shake of his head. He wouldn't entertain any notion of revealing its existence to anyone but Jay and Stitch. Even Cassie didn't know, and there was no way that he would allow a Reader to know about it, whatever her allegiances.

'You trust her?' Alf said, as they headed back into the shop.

Jay nodded. 'What she told me I've now seen for myself, it's all true. She's coming back to the Given. Isn't that what we hope for all Readers, eventually?'

Alf gave a gentle nod, and Jay motioned for them to head upstairs.

'See your family,' Alf said.

'Later,' said Jay, heading for the stairs.

On the top floor, Jay talked Alf through every step of her journey with Toyah. Alf rested back in his chair, taking it in. Buster curled up under the table. Alf didn't seem surprised at the extent of deterioration of Island 7 that Jay described. 'Colson has called on help from the London branch of your dad's *new resistance*,' Alf said.

'How will they help?' Jay asked, watching as Alf mumbled to himself, searching through papers. 'There was *something* back at the Interland about the...' He spread more papers over the table, next to the books already piled two feet high. 'There's something more in here about the source of the dark energy.'

'The London branch,' Jay said. 'What do they have that we don't?'

'Judith. I told you about her.' Jay nodded. 'And Hannah. Friend of Judith. They have a lot of knowledge. Your dad's gang has worked with them before.'

Jay looked at the mass of papers and picked up a single sheet from the table but could decipher less than 10% of the words, the rest either too faint or in a language she couldn't understand. She placed the soft, yellowing piece of paper carefully back on the table. 'We have to help them on Island 7.'

'First, we need to make sure we can protect ourselves,' Alf said, his expression grave.

'Their power comes from the core, channelled and controlled by their new sink-room. We need to destroy it.'

Alf shook his head. 'We've been here before,' he said. 'This time, we have to interrupt the flow of their power from the core permanently. Destroying the buildings clearly does nothing.'

Jay knew Alf was right. She could think of no means to stop the source of dark power. 'It might be impossible? Our Interland has been destroyed beyond all recognition, yet our power is just as strong.'

'I feel it too,' said Alf, resting back in his chair. 'It's not the source itself. The physical arrangement of the caves and rocks at the source is not important. We know that now. The rivers are still there, so the power comes.'

'What if it's the same for the energy from the core? What if there's no way of stopping the flow of darkness?'

Alf looked at the overwhelming pile of indecipherable papers on the table. 'There's a way,' he said, his tone unconvincing.

'What if I face him?'

Alf's expression hardened. 'From what you described to me about your recent encounter, that is the worst idea that's come out of you, my girl. Your suicide will not help the cause.'

'Not on Island 7, but *here*, where my power is the strongest?'

A noise from the stairs. Buster's ears pricked up, his eyes fixed on the top of the stairwell. Jay and Alf turned to see Colson stepping up the final stair and onto the top floor. Buster gave a single bark then settled as Alf raised a hand to reassure him. Colson was breathless, resting a moment, his hand on the door frame and two heavy books cradled in his other arm. 'I think it's you,' he said to Jay.

'What...?' Alf started.

'Maram,' said Colson, pausing again for breath. He moved closer and sat next to Alf. Buster growled, and Jay placed a reassuring hand on the dog's head.

Colson edged a little away from Alf. 'It's like we said. I've spoken to Judith. You remember her?' Alf nodded and stole a glance at Jay. 'And I've been reading this one.' Colson plonked one of the big old notebooks on the table. 'We thought Maram was simply a symbol, someone to give the true power of the Given a physical form. The ultimate 8C if you like. An 8C-plus.' He smiled.

'What are you talking about?' said Alf.

'A symbol. Like Atta is the symbol to represent the dark, Maram is the symbol to represent the power of the Given.'

'We know that but...'

'But,' Colson interrupted. 'What if Maram and Atta are not just fairytales? I cross-referenced the story in here,' he tapped the cover of the old notebook, 'with recorded historical events of the time, and I found something.' He sat back as if waiting for applause.

'What?' said Jay.

'Here,' Colson said, opening the second book, a contemporary encyclopaedia, its gloss cover in stark contrast to the other references on the table. 'The *Shamakhi* earthquake of 1667.' He paused again. Alf and Jay waited for explanation. 'I scanned current maps, and look here... At the recorded epicentre, there's a village. See what it's called?' He pointed to the full-page map in the encyclopaedia.

'Maramatta?' repeated Jay. 'As in, *Maram – Atta*?'

Colson nodded.

Alf leaned to get a closer look. 'What does it mean?'

'Over 1,000 people killed,' said Colson. 'They *say* it was an earthquake, but of course the records are sketchy, and much of the narrative around the event hints at a post-event desolation that sounds very much like what you get in a world of Readers – a withering environment, wide scale destruction of animal and plant life, deprivation, and famine.'

'So, what are you saying?' said Alf.

'I think this was the last clash of Maram and Atta, in whatever form they took at that time.' They were quiet for a minute as Alf and Jay took in the information. The words in the old notebook were barely decipherable. Interpretation was subjective. But the name of the village in the contemporary reference was clear. 'So,' Colson said, 'this confirms, in my mind...'

Alf finished Colson's sentence. 'The existence of the powers back as far as the 1600s.'

'Yes. And the power of the conflict between the Given – Maram – and the Dark, Atta.' Colson continued, 'The most recent incarnation of Maram was probably Sasha Colden. But, during her reign, the Readers were contained. And, thanks to Jay, were contained again. But now...'

'What?' said Jay.

'I think that the current incarnation of Maram is you,' Colson said. 'And Atta has returned. He has reached a point where the power of the core is sufficient to sustain him once more.'

'Oh no, it can't be...' started Alf, shaking his head.

'The earthquake,' said Jay, 'That was the ground-zero for the confrontation?'

Colson nodded. 'That's what Judith and Hannah think.'

'And Atta came out on top?' said Jay.

'We don't know. But the fact that it was contained to that single event, and no further spread of the darkness materialised, makes me think Atta was contained. Or destroyed.'

No one agreed or disagreed with Colson. They all just looked worried.

* * *

JAY NEEDED SPACE TO BREATHE. Back at her desk on the top floor, she tidied the papers and books into piles. She sat down and flicked through a book she'd already catalogued. She'd read it twice over the past few months, in shifts. It was one of the more progressive titles, delving under the surface of attitudes towards the powers, the already developing gender stereotypes, and the presentation of a vision for equality that could be written into the DNA of society, through education and policy, *before* the tendencies to prejudice surfaced and become embedded. It received little attention.

On the back cover was a picture of the author, a woman Jay's age. How could someone so young write a book of such authority? "The Three Pillars: A New Approach to Power". She pushed the words around inside her mind and allowed them to spill onto her tongue: 'Three pillars,' she whispered. Things always seemed to come in threes. Something clicked in Jay's memory, something she'd read, or something Colson had said.

She sprang from her chair and rejoined Alf and Colson. 'The darkness has been threatening,' she said, drawing their attention. 'But it hasn't arrived as such. It can't actually *come* here. Atta cannot venture into our land. We know that, because of the three conditions.'

Alf frowned and looked at Colson. Colson nodded thoughtfully. 'Yes,' Colson said. 'But how confident can we be that the conditions won't be met?'

'What conditions?' Alf straightened in his chair, looking mildly annoyed.

'Something Jay and I discussed before. You were there, Alf, don't look so surprised.' Alf slumped in his chair.

'Tell us again,' Jay said to Colson.

'We should take these words seriously. There is evidence

of their validity. But we need to remember the darkness cannot prevail where there is no firm connection to their source of power. And to create such a connection, as we have established, they need to be embedded here. So it's a chicken-and-egg situation.'

Alf shifted in his seat, impatient. 'The *conditions*?'

'Yes. Without their connection, as the legend goes, and this has been confirmed by Judith and Hannah.'

'Do they have power?' asked Jay.

Colson shook his head. 'Not that I am aware of. You don't need to *have* power to study and understand its history.'

'Carry on,' Jay encouraged.

'To move between lands, one must fulfil the three conditions, after which they are free to create their permanent connection with their power.' Colson sat back in his seat, making himself comfortable. 'So we need to make sure those conditions cannot be met.'

'And the conditions are...' Alf pushed.

'The first condition is that there must be a channel opened between the two lands, a channel that connects the darkness with the power of the Given.'

'What's that supposed to mean?' Alf asked.

'Your guess is as good as mine,' Colson said, becoming annoyed with Alf's impatience. 'That's as much as we can glean from the words. It's up to us to figure out what it means.'

'What do Judith and Hannah say?' Alf asked, a hint of mockery in his tone.

Colson ignored the baiting question.

'And the second?' asked Jay.

'The second condition is a little clearer. It says that there needs to be an *invitation* from the Given to the Dark.'

'Well, that will never happen,' said Jay.

'You'd think not, but the Dark is devious,' said Colson with a shrug. 'The third is more sinister. This one is right out of the witches' playbook. It says that for the last condition to be met, there needs to be a sacrifice.'

Jay sat up straight. 'Seriously? A sacrifice. At the altar or something?'

'The spill of blood in the land sacred to the Given.'

'The Interland?' said Jay.

Alf shook his head and leaned forward, placing his head in his hands. 'It's not clear.'

'It's pretty clear to me,' Jay said. 'We have a solid barrier. He can toy at the edges, but he can't come here. We just need to keep it that way.'

FLICK APPEARED in the doorway and fear spread across Colson's face. He slammed his books shut. 'Who's this?'

Jay introduced Flick, but Colson interrupted. 'A Reader,' he said. 'You shouldn't be here.'

'It's OK,' said Jay. This is Flick. She's been helping us.' Colson continued to back away from Flick, his two books clutched tight to his chest. He eventually stopped when he had placed Jay between himself and Flick.

'Hi,' said Flick, her voice little more than a whisper. 'Yes, I am a Reader.' She turned to Jay. 'I need you to *reduce* me.'

Jay looked into Flick and saw only pain.

Flick gasped, 'If you don't reduce me, I will die. I can't sustain myself here, and I won't go back to them. I want to be reduced.'

Jay and Alf exchanged a glance, and Jay turned to Flick. 'Tomorrow,' she said. 'We will do it tomorrow.'

18

A s Jay made her way to the hospital, she felt a message coming through the energy from her dad. She pushed a message back to say that she was OK, but before she could head home, she needed to see Angie. The sense she got on her way up to the sixth floor confirmed that Angie was awake. On the ward, there was no sign of her. A nurse approached. 'Who are you looking for?'

'The little girl, Angie?'

'She woke about ten minutes ago.' The nurse smiled at the good news. 'She's gone for some tests. Her parents are through here...' She motioned for Jay to follow.

'It's OK,' Jay said. I don't want to get in the way of family. I just wanted to see that she was OK.'

The nurse looked disappointed for a moment, then went back to her duties. 'Shall I tell her you were here?'

'Thanks. Just say that Jay was here.'

'Anything else?'

'No. Just say I was here.' She turned and headed back to the car park.

By the time Jay arrived home that night, the house was

asleep. She crept through the alleyway at the back and up onto her roof, slipping through the window and into bed.

She woke mid-morning, still half-clothed, to the sound of a bird squawking outside her window. Turning onto her back, she listened for the sounds of her family. They'd be worried about her. The muffled, low frequency of her dad's voice filtered through the floor. A faint smell of coffee.

She showered and made her way downstairs. Sonia startled at the sight of Jay entering the kitchen. Ben immediately held her, saying nothing. When her dad finally released Jay from the hug, she caught her mum wiping a tear from her face. Sonia turned her head away. 'We didn't know if you were dead or alive,' she said, and her voice turned stern. 'You should have told us where you were.'

'Hey,' said Ben. 'I told you she was OK.' Ben had a connection with Jay that prevailed when they were apart. 'I knew she was fine.'

'I'm OK, Mum,' said Jay, reaching for Sonia's arm.

Jay told them about her excursion to Island 7, about Flick, and about the possibility that the Readers were hunting for a route onto Island 8.

'So where is Flick?' asked Ben.

'With Alf at the shop,' said Jay, switching on the kettle to make tea.

'And what's she going to do? She's a Reader?'

'A reluctant Reader. She wants to be reduced, so that she can develop again as one of the Given.'

'Can she do that?' asked Sonia.

'Marcus did,' said Jay. The mention of Marcus's name brought a silence to the kitchen. The kettle clicked off. 'Where's Sammy?'

'In bed,' Ben said.

'I'll go see him.'

With tea in hand, she headed up the stairs to Sammy's room. Voices came through from the other side of his door. She recognised Toyah's voice and sensed tension. She knocked and walked in without waiting for a reply. 'Hey.' Jay smiled at her brother and Toyah, sitting upright, squeezed together in a single bed. An air of conflict between them. 'Look at you two, lovebirds.' She put a hand briefly on her brother's head before sitting on the end of the bed.

'I've been hearing about Island 7,' said Sammy. 'What are we going to do?'

'Not sure yet.' She sipped her tea.

Sammy's bedroom door swung open and Cassie appeared in the opening. 'Do about what?' She pushed the door closed behind her and took a seat on Sammy's bed, next to Jay.

'Seriously?' Sammy said, his pitch rising. 'This room is barely big enough for me.' Toyah slipped down against the wall to make herself small. Cassie nudged Sammy's and Toyah's legs out of the way so that she could sit and lean back against the wall.

Toyah edged out of Cassie's way. 'How's Otis?' she asked. 'Did you see him last night?'

Cassie answered, without looking at Toyah. 'He's upstairs actually, with Pinto.'

'In my room?' asked Jay.

Cassie nodded. 'On the roof.'

Sammy put a hand on Toyah's arm, but she refused to look at him. Whatever their disagreement, it hung in the air like a weight. Sammy looked at Jay and widened his eyes when he said, 'Why don't you guys go up and see Otis and Pinto? We'll come up in a minute.'

Cassie jumped off the bed and headed up without

another word. Jay followed, giving her brother a wink as she left his room.

Otis and Pinto were sitting together on the roof outside Jay's room. Jay climbed out to join them. Cassie peered through the window, leaning on the ledge. 'Hey,' she said. 'You want coffee?'

Otis nodded, and Pinto opted for tea. 'Hi Pinto,' Jay said, pulling him into a side-by-side hug as Cassie disappeared.

'We missed you,' he said.

'Heard you had an adventure,' Otis added.

'Something like that,' said Jay. 'Could have used you two, with your skills.'

Pinto smiled. 'Otis has been teaching me. Shall we show you?'

Jay nodded, and Pinto sat up, readying himself. 'There are some movements that are easier than others. If there's organic matter, carbon-based material, and it's light, then that's easy.' He looked at Otis for an encouraging nod. 'So those leaves, for example.' Pinto was quiet for a moment as he focused on transmitting his energy through the scattering of green leaves on the roof, fallen from the overhead sycamore. Within a few seconds, the leaves moved, then with a whoosh, they flew off the roof as if blown by a sudden gust of wind.

'Impressive,' said Jay.

'What about something a little more challenging?' said Otis.

'The same is true for bigger things, of organic constituents. Like the tree. It's bigger, but relatively easy compared to something smaller that's inorganic – like a wall, concrete or metal.' Pinto focused on the great sycamore rooted in the garden next door and towering above Jay's roof. The branches swayed for a moment before the entire trunk of the tree tilted to the side so that its leaves brushed the roof of Jay's house. He released his focus, and the tree sprang back into place, its leaves rustling and birds scattering.

'That's brilliant, Pinto. You've been practising. So what about other stuff that's not living. That's more difficult?'

'Takes more focus,' said Otis. 'But I'm getting the hang of it.'

Cassie appeared at the window, handing mugs of hot drinks out to Otis and Pinto. 'You controlled those guns back at the Interland,' she said to Otis.

'The energy of the other people there made a difference, especially as it was life or death.'

'It might have been the person you controlled,' said Pinto. 'Not the metal gun?'

'Maybe. The natural energy inside all of us, including the Readers, and those without power, makes it easier to manipulate people than objects.'

Jay sensed Pinto was trying something. His influence tugged at her. She smiled, avoiding looking at him. A pull on her legs made her slip a little on the tiles. A stronger pull, and she slipped onto her back with a squeal as Pinto erupted in laughter. The others laughed too as Jay righted herself. Otis gave Pinto a high-five.

19

L ater that afternoon, Jay arrived at the bookshop to find it locked up. She knocked on the door. Alf opened up from the inside. 'I heard Colson found something,' said Jay.

Alf raised a hand in a gesture, asking for patience, then closed the door behind Jay. He opened the blinds to allow just enough light into the dark bookshop for them to navigate to the stairs. 'Don't want anyone thinking we're open for business today,' he said.

'Where's Flick?' asked Jay.

'Out back. She was asleep. I'll check on her then we can head upstairs.'

As Alf left the room, Colson burst through the front door in a bluster, tripping over the threshold. 'Sorry,' he said, closing and bolting the door behind him. 'I found something. Where's Alf? Let's go up.' Without another word, he took the stairs two at a time. Alf returned, indicating that Flick was asleep, and that she was OK. They followed Colson, swept up the stairs in the wake of his enthusiasm.

The three sat at the table with the literature of the Given

spread out in front of them. Colson remained standing, and like a conductor, he began. 'So, what do we know?' Alf made to respond, but Colson held up a finger. 'We know that the balance has tipped, and Atta is here.'

'Well...' Alf began, his tone unsure.

'Yes,' said Jay emphatically.

'Good,' said Colson. 'And we know that whatever he is, he is powerful, and he channels the power of the Readers. He's like a super-Reader? Yes?'

Jay nodded. 'He's part of the dark power. He doesn't channel the power of the Readers, he has his own power, and it's on a scale like nothing else.'

'He's seeking a route through to our land here. We are the last stop on his railroad to complete power. He's looking to establish a base on each of the eight Islands, a link to the core in each energy centre, do you agree?' asked Colson.

'Yes,' said Jay. 'Ours might be the last remaining freedom for the Given.'

'We also know that we can't simply destroy the buildings and the infrastructure around the sink-room. It's the connection to the core that channels the power. The rest of it is just window dressing.'

'And they need electromagnets...' began Jay.

'Only to allow the Readers to remain *charged*,' interrupted Colson. 'But like the source at the Interland, the power is the power. It's there, as long as there is an environment, living things, to enable the power of the Given. And the Readers' power is there as long as there is a deep connection with the core.'

'Makes sense,' said Alf. Jay agreed.

'So the *only* way we win, the *only* way we can survive in the longer term, is by severing the connection with the core.'

'Agreed,' said Alf.

'Or we defend this place from the Readers,' said Jay. 'If they can't come here, if Atta can't come here, then they'll never overpower us.'

'Yes,' said Colson. 'In the short term, perhaps. But longer term, the risk is too great that they find a way through to fulfil the three conditions. Back in 1667, the so-called earthquake came *after* a period of hardship, not before. So it was the event of 1667 that *ended* the period of depravation, famine, and drought, not started it.'

Alf thought for a moment, then said, 'You think the period before this last earthquake was the period of Atta's control?'

Colson nodded.

Jay said, 'So the event, whatever it was, the earthquake, put an end to the Reader control, and an end to the desolation? What happened?'

'I don't know, but I *think* the Shamakhi earthquake in 1667 occurred at the location of the original connection to the core, and the place where the Readers drew their energy.'

'Is it on one of the Islands?' said Jay.

Colson nodded. 'And maybe this location is now free of the dark power, because they found a way to sever the connection between the core and the surface.'

Jay thought back to the vision of the Islands, connected in a circle of eight, all enveloped in darkness. 'But all the other seven islands are blackened. We saw them.'

'Are you sure? Absolutely? If I am right, then one of those Islands is free. Probably Island *One*.'

Jay shook her head. 'Island One is dark, if that's the other closest to our Island 8. Both seven and one are dark.'

Colson sat down. 'What about the others?'

'All dark as far as we could see...' Jay thought for a

moment. 'I'm not sure. There could be one on the far side that's not dark.'

'There must be. I don't know whether it's Island One or Four or whatever, but I *think* this place, Shamakhi, is the first to be free of Atta. The first to have severed the connection. So there is a way.'

* * *

Colson and Alf continued to debate the merits of Colson's theory as Jay sought solace back at her desk. She couldn't help but be drawn to her usual comfort that was the Sasha Colden book, her means to connect most deeply with the true power of the Given. If any of Colson's theories had merit, then surely she would have seen something in the Sasha Colden book, or felt something when the book took her to a higher plane. She was sure that this book held the answers to Colson's questions.

She returned to Alf and Colson, making a show of placing the book on the table between them before taking her seat.

'The biography?' asked Colson.

'Autobiography. It was penned by Sasha's hand. It contains her very essence, her energy. It's at the heart of everything I know to be true about the powers. You said it could be the key?'

Colson nodded. 'But you've read it all,' said Alf. 'More than once. There's nothing more in there that you don't already know.'

Jay agreed. She'd read it probably a hundred times, and each time had deepened her inner understanding of her world, and of the Given, in ways she couldn't articulate. She expected to read it another hundred times.

'There are elements that make no literal sense to me yet,' she said, thinking particularly of the last pages where the text deteriorated into a mix of languages. Jay had never worried too much about the literal meaning of those sections because the inner meaning came through in her subconscious. There was no reason for her to study the detail of the words. That wasn't the point as far as she could feel.

'What do you mean?' said Alf. 'You never said…'

'If there's an answer in here, then that's where it's hidden.'

Alf put a hand on the cover of the Sasha Colden book as if trying to feel its answers. Colson opened one of the old notebooks and pointed to the full-page map. 'See here,' he said.

'The village?' Alf said. 'Maramatta?'

'Yes, but look here,' he pointed to what looked like a reflection of the village outline in the space next to it. In very faint letters, the name of the village was repeated, but this time spelled backwards.

'*Attamaram*,' said Jay. 'Atta is a palindrome, and so is Maram.'

'So what? What does it mean?' said Alf.

Colson frowned, a bead of perspiration forming on his forehead as Jay watched him scour his mind for answers. She picked up the Sasha Colden book and flicked directly to the end section, where the words scattered more like a waterfall than the logical flow of a river. She studied the words and letters systematically for the first time, casting her eyes over their sequence, using logic instead of intuition for once.

'Turn it over,' said Alf. Jay looked at him quizzically. 'Turn the book over and read the words backwards.'

Colson peered over Jay's shoulder. 'These words mean little enough in the forward direction.'

'The palindrome,' said Alf. 'It might be the key. Try it upside down and backwards.'

Jay did as Alf suggested. She sat back and allowed her eyes to flow over the words, following their path backwards from the top of the upside-down page until the patterns emerged.

'Source... Stone,' Jay said, picking the letters from the sea of words on the upside-down page.

'What?' said Alf, leaning to get a look at what Jay was reading. 'Where?'

Jay tilted the book towards Alf but he simply frowned and shook his head, and Jay wasn't sure whether the letters she just picked out were actually on the page, or if they were in her head.

'What's the source stone?' asked Jay.

'Was there something at the source? A key-stone, or a central structure?' Colson asked.

Jay shook her head.

'There must have been something?'

Jay pictured the damp cave that was the confluence of the three streams of water at the Interland. The flows emerged from the rock and converged at a central pillar, into a bowl-like rock scoured from decades of flow from the three rivers, then out into the cracks in the rock floor. 'The bowl,' she said.

Alf and Colson waited for Jay to elaborate.

'The point at which the three streams converge.' She looked at Alf. He'd seen it. 'You remember?'

'I can't think what it's like down there. I was only there the one time.'

'It must be the *bowl*. It's a stone that's been battered by the magic of the unnamed river for decades.'

'We need to find it,' said Alf.

'We can't,' said Jay. 'The entire Interland has been destroyed. There's nothing left.'

'It will still be there, somewhere,' said Colson.

'I told you, everything's gone. The whole of the cave system is under water. There is no source.' As Jay said the words, a tingle of energy flowed over the surface of her skin. She faltered and rested her head in her hands. There was a chance that she'd sense the power of the source stone if it was near.

Colson seemed to read the energy in Jay. 'I think we can find it. We can go together and...'

'I'll go alone,' said Jay.

Colson looked disappointed. Alf shifted in his seat. 'Take Stitch, and Cassie, at least. You might need some help if you run into Readers.'

'No, I need the space to connect.'

'Then take Stitch...'

'I have to connect alone. With no interference.' She thought of Stitch. If he could hear her, he'd be annoyed. They'd drifted a little, and she couldn't figure if she should allow him space to find his own pathway, or if she should try to re-connect.

Colson and Alf looked at each other. Colson gave a slight nod, and Alf sighed in resignation. Jay felt a powerful need to be at the Interland without distraction. She would connect once more with the source on her own terms, with no compromise. She would connect with her roots, and if the source stone had survived, she'd find it.

20

J ay locked the door behind Colson and, as she turned to head back up to Alf on the top floor, she caught sight of Flick standing in the shadows. 'You scared me, standing there like a ghost.'

'Are you going somewhere?' asked Flick.

Jay hesitated. 'Not sure yet. How are you feeling?'

Flick sighed. 'Tired.'

'Come up. We can sit with Alf.' Jay held out a hand to Flick, who instead took the banister. They ascended slowly, Flick taking regular rests.

'You need to do it now,' Flick said. 'I can't go on like this much longer.'

'Cassie and Otis are on their way,' said Jay. 'Alf and I will reduce you, then you can go with Otis to Highdown to re-build.' Highdown was one of the strongest sources of energy for the Given, along with the hilltops at Chanctonbury and Cissbury.

As Flick and Jay stepped up to the top floor, Alf saw them and moved to help Flick.

There was a bang on the door downstairs.

'That'll be Cassie,' said Jay, leaving Flick to Alf as she bounded back down the stairs. She swung open the shop door and caught Cassie and Otis in each other's arms. 'Sorry to interrupt,' she said with a smile. Cassie rolled her eyes and pushed past Jay into the shop. Otis, her unlikely partner, shorter and more upbeat than Cassie, followed.

Jay felt a momentary pang of sadness. She'd always assumed that *Sammy* and Cassie would be together one day. It was written in the stars. A year on from when Otis almost died at the battle for the Interland, and now he and Cassie were tight. And they were good together. Life was full of surprises.

Upstairs, Flick sat on a chair with her back to the window facing Alf. Cassie and Otis stood, waiting for Jay. 'If we work this together,' said Jay, 'we can control it better. We need to go easy. Too much infiltration and we'll do damage.' She turned to Flick. 'Are you sure?'

Flick nodded. 'Just be careful.'

Jay held Flick's hand, then reached for Cassie, motioning for Otis and Alf to complete the circle. 'Follow my lead,' she said, 'and go slowly.'

Flick closed her eyes and leaned back in her chair. Faint wisps of grey emanated from Flick, the remains of the darkness leaking from inside her. Cassie's energy flowed in support. Otis and Alf too, contributing, edging up the pressure as the last of Flick's power flowed from her body and into the room. *Slow down*, Jay said without speaking. The energy from the others eased off in response and Jay could bring Flick to a neutral state in a controlled manner. Flick slumped as Jay released her hand, then moved to support her to stop her from slipping onto the floor.

'Did it work?' asked Otis.

Jay nodded, placing her hand on the scar forming on the

side of Flick's face. It wasn't the first scar that had marked Flick's cheek. An older scar was clear, running alongside the new. Jay frowned as she studied the scars. It looked like there was a third scar, faded but visible. The poor girl had been reduced several times.

Flick twitched to consciousness and pulled her head away from Jay. They exchanged a glance and Jay read that Flick was uncomfortable with Jay studying her face.

Flick's eyes darted from Jay to the others and back to Jay. 'What happened?'

'You're safe. We reduced your power, the dark is now gone.'

Flick seemed to remember where she was and the process she'd been through. She puffed out her cheeks and leaned over with her hands on her knees. 'That was painful,' she said, staggering then leaning on the back of the chair.

'Slowly,' said Alf. 'There's no rush.'

'I need to get up to Highdown.'

As if this were his cue, Otis stood. Cassie asked if Otis wanted her to go too, but he shook his head. 'You need to go home, and there's only room for one on the back of the bike. Come up to see us tomorrow.' Otis put a hand on Cassie's shoulder and she placed her own hand on top of his.

Otis led Flick to the stairs to begin their journey to Highdown, where Flick would at last be able to leave behind the life of a Reader, and once again welcome the power of the Given.

* * *

AT HOME, Jay packed a small rucksack with some basic supplies – a change of clothes, waterproofs, and some cash.

In the kitchen, she filled the pockets of the bag with food from the cupboard – bananas, chocolate and cereal bars.

As she slung the rucksack onto her back, Sammy walked in. 'You're leaving again?'

'Not for long. I'm not leaving the Island.'

Sammy looked visibly relieved that his sister wasn't planning on heading back into the lair of the Readers. He pushed his hair out of his eyes. 'Where, then?'

Jay contemplated what would be the short version of the story. 'I've been working with Alf and Colson on...'

'Colson?'

'Dad's friend at the club. We have a theory. I need to check it out.'

'You're heading to the Interland?' Jay nodded, and Sammy said, 'I thought it had been destroyed? There's nothing there?'

'It's still the source of the power. We think there's a *source stone*, something with the power to sever the Readers' connection to their own source, the connection to the core.'

Sammy frowned. Jay turned away from him, not wanting to be influenced by any of Sammy's scepticism. Not now. She needed to be focused. Sammy's frown broke, and he smiled. 'You need help?'

Jay relaxed. 'No, I need to do this on my own. If this thing is there, I'll find it.'

Sammy flung his long arms around Jay, and she allowed his gangly body to swallow her up for a moment.

'Tell Mum and Dad I'm fine,' said Jay. 'I'll be back in a day or so.'

'They're in there.' He motioned towards the lounge, where Jay could hear the muffled sound of the TV. 'Tell them yourself.'

Jay shook her head. 'Please? They'll start up again. I

don't need to debate this right now. And can you speak to Stitch?'

'Why can't *you* speak to Stitch?'

'I need to go. Tell him not to worry. I'll be back before he knows it.'

Sammy agreed. 'You taking the Beast?' Jay nodded and checked her pocket for the car keys. Sonia shouted for Sammy to come into the lounge. He smiled, and Jay turned and headed out, quickly dissolving into the darkness as she broke into a run.

21

U p on Highdown Hill, Flick and Otis rested on a log by the fire inside the ring of trees. Flick already felt the energy of the Given flowing through the ground and into her body. Despite having experienced it before, it was a strange sensation. The tingle over her skin was different to that which came from the power of the Readers. Dark power from the core seemed to penetrate her bones. The power of the Given was superficial, flowing only over the surface of her body.

'You feel anything?' Otis asked.

'It's coming.'

Otis put a hand on Flick's shoulder, and she sensed his trust and affection. He was loyal to the Given. He *belonged*. These people were his family. She felt compassion, a sense of belonging to Otis's circle, and it caught her off-guard. She leaned away from him so that his hand slipped from her shoulder. The tightness of the community of the Given repelled her. She had experienced the power from both sides, and it was the power of the Given that most unsettled her. The power of the Readers was more direct, simple, and unambiguous. It came from the centre of the earth and radiated without discrimination. The power of the Given was selective. It chose its subjects, anointed the few.

She shook herself from contemplation and reminded herself of her mission. The triangle of conditions would soon be met. The pathway for Atta could be completed.

* * *

OTIS'S EXPRESSION WAS GRAVE. He sensed something shifting in Flick. She looked up into the trees, the grey sky visible between the branches, and the wind creating a chorus of rustling leaves. As Otis followed her gaze, she pulled her knife from its sheath strapped around her ankle. She leaned down and dragged the knife across the back of Otis's left heel, slicing deep across his Achilles tendon.

A second passed before the pain registered, and in that time, he leaned down and pulled up the leg of his trousers to see blood seeping from the cut. His face was twisted with pain and confusion.

He screamed and pushed himself away from Flick, but when he tried to stand, his leg gave way. He landed headfirst in the leaves on the woodland floor. As he struggled, Flick approached him once more and sliced his other Achilles. He screamed again before he began whimpering.

'Shh,' Flick said. 'Be still.' She tore a strip of cloth from her own shirt and tied it around his bleeding cut. Then another, tying both of his wounds in makeshift bandages to slow the bleeding.

'What...? Why?' Otis stammered.

'Atta will decide your fate now.' She again looked up into the trees. There was a whoosh and rustle of the wind in the branches and leaves. A wisp of darkness circled, the grey sky darkening by the second.

'Atta...' Flick said to herself.

Otis panted and groaned in pain. 'What's happening?'

'This is the final stage,' Flick said, brightening as she felt her master. Atta was close now. 'This is the last remaining Island. The ultimate destination.'

Otis turned over and pulled his knees to his chest. He reached down to feel for the wounds on his heels. Flick looked at him with some sympathy. She cleaned her knife on her shirt and slipped it back into its sheath. 'It won't be long now.'

The swirl of wind picked up again, collecting the leaves scattered over the floor inside the ring of trees and flinging them into the surrounding air.

Flick raised her hands, feeling the power of Atta in the air.

The wind seemed to take a physical form. The darkness mixed and merged with the scattered leaves. A swirl of energy. A shape appeared.

Atta.

The wind dropped.

Silence enveloped them like a heavy blanket.

As the leaves drifted to the floor, the figure of Atta stood in the forest like a ghost – the serenity belying the evil. He looked up and around himself, taking a deep breath, taking no notice of Flick or Otis.

After a moment, his gaze settled on Flick and he smiled. Without looking at the shivering Otis, curled up on the floor, he stepped up to Flick and put a hand on her shoulder. She immediately felt the weight of his power. The air caught in her throat and it was as if she were breathing thick treacle.

As he released her from his spell, she breathed again, stepping back from his great presence.

'You've done well,' he said, now looking down at Otis. 'For the third time, you don't disappoint.'

The first time Flick had facilitated Atta's movement between Islands was from Island 5 to Island 6. Then on to 7 and now, finally, to 8. How he had moved across all the Islands that were now dark, Flick did not know. She would surely hold a position of power in the new world. She would receive her thanks for the three scars on the side of her face – the sacrifice she had made in three times losing the power of the Readers, only to re-energise as the Given to facilitate Atta's movement between Islands. The three conditions had once more been met, thanks to Flick's manipulation of Jay and her friends.

'What now?' asked Flick, knowing that their destination was to be the prison, to finish the job the Readers had started. They would commission the final electro-magnets and begin the process that would ensure the balance towards Reader power would be maintained on Island 8. Then Atta could remain, and move freely between all the Islands. His power and his control would be unopposed.

'We leave,' said Atta, his words seeped from him - slow but controlled.

'The sink-room? The prison?'

'First, we have to head south. The bookshop.'

Flick looked down at Otis.

Atta said, 'Take off those bandages. We will leave him to the mercy of his environment that he so loves. He will see how it cannot protect him.'

Atta stepped away towards the outer ring of trees as Flick leaned down to release the makeshift bandages tied around Otis's ankles. The blood flowed as soon as she loosened the knots.

'Please...' said Otis, trying to make eye contact with Flick. She shielded him, sensing that he was trying to get inside her head. 'Don't leave me here to die.'

Flick blocked out his words, standing with the blood-soaked bandages staining her fingers red. Fate would play a part in whether Otis lived or died. If he was meant to live, then he would find a way to those bandages, a way to stem the bleeding. But if it was not meant to be, then his end would come inside the inner circle. She threw the bloodied bandages into the bushes, and looked back just once, seeing that Otis had not moved from his foetal position on the floor, and she judged that his fate was decided.

22

J ay pulled open the garage door and secured it on its latch before climbing in to the old Ford, taking a breath of its familiar musty interior. It started first time, and she pushed it into gear, hesitating a moment as she thought about Stitch and Cassie, before releasing the clutch.

As the car edged forward, a figure appeared at the end of the bonnet. She slammed on the brakes and rocked back in her seat, straining her eyes to see who it was. 'Stitch?' She said under her breath.

He moved around and climbed in to the passenger side of the car, a small rucksack on his back. 'Ready?' he said.

Jay switched off the engine. 'What are you doing?'

'Coming with you.'

'How did you know?'

Stitch pulled back his sleeve to remind Jay of his marking, of their connection. 'And Alf told me.'

Jay huffed and looked away. 'I didn't want...'

'What is it, Jay?' Stitch interrupted. 'Why are you freezing me out? You think you're the only one who can do this, and you have to do it all on your own? What are you trying to prove?'

'I'm not...'

'And who are you trying to impress?'

'Come on, Stitch. I just don't want anyone else to get hurt. We don't yet know what this new darkness is capable of. We don't know how long we can remain safe here. I need to figure this out.'

'Not *you*, Jay. *We* need to figure this out.' He yanked back his sleeve once more and shoved his wrist forward. 'Connected.'

'Fine,' Jay said tersely, and started the engine. The car jolted forward and out into the streetlamp-lit side streets.

It was almost ten minutes of aching silence before either spoke. Some of the tension had leaked from Jay's body and she looked over at her friend, his head up against the side window and his eyes flickering with the passing trees on the side of the road. She glanced down at her exposed wrist and studied the 8C for a moment before returning her eyes to the road. She wondered what it meant - the 8C and the C. Were she and Stitch *meant* to be together, both in their connected power, and in every other way? Or was the opposite true? Perhaps their relationship should be focused entirely on the development of the power for the safety of their homeland.

Stitch seemed to sense her muddled thoughts and looked at her. 'Look,' he said. 'Can we be honest with each other?'

Jay tensed once more, bracing herself for an argument. 'Always,' she said.

'I just need to know what this is,' he motioned between them. 'Me and you.'

'I love you, Stitch. You know that.' Jay kept her eyes on

the road and her shield raised. She didn't want Stitch to read the confusion in her mind over her feelings for him. There was love, for sure. The confusion came with how those feelings twisted and turned as she tried to pin them down, understand them. What kind of love? Was it love driven by the connection, or despite it?

Stitch let out a deep, frustrated sigh and turned back to the window. A minute passed. 'I know,' he said. 'I love you too.'

'That's all that matters right now,' said Jay. 'We can figure the rest out later.' She turned into River Road and headed for the village to the south of the Interland. The road narrowed and Jay sensed a change in the energy in the air. The atmosphere near the Interland was charged. She felt the static on her skin. This was her spiritual home.

She looked at Stitch and knew that he felt it too. He smiled and straightened in his seat. 'We're close,' he said.

They pulled into a small car park by the river. Jay stepped out of the car, slammed and locked the door. Across the green, a row of Vespa mopeds lined up outside the cafe. Stitch looked over and smiled. 'Is that where Cassie *borrowed* that moped from?'

Jay nodded, recalling how Cassie had turned up to save her, collecting her in the woods where she'd fallen. She was sure that they'd never have been able to defeat Marcus if it weren't for Cassie's determination to get to Jay. That all seemed so long ago, and so much had changed. They turned away from the village centre and slid down the river bank to the tow-path.

'Are you sure we can get through this way?' asked Stitch.

'As sure as I can be.' The new Interland was no longer characterised by hidden caves, secret routes through to deep underground. The caves were gone. When she and Toyah left there a few days before, it more closely resembled a flooded quarry than a magical centre of power. There was a bonus, however: an easier route in. There was no longer a need to trek through the undergrowth to approach from the north or the east. The route in from the south, along the River Arun, would take them to the lake, where they'd find whatever was left of the source.

They were quiet as they pressed forward along the river bank. Jay caught the occasional wave of thoughts through the air from Stitch, but nothing she could get a hold on. She sensed that he too was keeping his thoughts hidden.

'You know the other day?' Stitch said. 'When the darkness, or whatever it was, attacked the shop?' Jay nodded for him to continue. 'I got nothing. No energy when I tried to heal Angie. Not even a bit.' His expression was pained.

'It'll come,' said Jay.

'It's gone. It came and went. I don't know what's happened.'

'Hey,' Jay said. 'Calm down. You know how it works. You don't control the power through sheer determination. You control it through here.' She pointed to her chest. 'Through your emotions.'

'I know, but whenever I focus in on it...'

'Don't *focus* in on anything,' Jay interrupted.

'But that's how we used to build up the strength, by channelling the energy.'

'Not with your mind.' Jay stopped on the footpath and turned to face Stitch. She held out both of her hands. 'Close your eyes.'

Stitch did as he was asked. Jay opened to the power of the Interland, allowing the energy to flow through her and connect her with Stitch. She too closed her eyes and couldn't help but smile at the sensation - the intensity of the power so close to the source. Stitch gulped a breath, as if coming up for air. He swayed a little. 'Relax,' said Jay, keeping her voice low. 'Just *feel* it for a moment, in your body, not in your mind. Don't try to do anything with it.'

Jay opened her eyes and watched Stitch as he opened to the flow of the energy. He swayed and twitched as it passed through Jay and into him. Gradually, his movements became more steady, more cyclical as he tuned into the waves of power. His shoulders relaxed and Jay could feel the energy flowing back into her from him. At last he was connected. Still holding his hands, she turned her arms slightly so that she could see the markings on their wrists. She let go of his hands for a moment and brought her left hand to his so their markings became physically connected.

She closed her eyes once more.

Together, in their minds, they sank into the ground beneath their feet, into the banks of the river, below the deep river channel and raced through the tangle of tree roots stretching deep into the earth. Stitch's strength of power matched Jay's own energy as they flowed through the land, expanding thorough the soil and integrating with their environment until there was nothing between Jay and Stitch and their surroundings.

As they snapped out of their trance, Stitch stumbled backwards, falling into the long grass before Jay could reach for him. He came to and stood, laughing, brushing himself down. 'Wow,' he said. 'Haven't felt that level of connection for a while.'

'Me neither to be honest.' Jay turned to continue along the pathway. 'Come on. Before it gets dark.'

Twenty minutes later, the pathway petered out to nothing. They fought their way through thick undergrowth. Jay stumbled. Something washed over her like a wave of dark energy. She glanced at Stitch, then up to the hills. Wisps of black cloud circled above the Interland, then away. She steadied herself. Her breathing regulated once more, and they pressed on.

A further twenty minutes and still no sign of the sunken lake. The energy of the Interland was waning, and she considered for a moment that they could be walking in the wrong direction. She craned to see over the tops of the wild undergrowth. 'Can you see the river?'

Stitch jumped up to see. 'No.'

'I think we're lost,' said Jay.

Stitch turned full circle as if taking in the energy around them. 'Do you feel anything?'

'I'm getting mixed signals,' said Jay. 'I can't home in on the location.'

'Something moving,' said Stitch, his eyes closed.

Jay looked up into the air. A bird came into view. It looked like the falcon from the Interland. Before she could say anything, Stitch opened his eyes and said, 'There. Our guide. The *phoenix*.' The bird that had taken to Cassie, flown to her. The same bird that had flown to Cassie's grandad years before. Jay was sure of it. The markings on the wings. It circled once, twice, three times before heading away towards the hills in the distance.

Jay laughed. 'I thought birds were Sammy's special talent?'

'I'm feeling a little more connected,' Stitch said as he linked arms with Jay and they adjusted their course and moved off in the falcon's direction. Within a few minutes, the falcon re-appeared to guide them once more. It swooped down to just twenty feet above their heads and off again.

The sky had darkened as they stepped out of the wood-land and onto the lake shore. Stitch looked around, open mouthed. He'd not before seen the changed landscape. 'Looks different, eh?' said Jay.

'I'll say.'

Jay flopped onto the stones at the water's edge and pulled off her shoes. She stretched out her legs and dipped her feet in the water, the cold immediately relieving the aches and pains.

'How's that foot?' Stitch said.

Jay looked down and squeezed her foot where it had been burned in the darkness of the water between the islands. It was a little red. 'It's a funny colour, but it doesn't hurt.' She leaned to take some water in her hands, letting it flow away through her fingers. She felt its energy. Closing her eyes, white light entered her head, warming her body.

The lake was the point of confluence of the three sources – the three rivers. But the location of the river entry points was not clear. There was nothing obvious above the ground, and it was likely that the three sources connected below the surface of the lake. It was the unnamed river that brought the power, the magic they would need to tap into to find the source stone. If indeed the stone existed.

'Where do we start?' asked Stitch.

Jay shrugged. She stood and squeezed on her shoes. Together, they walked along the shore of the lake, taking some minutes to travel a short section of its circumference. The light faded further and little was visible beyond the immediate shore. Jay hugged her arms to her chest, feeling the chill that came with the dark. 'I think we need to do this at first light. We have no hope of seeing anything tonight.'

'Over there,' said Stitch, pointing to an alcove in the cliff face. 'We can shelter in there.'

There was enough wood scattered across the shore of the lake for a hundred fires. Much of the woodland that sat above the caves had been deposited on the lakeside by the explosions. Stars appeared in the sky. The fire warmed Jay's cheeks and the darting orange flames intermittently illuminated the surface of the lake just twenty feet away.

Feeling the cold on her back, Jay pulled on a hoodie and edged a little closer to the fire as Stitch fed it with wood. Without sleeping bags, they would have to make do with limestone beds and their rucksacks for pillows.

'Thanks,' said Stitch.

Jay looked up. 'What for?'

'I needed that re-connection.'

'Me too.' Jay smiled into the darkness.

A RELENTLESS STREAM of light pierced Jay's mind, bringing haphazard images and feelings from her subconscious. Tiago was there, but he looked different. Each time she moved to look him in the face, he turned away. Then he fell, with darkness circling him and the space where his face should have been, a blank, faceless mask. She asked his name. 'Maram,' he said, as the darkness entwined his neck. But that wasn't his name. It squeezed. 'Maram,' he gasped. It squeezed tighter, flowing around Tiago and then in through his nose, his ears, his mouth. Then came a wail of pure fear, like a scream of a baby caught on the wind.

Jay woke to the call of the falcon, a whistle in the distance bringing her out of her dreams. The fire had all but died, the last wisps of smoke carried in her direction by a morning breeze coming off the lake. She coughed as smoke caught in her throat. Stitch was still asleep.

She tried to get a hold of her dream, to remember it, but

it slipped away like water through her fingers. The morning air was fresh, not too cold, but her toes were frozen numb.

Up on the distant cliff face, the falcon preened its feathers, all the while closely watching Jay and Stitch. Energy fizzed through Jay's body, giving her a sense of invincibility. Her fingers tingled, and she looked at her palms, expecting to see them sparkle.

In the lake, currents rippled the surface, moving in tidy sequence. Leaving Stitch to sleep, she stepped into the shallows up to her shins to get a better look. The green sparkle of the unnamed river was clear in the three converging colours. She was drawn to it, the tingling in her body intensifying, and the surface of her skin becoming warm.

Finding the stone in the vast space left by the destruction of the Interland felt like an impossible task. Where would they start? She turned to look at the cliff face, her eyes hunting for a clue, something out of place, an energy signal that she might lock on to. Stones crumbled and fell from the cliff face as if to wave her away.

Nausea hit her stomach, and, in a beat, Angie was with her. She straightened, her eyes half closed as Angie's smiling face came into focus in her mind. Before Jay could speak, her image faded and disappeared, leaving Jay confused and light-headed.

The falcon swooped. It flew past just a few feet from Jay, then circled to pass again. Jay looked over to see if Stitch was watching. He stirred and sat up. The bird touched the surface of the lake. Jay expected its claws to emerge clutching a fish, but there was nothing but the spray of water as the falcon rose and circled again. Stitch stood, stepping closer to the edge of the lake. The falcon whistled as it powered back towards Jay like a bomber, turning at the last and diving into the lake.

This time, the falcon had something clutched in both claws. Its wings beat the water as it struggled to free itself, the force of the surface tension holding it back for just a moment, as if it were frozen in time. The falcon broke free of the water and turned immediately towards Jay, releasing its boon as it passed overhead. Jay caught the rock in both hands and turned, grinning, to Stitch. They watched after the falcon as it returned to its perch on the cliff face where it rested and dipped its head as if to say *there you go*.

Jay looked at the stone. 'Thanks,' she said, smiling up at the bird and thinking of Angie. The stone was smooth, the shape of a large bowl. Into its hollow, the three river sources deposited their flow deep in the underground cave of the Interland. She stroked the smooth surface and turned it over in her hands. It was heavy given its size, like it was made of something denser than rock. She felt the energy in her hands, like this piece of stone had for years absorbed the energy and power of the Given.

'Thank you,' she said again, to the falcon.

23

A   tta towered over Flick, an expressionless sculpture. He looked up at the bookshop's façade and then stepped towards the door. Flick felt power ripple from his body before the door gave way. He entered ahead of her. His presence sent chills through Flick. Her fear of him was stronger than any sense of allegiance. His power was stronger than ever before, growing with every Island conquest. When Island 8 was his, his power would be absolute. No one could challenge him again.

With a wave of his hand, the books along the back wall of the shop flew from the shelves and scattered across the floor. Flick stepped through the book debris towards the stairs. 'What you want is upstairs.'

Without looking back at Atta, Flick headed to the top floor. She heard the sounds of scattering books, smashing of shelves on the ground floor, and then the middle floor, as Atta destroyed all in his path.

As she stepped up to the top floor, Alf was nowhere to be seen, and Flick felt relief. She'd rather not look Alf in the eye and acknowledge her betrayal before his death. It was

Alf's work, with Jay at the bookshop that had made the passageway to Island 8 more challenging for Atta. The power of the Given on Island 8 was greater than on any of the other Islands, and the bookshop was no small part of that. It provided structure for the Given, a means for them to learn and develop. The destruction of the bookshop was Atta's priority on entering Island 8, a greater priority even than the destruction of the Interland, and the completion of the sink-room.

'He's here,' Atta said. 'I feel him.' He walked the length of the top floor, running his fingers along the books as he went, as if he were taking in their contents, identifying those that he would mark for destruction.

He reached the fire escape at the far end and pushed open the door, stepping out onto the landing for a moment and breathing in the air, like a dog searching for a scent. Flick watched as he returned and made his way to the back wall. She followed. As she turned the corner of the book-shelves, Atta stood still, gazing at a wall of books. He flung open cabinet doors to see more books on the Given. His anger bubbled to the surface, and the books fell. Book after book slipped from the shelves, the cupboards and onto the floor.

Atta groaned as if in pain. The energy of the Given enveloped and supported the top floor of the bookshop, created conflict with the opposing power of the darkness that flowed from Atta.

Flick sensed Alf; he was nearby. Knowing how good he was at shielding, that she sensed something of him let her know he was close. For reasons she couldn't untangle, she didn't mention his apartment to Atta.

'Where is he?' Atta growled.

For reasons she couldn't figure, Flick kept silent.

Atta's speed increased as he made his way along the wall of books. Wisps of smoke rose from the books piled onto the floor, as if the friction between Dark and Given generated sufficient heat to burn.

Flick stepped aside as flames flickered on the shelves and on the floor. Atta shouted as he pulled the last rows of books onto the floor and into the growing flames.

'Let's go,' said Flick, backing towards the fire escape.

Atta stared at her. She was still one of the Given. She had not yet been reduced and returned to the tribe of the Readers. She felt the power of the Given within her, fighting against the energy of the darkness, against Atta's destruction of their history.

The flames rose and licked the walls and ceiling. He stepped towards Flick, and past her to the fire escape. Without words, he flung open the fire escape door and out onto the steps.

STITCH CRADLED the source stone as Jay steered the Ford through the streets towards Cassie's house. Jay was jittery. She felt darkness all around as if there were Readers on every corner. With no response to Jay honking the horn, Stitch went in to find Cassie. By the time they returned, Jay was beside herself.

'Hurry,' Jay said, a tightness in her voice. The darkness had infiltrated, and the energy of the Given was threatened.

'What's the matter?' Cassie said as she slid into the back seat and leaned through to the front.

Stich fell into the car as Jay pulled away. 'Something's wrong. We need to get to Alf,' she said.

In the short journey to the bookshop, Jay described her

fears to Cassie. She told them both about Colson's theory, and the three conditions. And she told them she was determined to ensure the darkness would never take their homeland again. What she didn't tell them was what she felt deep down in her bones - that the darkness had already arrived.

They saw the smoke rising from more than a mile away, and when the car screeched to a stop outside the bookshop, there was already a fire engine in the street, its hoses trained on the windows of the top floor. Flames licked the window frames. The glass in one of the windows shattered, raining shards down onto the street below.

They leaped from the car. 'Alf?' Cassie said.

Jay sensed Alf. Their connection had strengthened over their time working together. She felt his fear, his uneasiness. He was afraid, but not in immediate danger. 'He's alive. He's here. Panic room,' she shouted above the background noise. Alf's panic room in his apartment was built into the refurbishment of the bookshop to protect from attack. Alf was determined that his first experience of being taken by Readers wouldn't be repeated.

Without explaining further, Jay took off around the side of the building to the back entrance, with Cassie and Stitch following close behind. She kicked open the door of the outhouse in the rear car port and lifted the floor hatch that led down to the back entrance to Alf's panic room.

She pounded on the steel door at the bottom of the steps. Cassie and Stitch perched on the steps above her. 'Alf!'

A clunk and a click came from the door and it swung slowly inward. Alf's face appeared, Buster at his feet, agitated. Jay almost broke down with the relief. 'Thank God,' she said.

Alf took Jay into a hug. 'I thought you were them,' he

said. 'Readers. They were here. Their power was strong. I was sure they'd sense me down here.'

'We need to leave. The top floor is on fire.'

Alf's eyes filled with dread. 'The books. *Your* books?'

Jay nodded.

A second fire engine arrived and doubled the flow of water aimed at the top floor. Jay begged to be allowed in but the fire department formed a barricade and pushed them back. There was nothing they could do but watch. With a sigh of sadness, Alf beckoned Jay, Cassie and Stitch to the pub opposite.

THEY FOUND a seat by the window from which they could see the bookshop. Cassie and Stitch placed drinks on the table and they sat in silence, watching the streams of water blast into the shop's top floor. Beneath the table, Buster whined.

The smell of cigarette smoke and beer turned Jay's stomach. She sipped her iced water and looked out at the burning building. A firefighter trained a powerful hose on one of the top floor windows. He was joined by another, who shouted something in his ear and took a turn with the hose. Jay imagined the valuable, irreplaceable material on the top floor being destroyed, either by the fire or by the water. She instinctively looked towards her bag, thankful at least that she'd kept the Sasha Colden book with her.

Alf stared at the spectacle beyond the window. A reflection of the orange flames danced in his eyes.

'I'm sorry,' said Jay, breaking the silence.

'What for?' said Stitch, not averting his gaze from the burning building.

'It's my fault,' she said.

Cassie shook her head. 'It makes no sense. If this is the work of Atta, like you said in the car, then how has he gained access? You said that there were conditions?'

Alf and Jay exchanged a glance. They had both felt the power of the dark energy.

Jay thought back to what Colson had said about the conditions for the opening of the channel to the darkness. She'd connected with the darkness herself, up on the roof outside her bedroom window.

'It could have been me,' Jay said, pushing the thoughts around her head. 'That time on the roof.' She looked at Stitch. 'Condition 1. Maybe I opened the door?'

'How?' asked Cassie.

'Something Flick said.' Jay paused. 'I have to protect this place. If I can't do it then who…'

'What are you saying?' Cassie interrupted.

'If I stand any chance of keeping the darkness out, then I need to control it. The power of the Given is just half the story. True power will only come from the integration, the joining of the light and the dark. Maybe that's the answer.' Jay's confidence in her own words waned. She looked defeated.

'What have you done?' Cassie stood, her mind searching, links connecting.

Alf held up a hand. 'Hold on,' he said. 'You never *invited* Atta through. The second condition requires an invitation from the Given to the darkness to use the channel.'

Cassie shuffled on her feet, unable to sit back down. 'Well, something's going on,' she spat, accusatory.

'Even if Condition 2 has been met somehow,' said Stitch. 'Then the sacrifice, the spilling of Given blood? No way.'

'He's found a way,' said Jay, looking at Alf. He knew Jay was right. 'Colson might not have it right.'

'Where is Flick now?' said Stitch.

Alf, his voice low, 'We reduced her.'

Cassie paced up and down. A noise from outside drew Jay's attention. A piece of the roof of the bookshop had dislodged and fallen onto the pavement below. Firefighters stepped back, then re-positioned to direct their water into the hole in the roof.

'She's re-building as the Given, said Cassie. 'She's with Otis.' Cassie stopped her pacing and looked at Jay.

'So Flick is one of the Given...' Jay said.

Alf leaned forward in his chair. 'What have we done?'

'Otis,' Cassie said and bolted for the door.

'Wait. I'll come with you,' Jay stood.

'You've done enough,' Cassie shouted before she stormed out.

PART III

24

A t the sight of the bookshop's top floor, Jay's heart sank. More than half of the books were burnt and charred, those that survived the fire were sodden pulpy lumps. Irreplaceable books –gone forever.

Fire had ravaged Jay's special collection on the top floor. Wet, black soot and ash clung to everything. The smell fizzed in her nose like a chemical burn with every breath. Three out of the four cupboards of papers and notebooks had fallen off the wall, their contents unsalvageable.

The fourth wall cupboard remained hanging from its supports. The cupboard door was blackened, but it remained closed and relatively intact. She held the side of the cupboard to support it as she carefully pulled open the door. Inside, the papers were virtually untouched. She allowed herself a half smile as she ran her fingers over the spines of the notebooks. Then she opened her backpack. The source stone rested at the bottom, next to the Sasha Colden book. She placed the rucksack on the floor and ran her hand over the smooth surface of the source stone. The bowl, worn down by the action of the three river sources, was so soft it felt like soap-stone. She pushed it to the side in her bag and began slotting in the books from the shelves.

Alf knelt by the shelf of books on the Given that looked least touched by flame. He carefully packed his own ruck-sack, then turned to Jay and opened his arms. 'Load me up,' he said. 'We can take as much as we can carry, then come back later.'

'Where to?'

'I was thinking about your dad's pub. The basement. Will you call him?'

'Of course. We can get a taxi,' she said, feeling the weight of the books and the source stone on her back.

JAY AND ALF edged down the steps into the basement of the pub, their arms laden and backpacks full. The room was empty but for her dad standing at the foot of the steps, and Colson at the table. When Ben saw them, he rushed to help Jay with the books, taking an armful and stacking them on the far side of the basement. 'Are you hurt?' he asked.

'Not physically,' said Jay. 'Atta has destroyed most of the books.' She unloaded her backpack, leaving the source stone and Sasha Colden book in the bag.

Alf stacked his books next to Jay's and turned to an expectant looking Colson. 'The conditions have been met,' Alf said, sitting heavily in a chair at the end of the table.

'How?' asked Colson, pausing from his tobacco rolling and leaning forward.

'We think it was Flick.'

Jay's legs wobbled as she staggered to sit, her dad's hand guiding her. She felt light-headed, as if dehydrated. She was sick to her stomach for allowing this to happen. 'It was my fault,' she said.

'Don't,' said Alf. 'This is no-one's fault.' Alf explained to Ben and Colson what had happened at the shop, and their theory about Flick.

'What happened to Otis?' said Colson.

'Cassie's gone to Highdown to find him.'

'Alone?' asked Ben, looking fearful.

'Stitch is following,' said Jay. 'I'll know if they hit trouble.' She lowered her gaze, trying to hide her shame. She was responsible for Flick's betrayal. Cassie had barely looked at Jay.

Colson moved to open the hatch from the bar above, bringing back four steaming bowls. Jay's stomach turned at the meaty smell and she pushed her bowl away. Alf had already tucked in, reaching to rip a hunk of bread from the loaf that Colson placed in the middle of the table. Colson returned to the hatch and brought back four glasses of water.

Ben handed a drink to Jay, along with a spoon. 'You need to eat,' he said.

Colson couldn't eat either. He was distracted. He grabbed himself a crust of bread and stood. He paced the floor of the basement. 'Even if the conditions were met, Atta...' He paused, rubbing his temples. 'I can't believe I'm saying his name. He has been nothing but a myth and now he's here, in our world.'

'He exists. I've met him,' said Jay. 'And he has power like I've never felt before. He controlled me.'

Colson nodded. 'But he can't sustain power without the energy of the core, the sink-room.'

'They will build a new sink-room here,' said Jay. 'We destroyed the building, but not the connection to the core.

We saw the construction on Island 7. They've built over the core, created some kind of power station, a means to amplify the power coming from below.'

'What was it like?' asked Colson.

'A huge warehouse over the top of a massive crater, like an alien landing site or something. In the hole were three rotating electromagnets, connected into the central column. The power was obvious. I felt it. They'll plan to replicate that here.'

'We don't know that...' started Ben.

'What else would they be here for?' Jay snapped.

'Well, it's not the first thing they did, is it? They took out the shop,' said Ben. 'It's the centre of all things relating to the Given. They've hit the central knowledge source.'

'So now they'll just leave it at that? Conquer all the other Islands and leave this one? Be serious, Dad.'

'And they've destroyed the Interland,' Ben added.

'Surprised they haven't taken out the new resistance,' Jay said, losing patience. She immediately felt bad for belittling her dad's group. If it weren't for the basement of the pub, and for Ben and Colson's help, things would be even worse.

'I'm sorry,' she continued. 'The caves have gone, but not the power. The Given power is still strong. Taking out the Interland, and the shop was just a message, a sign, something for them to let us know that they're strong, and that they can come in and destroy what's dear to us. He won't stop there. He's just warming up.'

'Then we have to stop him,' said Alf. 'Tell us about what you found at the Interland.'

Jay retrieved her rucksack from the floor, feeling the weight of the source stone. She unzipped the top and reached inside, lifting out the lump of stone with both hands.

Colson gasped at the sight of it, holding out his hands to take the bowl from Jay. He held it in both hands.

'What is it?' asked Ben, looking at his daughter.

'The stone at the centre of the source, in the underground, from the Interland.'

'How did you find it? I thought the place had sunk into the earth.'

'A little bird helped me.' Jay smiled.

'This is it,' Colson said, his eyes wide. 'I can feel it.'

'Maybe you should put it down?' said Alf, getting jittery as Colson's hands shook.

Colson seemed not to hear Alf. 'Was this in the location of the confluence? Where the three sources joined?' Without waiting for an answer, he placed the bowl on the table and took two books from his own bag. Looking at the big notebooks that Colson placed on the table, Jay was momentarily annoyed he'd taken them from the bookshop, then immediately thankful he'd saved them from the fire.

'What now?' Ben asked, looking at Colson.

'That's what we need to work out,' Colson said, taking another mouthful of bread before opening the cover of the notebook.

25

Otis had been lying beneath the circle of trees for what felt like forever. He was exhausted from moving the bandages telekinetically towards his outstretched hands before tying them around his still seeping ankles. The ground around him was soaked with his blood. Above, a breeze gently rustled the leaves in the trees.

He sent out messages of desperation to Cassie and to Jay, but his energy levels were so low he was sure they would never hear.

The darkness overhead was oppressive. There were no stars in the sky, as if Atta had wiped them away.

He floated in and out of consciousness, shivering one moment, burning with heat the next. Nausea drifted from his stomach through to his chest and into his throat. He wasn't sure if he'd have the energy to survive throwing up.

Otis wished for the end. When he heard footsteps approach, he didn't lift a hand to defend himself. If it were to end his pain, then the re-emergence of Atta and Flick was welcome.

The crack of sticks, the rustle of leaves as two people approached. Otis closed his eyes.

'Otis!'

He recognised Cassie's voice and his body stopped fighting to survive. He slipped into unconsciousness.

* * *

CASSIE REMAINED CALM, slipping into autopilot. As soon as she crouched beside Otis she felt her hands sink into his warm blood. 'His ankles,' Stitch said. 'They're cut.'

Without a word, Cassie inspected the bandages. She used the bottom of her t-shirt to wipe away some of the blood so that she could see how bad he was. Blood seeped from deep wounds to both heels. 'How could she do this?' She re-arranged the bandages and pulled them tighter. 'We need to get him down to the car park.'

'I can carry him,' said Stitch.

'I'll do it,' insisted Cassie. 'You run down to the phone box in the car park. Call an ambulance.' The nearer of the two car parks was only a fifteen-minute walk. Cassie wiped blood from her hands onto her t-shirt and reached for Otis's arms. Stitch helped her drag his body diagonally over her shoulder, careful as he manoeuvred his legs into position.

* * *

AFTER SOME TIME, Colson looked up from the notebook. He had a sparkle in his eyes. He picked up the Sasha Colden book once more, flicking to the back pages where Jay had read the coded message about the source stone. He placed the Colden book gently on the table and picked up the source stone itself, turning it over in his hands, inspecting every inch of its surface as if looking for something.

'What is it?' asked Jay.

'This is it,' said Colson. 'This little packet of power is what will break the flow of dark energy.'

'How?' asked Alf, straightening in his seat.

'We simply need to position it within the channel.'

'*Simply*...' scoffed Ben. 'You're talking about getting that stone into the hole beneath the sink-room, if it's even possible to get to it?'

Alf reached for Jay's hand. 'If Atta is on our Island, then won't he be there, waiting? You can't just walk in there and throw this into the hole.'

'That's exactly what I can do.'

'What if the hole isn't there?' said Ben.

Colson placed the source stone down on the table with enough of a thump to draw attention. 'It must be,' he said. 'We've already agreed that Atta and the Readers cannot be here without a source of power. It's wishful thinking to believe that he's here because of the power on Island 7. We need to get real. He's here, there is a channel to the core, and they're probably building one of those big sink-rooms like Jay saw on Island 7.'

'I'll go,' Jay said. She looked at her dad, and then at Alf. 'I can do this. He might be strong on Island 7, but this is *my* home.'

'This isn't Marcus,' said Alf. 'Or even Hinton. This is a whole new level.'

Colson reached for the source stone and pulled it towards him. He nodded. He stood and placed a hand on Jay's shoulder. 'We know nothing for sure,' he said. 'But if you can get that thing deep into the core, then I think there'll be no coming back for the darkness in this land.'

'How deep?' asked Alf.

Colson shrugged. 'As deep as it goes.'

'What happens then?' said Alf.

Colson looked at Jay. 'You run.'

* * *

BEN LEFT WITH COLSON, and a few minutes later, Stitch appeared in the stairwell. He edged down the last steps and slumped down opposite Jay.

Jay startled at the sight of him. 'Where's Cassie? Otis?'

'Hospital. He's alive. Lost a lot of blood, but he's alive.'

'What happened?'

'Flick. That's what happened.'

Alf stood and paced. 'Otis was the third condition. The sacrifice.'

Stitch nodded.

'The spilling of blood wasn't at the Interland then? It was at Highdown.'

Jay said, 'The legend said it needed to be at a sacred place of the Given, which could have been any of the hill forts, or the Interland.'

'I couldn't do anything. Couldn't help him,' said Stitch, looking at his open hands and then wringing them together as if trying to scrape off the surface of the skin. '*Fricking* useless.'

'You tried to heal?' Asked Alf.

Stitch nodded. 'I've been working on it. A lot. So much for all that.'

'It's coming, Stitch,' said Jay. 'Earlier, your power was strong. Keep going.' She leaned towards Stitch across the table and rested her hand on his. He pulled it away, and Jay thought she could see tears in the corners of his eyes. They were quiet for a moment.

Stitch turned back to the table and the source stone drew his focus. He reached for it, touching it gently with the tips of the fingers on one hand. He seemed to get a spark of energy from the contact and drew his hand away.

'Colson worked it out,' said Jay. 'I need to get it into the channel to the core.'

Stitch shook his head but said nothing.

'Hey,' said Alf, drawing Stitch's attention. 'We need you on this.'

'No,' said Jay, before Stitch could respond. 'This is my responsibility. I won't have anyone else getting hurt.'

Stitch was silent, staring at the source stone. Jay knew that his confidence had taken a hit, and his faith in the power was waning.

'Stitch,' Alf continued, ignoring Jay. 'There's a reason you're branded a "C". You're Jay's connection. Together, you two...'

'Leave it, Alf,' said Jay. 'This is not up for discussion. This is just something I need to do. No casualties on this one.'

'Except you?' Alf snapped. 'What makes you so invincible?'

'Look,' she said. 'There are too many unknowns. What if we go in there together and it's a war? We face an almighty battle and none of us survives? I go alone, under the radar, see the lie of the land and get the stone into position. No-one gets hurt. I come back.'

Alf sighed. 'You remember when we first met?' Jay shook her head, trying to recall the first time she saw Alf in the bookshop, back when she was only six or seven years old. 'Well, I remember it well. You came in with your dad, and I felt the energy. I'd seen your dad before and I knew he had a little something, but that day the energy flowed into the shop like something else.'

'Not when I was *that* little?' said Jay.

Alf nodded emphatically. 'For sure. I knew. Probably before you did, or your dad. I knew you'd be something special.'

'Took a while before I really felt it...'

'But that was nothing,' Alf interrupted. 'Compared to what happened when you made the connection.' He looked at Stitch. He reached for Jay's arm, taking her by the hand and pushing her sleeve back to see her marking. 'This is a gift. And a responsibility.'

'I know,' snapped Jay, pulling her hand away. 'I'll *take* that responsibility. I've caused enough pain already; it's time now for me to finish this.' She picked up the source stone and fed it back into her bag with the Sasha Colden book. She slung the bag onto her back and left without looking back.

* * *

JAY LEFT her house by the back alley, avoiding Sammy and her dad, to head to the hospital. She needed to see Otis. The Beast, the old Ford, was there for her as always. It had become like an old, reliable friend. She turned the key, and it kicked in first time.

The lift doors at the hospital opened. There was a smell from the toilets in the lift lobby mixed with that of bleach to give it a sweet, corrosive flavour. She resisted the urge to pull her top up to cover her nose and stepped into the corridor.

She crossed the reception area and headed for the ward, seeing Cassie as soon as she entered. Jay moved slowly towards the bed. This would be the second person in this hospital with serious injuries resulting from Jay's own failure to protect them. Angie was clear of danger, out of the medically induced coma but still poorly. And now here lay Otis.

As she drew closer, she saw Cassie had Otis's hand in hers. She glanced at Jay.

'She sliced both of his heels. He lost a lot of blood.' Cassie nodded towards the machine at Otis's side with a drip and blood supply. 'He was in the ICU but he's stable now, so they brought him out here.' Cassie looked around the empty ward. 'It's like a morgue.'

Otis lay asleep in a hospital gown like a straitjacket, bandages covering both of his ankles. 'I'm sorry...' Jay said under her breath. It was she who insisted they trust Flick. It was she who swallowed Flick's story about the reduction and re-building as one of the Given. She hadn't even questioned the third scar. She had allowed the most powerful agent of the darkness a path straight into their world. 'I'll make it right,' Jay said. 'I promise.'

Otis's eyelids flickered and Cassie lifted herself in her chair to see into his face. 'Otis?' she said. He opened his eyes and smiled at Cassie, then looked at Jay, his smile remaining fixed.

'Thought I was a goner,' he croaked.

'Shh,' said Cassie, holding a finger to her lips. 'Take it easy. The nurse said you need to go slow.'

He looked over at Jay. 'That friend of yours...' He took a breath. 'She's quite something.'

'I'm sorry, Otis. She took us for a ride...'

'Took *you* for a ride,' Cassie said. Jay nodded solemnly, looking away from Cassie and Otis.

'Hey,' said Otis, turning back to Cassie. 'Don't blame Jay

for this. None of us saw through her. How was Jay to know she was a psychopath?'

Cassie shrugged. 'If there's one person on this planet who should have known exactly who she was and what she was planning...' She turned to Jay, her eyes stony.

Jay avoided Cassie's eye and looked back at Otis. 'I'm going to put this right.' She turned to leave. No one called her to come back.

* * *

AS JAY TURNED the corner into the lift lobby, her mind shifted to little Angie. She had been in this same hospital and last she knew was still here. She looked at the hospital map on the wall next to the lifts and searched for Angie's ward. 'Sixth floor,' she said to herself and slapped the button to call the lift.

With both lifts stopped on the ground floor, Jay turned and pushed the door into the stairwell. She took the two flights of stairs two steps at a time and spilled out into the corridor on level six. Following signs to the wards, she picked up speed, breaking into a run as she felt a genuine sense of urgency to see Angie.

Turning a corner, she narrowly avoided a head on collision with a nurse. 'Hey! Slow down.'

She caught the door before it snapped shut and strode through Angie's ward, looking left and right at each bed as she passed. In the middle of the ward on the left-hand side, there was a couple sat at Angie's bed, one on each side. Angie's parents looked too young, but when they turned to look at Jay, she saw that pain and worry had etched years into their faces.

'Jay!' Angie shouted, waving her over.

'Hey, little one...'

'Who's this, Angie?' her father asked.

'This is the most powerful of the Given... ever,' said Angie, a smile from ear to ear.

'Oh, I see now,' the man said, his expression hardening.

Angie's mum stood and held out a hand. 'She hasn't stopped talking about you,' she said.

'How is she?' Jay asked.

'She's had a bit of a scare. We think it was a shock more than anything else. The coma was a precaution, to enable them to do some tests without fear of damage. She's strong.'

'She's a determined soul,' said Jay. 'I'm sorry,' she said again.

'Bit late for that,' Angie's dad said, standing but not looking at Jay. 'I don't know what you allowed to get to our little girl, but whatever it was, it nearly killed her.'

'Dad...' Angie's face dropped. 'It wasn't Jay, it was Readers.'

'I don't care what...'

'Phillip!' Angie's mum cut him off. 'Take a minute.' She motioned for him to leave. He turned and made for the door without resistance.

'He's just scared. We both are. We don't understand all this...' She trailed off as she waved her hand about. 'We are helpless here. Maybe you can tell us what is going on?'

Jay sat in the seat vacated by Angie's dad. Angie reached for her hand and gave her a warm smile. 'We don't know everything,' Jay said. 'Not yet.'

'It was Readers though,' said Angie, as if she were excited by it. 'Readers attacked, and we fought them off.'

Jay smiled, enjoying Angie's version of events. Her smile faded. 'But I promised I'd keep you safe. And I failed.'

'It wasn't your fault. If it wasn't for you, the Readers would be in charge already.'

'I won't let it happen again,' said Jay.

'Well, it's not all up to you, is it?' said Angie. 'It takes all of us.'

'I hear you,' Jay said softly.

'Do you, Jay?' said Angie. 'You know, it's a sign of strength to ask for help.'

Jay nodded, her eyes downcast as she took in the words.

'You taught me what makes the Given different from the dark power,' Angie continued. 'It's all of us. Together. You, and Stitch. And me.' She smiled and looked over at her mum. Her mum nodded. 'And Alf, and everyone Given. Like when I found you and helped with the phoenix.' Angie smiled.

'Yes, you're right...' Jay started.

'Not just that though,' said Angie. 'Remember you said the most important thing you taught me is the *total* connection. The animals. The sea, and the hills.'

Jay shook her head with a smile. For someone so little, Angie had deep wisdom. She had soaked up so much information on the Given in so little time in the bookshop. Every time Jay saw her, she was full of questions that she'd stored up through her reading time. And her thoughts were always insightful. Angie had great potential.

Angie was right about her needing to connect. She'd never felt so distant from her closest allies, Stitch and Cassie. Jay pictured Otis, his face pale, his body so weak. It was Otis who had been closest to Davey, before Davey met his end in the crossfire in the fight between the darkness and the Given. And Reuben, who was Cassie's first love, killed by Readers. Seeing Otis in that hospital bed, so close to death himself, and Angie, so little, just reinforced the resolve in Jay to put things right while endangering no one else.

'So you need to step up, Jay,' Angie said with a grin. 'Get everyone together for a big fight.'

Jay nodded again but her face was set. She wasn't listening anymore.

26

W hen Jay arrived home, the atmosphere was frosty. Her mum and dad had been arguing. The tension hung in the air and there was no sign of Sammy. She hooked her jacket on the end of the banister, and out of the corner of her eye, she spotted her dad in the kitchen. He was deep in thought, gazing into a bubbling pan on the stove.

Ben looked up as if nudged by Jay's intrusion into his thoughts. He smiled. 'Hey,' Jay said, stepping off the stairs and entering the spicy, humid kitchen.

'You look tired,' Ben said. Jay rubbed her forehead. She dumped her rucksack in the hallway and lifted herself up to sit on the kitchen worktop. Ben looked at her bag. 'Is the stone in there?'

Jay nodded. 'It pulses. Can you feel it?' He shook his head and turned back to the stove. His eyes glazed over as he stared into the broth. 'Everything OK?' asked Jay.

Her dad smiled and straightened, as if to pull himself out of his ruminations. 'Sorry if I've been difficult recently,' he said, taking Jay by surprise. It was true he'd been a little more insistent that Jay be careful, but she wouldn't have called him *difficult*. 'It's been a weird time.' He looked up. 'With your mum and all that. Getting through and coming to terms with what's happened. Figuring out our future. You know?'

Jay nodded. 'You've been doing really well. None of this is easy.' Her mum's affair with the Reader Marcus, an affair that created Sammy, had only come to light last year, even though Jay suspected her dad had known about it. He'd raised Sammy. The biology of a child ceases to be important when the baby arrives. How could anyone resent an act that produced something so perfect? Her parents' decision to make a go of their complex relationship when Ben returned from the Interland would never make for a smooth ride.

'You remember the stories? Back when you two were little?'

Jay smiled. 'Always. Those stories are in my DNA.'

'Who'd have known how it would turn out?' He glanced towards Jay's wrist where her marking seemed so dark as to absorb the light from around it.

'We wouldn't be here if it wasn't for you, Dad. It was your insight that got us to the Interland, got us to where we built what we have now.'

Ben laughed. 'I pointed the way, but you took the lead in that journey, my love.' He put a hand on Jay's arm for a moment, then turned to lean against the kitchen side. He looked at the chessboard on the fridge, its magnetic pieces arranged in a battle not yet played out to a conclusion. 'Is this our game?'

'Me and Sammy's. He's getting the better of me this time. It's been a while. I don't even know whose move it is.'

'You used to let him win,' Ben said with a smile.

'Wish I had that option now,' said Jay.

They were silent for a minute and the only sounds were the distant noise of the television in the lounge and the bubbling stew on the stove. The windows in the kitchen had steamed up and the orange glow from the streetlamp outside sparkled in the moisture on the glass.

'I get a sense that something bad is coming,' Ben said. 'Whatever happens, I want you to know that I'm proud of you. Proud of what you've achieved, for sure, but mostly I'm proud of how you've done it.' He leaned back and took in a deep breath before letting it out slowly, as if trying to calm his nerves. 'Back when the Given were forming as a collective, at the Interland, people gravitated to your way of doing things. You have a way about you that garners a consensus. Looking back, I didn't always do things right. And I'm sorry for that.'

Jay made to interrupt, but Ben raised a hand for her to allow him to finish. 'Whatever happens with this...' He looked up at the ceiling. 'With this resurgence of the Dark, or Atta, or whatever it is, I want you to know that I love you. I'm proud of you, and I've got your back. Whatever you need, I'm here.'

'That means so much, Dad,' Jay said. They hugged.

Her dad pulled away and turned off the stove, removing the pan and placing it on the side. 'You want some?'

'No thanks,' Jay said.

Sammy spilled into the room from the bottom of the stairs. 'What is it?' he asked.

Ben smiled at Jay. 'He only comes when he smells food.'

'Not true,' said Sammy, taking a bowl from the cupboard and ladling stew into it.

'Dish some out for me and your mum,' said Ben. Sammy did as he was asked and Ben took two bowls out to the dining room where he'd eat with Sonia. Sammy pulled himself up to sit on the kitchen top opposite Jay, spooning food into his mouth.

'Good?' asked Jay.

'Not bad for Dad.'

Jay looked at the chess set stuck to the fridge. 'Whose go is it?'

'Yours,' Sammy said between mouthfuls. 'It's been your go for weeks. Anyone would think I scared you off.' Jay studied the board with little recollection of the game. 'You're black,' Sammy said. They were down to a few remaining pieces and with Sammy's queen already gone, Jay was in a commanding position.

She moved her rook into attack. 'Check,' she said.

'Give me a couple of weeks and I'll get back to you,' Sammy teased.

Jay picked up the empty pan from the stove and put it in the kitchen basin, filling it with water to soak. 'Where's Toyah?'

'No idea. She's like a ghost. I thought you'd know better than me. You've spent more time with her than I have recently.'

'I'm not sure we would have got away so cleanly from the Readers if it wasn't for her,' said Jay.

'Yes, she told me about it,' Sammy said, finishing his food and handing Jay the bowl to put in the sink. 'What's going on with that? She says we are safe here, is that true?'

'Yes,' Jay said. 'As long as we take measures.'

'What measures?'

'We're working it out. But don't worry.'

'You could let me in, you know?'

Jay turned to her brother with a frown.

'Come on,' said Sammy. 'This is *me* you're talking to. I know you. And you should know that I'm on your side. You shouldn't need convincing.' He jumped down off the kitchen surface. On the fridge, he moved his king out of reach of Jay's rook and headed for the door. 'I know you'll do it right, Sis. I'm here if you need me.'

Jay looked at the chessboard as Sammy disappeared into the lounge. 'Stalemate,' she said under her breath, seeing that Sammy had manoeuvred into a no-win position for both of them.

* * *

BACK IN HER ROOM, Jay pulled open the Velux and climbed out onto the tiles, only to startle at the sight of Toyah walking away across the roof towards the back alleyway. 'Hey!' she called.

Toyah turned, looking disappointed to be seen.

'What are you doing up here?' Jay asked.

'Just leaving.' Toyah turned again to continue away from Jay.

'Hey!' Jay repeated. 'You can't just...'

Toyah edged back over to Jay and sat down on the tiles, nodding for Jay to join her. 'I sit up here sometimes.'

Jay smiled, trying to draw Toyah's eye. 'On your own? When I'm not here?'

'Sometimes.'

Jay laughed. 'Well, I'm glad to provide a facility for you.'

Toyah remained silent and Jay asked: 'Are you OK? I've hardly seen you since we got back.'

'I've been keeping out of the way.' She nodded back towards the house.

'Sammy?'

Toyah nodded. 'It's complicated. It's nothing to do with *him*.'

'It's not him, it's you? Heard that one before.'

'I need to sort my head out. It's not fair on him until I do.'

'So why are you here?'

Toyah let out a humourless laugh. 'Ask my psychologist. I don't know, to be honest. I'm drawn here, to you as much as to Sammy.'

'I'm flattered.'

'More a draw to the *place*, I think.' Toyah laughed to herself. 'Sorry. I know I'm not making sense.'

'Sammy's downstairs.'

'I guessed as much. I saw him yesterday.'

'Why don't you...'

'Can we leave it?' Toyah said, a tone of pleading in her voice.

Jay left it. 'How's Pinto?'

'Still struggling at school. He told me you went to see him. He appreciated it. Thanks.'

'He's strong. He needs to see those boys off. He's too nice.' Jay pictured the boys throwing things at Pinto at the school gate. She remembered that feeling of isolation, and her heart ached for Pinto. She resolved to see him again, and this time she wouldn't stick to the sidelines. This time, she'd make sure the bullies knew what they were dealing with. 'And what about you? Is home OK?'

'That place has never been my home. Not sure I know where my home is, maybe that's the problem.' Toyah looked out and up to the hills. The dark clouds that had gathered over the past few days lingered, ominous.

'I think you need to do something for *you*. For your future. Pinto will work things out.'

Toyah dragged her focus from the horizon to look at Jay like she'd suggested something crazy. Emotions flickered across her face, intrigue, even hope. 'Maybe,' she said, returning her gaze to the hills. 'So what's going on? What does the oracle say about this darkness?'

'Alf?'

'And the other one, what was his name?'

'Colson. We think there's a way to protect Island 8. For good.'

Toyah nodded, like she knew Jay would already have a solid plan. Her confidence energised Jay. Cassie and Stitch had offered little in the way of support and solidarity in recent weeks, so Toyah's positive energy had become important.

'Thanks,' said Jay.

'What for?'

'Lots of things. Thanks for getting us out of that place, Island 7. At one stage I wasn't convinced we'd make it back.'

'Never in doubt.' Toyah smiled. 'Can't help worry about Tiago and his family. You think the Readers will get to him in the end?'

'He's made it this far. He has some means of shielding they haven't cracked yet.'

'You cracked it.'

'I'm Given. It's different.'

Toyah shrugged. 'I guess. You'd know.' She stood to leave. 'Let me know if you need anything. Whatever your plan is.'

'I will.' As much as she valued Toyah's ingenuity, she had no intention of dragging her into her journey to the source. This one was meant for her alone. 'And don't worry. You'll work it out.'

Darkness hung like a cloak over Highdown. The hilltop seemed to emit tiny sparks of light, like a thundercloud. With each spark, a picture came to Jay's mind. 'The channel,' she said to herself, her words drifting on the light breeze off the sea.

It was Flick's deception that tricked Jay into opening the first channel to the darkness. What she now saw was a consequence of Flick's attack on Otis. The pathway for Atta was wide open. There was no way of telling how much time she had. Atta could already be at the sink-room, building, preparing to take the final Island, the last remaining stronghold of the Given.

Looking into the darkness, Jay felt the power of the Given flow through her body. The sea whispered. The power was as strong as ever. Jay was as strong as she'd ever been. A spark pierced the darkness and shot through the distance between the house and the hills in a fraction of a second. This time, Jay opened and saw a vision of Atta. She sensed his weakness, that his eagerness to get to her would be his downfall. She was far more powerful.

She stood, opening to the waves of dark energy, matching their force with her own Given energy. She felt no fear. The sparks became a stream of white light, a pathway between Jay and the dark. The light expanded to encompass the whole of the grey sky so that nothing was visible but for a figure in the distance, heading towards Jay as if crossing a bridge. Jay beckoned. This was Atta, yet, still, she felt no fear.

The physical form of Atta came into view as the white light cleared. Jay stood on the shore of Island 8, looking over the water to Atta, on the shore of Island 7. Neither moved.

'Very brave,' Atta said, his voice low, steady, and calm. 'Bringing me here like this.'

Jay's energy outweighed her fear. While she hadn't intended to summon Atta, she was surprised at how easy it had been. She sensed she would have the upper hand if they were to fight. Could he be defeated here, in interdimensional space?

She wasted no time. Jay attacked with all the power she could summon. Atta rocked back, stumbling into the trunk of the tree in the centre of Island 7.

She reached deeper into the Given lake of power, directing a growing stream of attack. Then she paused. Atta recovered, slowly standing tall again. He niggled at the edges of her defences, but she chased away his infiltrations like batting insects buzzing around her head.

Jay took a deep breath and opened fully to the energy in the environment, the tree at the centre of her Island, the ground beneath her feet, and the three streams of water from the rivers flowing into the foot of the tree. She dug deep into Atta's mind, pushing his consciousness around as easily as if she were sweeping leaves. He lost his footing for a moment and fell to the floor on all fours.

The full power of the Given flowed through Jay. She sensed the energy of the source stone and made one decisive attack on Atta as he struggled to get to his feet.

The energy knocked Atta flat. White light filled the sky and descended once more on the Islands. Jay kept up the flow of her attack, determined to finish Atta here, now. He seemed to shrivel under the weight of the white glare of the light from the sky. Then everything went white and Jay stopped, crouching to rest. She breathed heavily for a minute, peering into the light to see what remained of Atta.

As the light eased, like a clearing mist, she saw the prone figure of Atta on the shore of Island 7. She sensed no dark energy from him, and for a moment she dared to hope that he could be dead, or at least reduced. Then his leg moved.

She drew a deep breath once more. He was weak. She would finish him. She thrust her power into his mind. He squirmed, turning over on the shore. He seemed to gather whatever remaining power he could and fired dark pulses of energy at Jay, but it was a distraction more than a concern.

Atta raised himself to his knees and looked into the sky. The white mist intensified, swirled around the Islands mixed with black smoke-like swirls of darkness. The light intensified until Atta was nothing more than a dim outline across the water. He turned then, away from Jay, and the light filled her head until there was nothing else.

Jay woke face down on her bed, with no memory of how she'd got from outside on the roof to her room. She shook her head clear and sat up.

She'd taken on Atta and got the better of him. His attacks had been feeble. His attempts to fight her off ineffective.

But he was alive. She felt him still.

So now she knew she couldn't defeat him on the Islands. She would need to finish him in the physical world. But any vestige of fear was now gone. Jay knew her power was enough.

27

At first light, Jay climbed in to the front seat of the car to head to the prison. She threw her rucksack with the source stone onto the passenger seat. Before she turned the key in the ignition, she paused, sensing something. She looked over her shoulder and jumped when she saw Stitch laid out on the back seat, his legs folded over one another and a coat over his body for warmth. He stirred.

'Sorry to wake you,' Jay said, sarcasm in her tone.

Stitch croaked a reply. 'Ah, you're here. I figured you'd slope off early.'

'You could have come in to the house?'

'Didn't want you to talk me out of it. I'm coming with you.'

Jay stifled a laugh at Stitch's bedraggled look. She was relieved to have him with her. She needed him. As much as she tried to push the fear from her mind, she was scared for sure, and she didn't yet know how much resistance she would get from Atta and his Readers. With Stitch, she was stronger. She knew that now. He clambered into the front seat, knocking Jay's bag onto the floor.

'Careful,' Jay said. 'That's only the most valuable and powerful piece of rock you'll ever come across.'

'Sorry,' Stitch said, pulling his seatbelt on. 'Let's hit the road.'

Jay drove with her window rolled down and sea breeze blowing through the car. She glanced over at the bag on Stitch's lap, the source stone safe inside. With their combined strength of power, they'd get the stone into the channel to the core. Where uncertainty fluttered at the edges of her mind, she pushed it away. There was no time for second thoughts.

She shifted the car down into second and turned into Northtown, taking the route along the river. She pulled over, pausing for a moment on the river road. It was here they'd scaled the river wall and entered the storm water system to free Cassie from Hinton. 'This time we take the front entrance,' she said.

'Go in fighting,' said Stitch.

She looked up towards the alleyway between the houses and wondered about Sebastian, the guardian of the house that was their overnight resting place before moving in for their rescue of Cassie. Sebastian had been twitchy, nervous of their presence, fearful of capture by Readers. The estate had improved since then. More of the houses were occupied. There were people on the streets – families heading home, teenagers on their way out. She looked through the windscreen towards the prison.

'What are you thinking?' asked Stitch.

'That we see if Sebastian is there, check he's OK?'

'You sense something?'

'No,' said Jay. 'That's the thing. I don't feel him.' She turned the car around and headed for Sebastian's place.

The windows of Sebastian's house remained boarded, much as they were before, but now the windows on each side showed life. Jay pulled on the handbrake and they slipped out of the car, the rucksack with the source stone over her shoulder. They hopped over the low front wall and around to the side alley, which led to the back door of the house. Jay cupped her hands on the glass to look for any signs of movement. Sebastian should be less reclusive now that the Given were accepted in society.

She knocked, waited, then tried the handle. The door clicked open and Jay pushed it far enough that they could squeeze through. Stitch closed it behind them. The kitchen was dingy. The smell in the air was of a house left empty - no scent of human activity. She opened the fridge, which stayed dark and held nothing but a half-empty container of milk, solid at the bottom. She exchanged a look with Stitch. Her heart sank at the thought that Sebastian had been taken by Readers, and that it could have been payback for sheltering her and Stitch.

In the middle room, Sebastian's belongings were scattered all over the floor. She feared the worst for him, but retained hope that he'd moved on, and not fallen to the mercies of the Readers.

Stitch sat on the bed as Jay sifted through his scattered belongings, organising them into piles as she tidied. A drawer full of papers had been upended onto the floor – correspondence, bills, old bank statements, and a few personal effects. She stacked them neatly back in the drawer and returned the drawer to its cabinet.

Opening a photo album, she recognised Sebastian as a

younger man, standing with a woman Jay figured was his partner, and two children, girls both under five.

'What's that?' asked Stitch.

'His family.' One of the little girls hung onto his arm, pulling him towards the floor. She was crying in the photo. Sebastian looked young, maybe not much over twenty. 'I wonder what happened to them.'

Stitch stood. 'We should go.'

Jay felt an urgent need to find out what had happened to Sebastian, but she knew Stitch was right. She closed the photo album and pushed it onto the table beside Sebastian's bed, knocking something onto the floor as she did so.

'What's that?' asked Stitch.

Jay leaned down to pick it up. 'His old staff pass for the prison. He used to work there.'

'Any use?'

'No. It's more than two years out of date and, anyway, the prison's been closed for months. But this...'

'What?'

'The pass is for a staff entrance on Southdown Road. I didn't know there was a staff entrance. That will be a better route in than the main entrance.'

JAY KEPT THE ENGINE RUNNING. The guard's box was occupied, just like the one at the main gates which they had passed by on their way through. It made no sense for security to be in place if the prison had long been abandoned.

She pulled up to the lowered gate and shielded. A Reader stepped out of the security hut and approached the driver's side, pulling his hood up against the gathering wind and spotting rain. Jay looked at Stitch, then wound the window down halfway.

'The prison is closed,' said the man, speaking slowly, his voice low and his breath steaming the outside of the window. Jay felt his power and immediately directed more energy into her shield. He scrutinised her, then Stitch, his grey-blue eyes reflecting the colour of the sky. His expression was neutral - not suspicious, not interested.

He was a level seven, strong, but still no match for Jay and Stitch. She looked over his shoulder at the other guard in the security hut. His level was lower, perhaps a four or five. The Reader at her window would be the one to focus on. 'Ready?' she said. Stitch nodded.

Working together, they entered the Reader's mind. They twisted the level seven's thoughts. His expression turned from neutral to confused. He straightened, staggered a little and then leaned with his back into Jay's window. Jay doubled her effort, and the Reader shook his head as if trying to rid himself of their influence.

The other Reader called out, 'Hey?'

Jay and Stitch turned their attention to the Reader in the booth. He went down with little resistance. Without taking her eyes off the level seven, Jay reduced the weaker Reader to the point of unconsciousness. The level seven saw what was happening and turned to run. Jay and Stitch entered his head, digging, manipulating. He stumbled, then fell over his own legs, hitting the ground with force where he remained prone, unmoving.

Both Readers incapacitated, Jay stepped carefully from the car to the booth and opened the gates, looking towards the prison complex for any movement.

Jay followed her intuition, guiding the car through the

old prison access roads, her senses tuned to the presence of more Readers. It was eerily quiet.

There were few buildings remaining from the old prison complex. Most of the area had returned to its natural state, with grass and foliage weaving through the rubble. In the distance, she saw one of the few structures still standing, the main building, which sat above the old sink-room.

28

The tarmac surface of the old staff car park had deteriorated over time, making way for weeds and grass impatiently pushing up from below. They could see the remains of the sink-room building they had destroyed, the building where the Given were led to have their powers ripped from them by Readers.

'You feel that?' Jay said. She sensed dark power emanating from the building and knew that the connection with the core was active. The strength of the power shocked her, given that the electromagnets, like she'd seen on Island 7, couldn't yet be operational. It crossed her mind to turn around and head as far from the facility as possible.

'I can feel something,' said Stitch.

Forcing the fear from her mind, Jay pushed open the car door. They strode across the car park to the outside of the part-demolished building. The hum of the facility grew louder as they approached, reminding Jay of the noise that came from the sink-room on Island 7. The closer they got, the surer she became the electromagnets were more advanced than she'd expected. Jay shuddered, thinking how

Flick had played her. Atta was closer to taking control than she'd let on.

Not one door to the main building was intact. The rehabilitation of the sink-room by the Readers hadn't included repairs to the superstructure. This was a functional repair, no time for the aesthetics. They passed through an opening and into the building. As they turned a corner, they were faced by a lone Reader.

'What are you doing here?' he said. 'How did you get in?'

Before Jay or Stitch answered, the Reader seemed to recognise who they were, and he reacted. A sharp pain entered Jay's head, knocking her off balance. She staggered against the wall of the corridor, her bag dropping to the floor by her feet. She shielded, resisting his influence. Stitch reacted, launching a counterattack on the Reader. The Reader intensified his digging, piercing Jay's mind and disorientating her. Stitch struggled to penetrate the Reader's mind. As Jay wobbled on her feet, he came at her. His switch to physical attack took his concentration and Jay was momentarily released from his grip. She ducked, and he stumbled past her into the wall. When he turned, Jay and Stitch were ready.

He hit the ground with the force of their combined attack. On the floor of the corridor in front of them, he writhed in pain, holding the sides of his head. Jay saw through the darkness to the fear in the level eight Reader. He'd not experienced the Given with the connected strength of Jay and Stitch's power before. She preyed on that fear, used it as a door to the deeper parts of his mind until she dug into his subconscious.

He let out a defeated gasp of air and his arms dropped from the sides of his head as he slipped over onto his back, unmoving, unconscious.

With her foot, Jay pushed back the Reader's sleeve to confirm her sense that he was a high level. The black figure of 8 stared back at her, a marking she'd seen only a few times, including her own. She looked at Stitch and his jaw dropped open. 'This is bad,' he said.

Jay picked up her rucksack and pressed on towards the source of the hum, her confidence growing with each step. The level 8 Reader had caught them off guard, but proved little resistance in the end. She would find the opening to the core and free this place from Atta's darkness.

They turned the last corner into an atrium. A deep tomb opened in the ground, not as wide as the hole on Island 7, but deeper. It fell away into darkness as Jay neared the edge.

The hum emanated from the depths. As she came closer, a glint of light emerged where the three heads of the electromagnet rotated around a central core.

It's complete, Jay thought with shock. The system was already fully functional, much like the system on Island 7. She looked around, her eyes darting between glints of light in the depths of the hole, looking for Atta.

'What is this?' Stitch said, staring into the darkness.

'Like I saw on Island 7. This is the sink-room.'

Atta was close. Jay could sense him. He was already channelling the power from the core. Feeling the dark energy, Jay knew that this facility was powerful, more so than that on Island 7.

Jay's heart raced as she scanned the room. Near the far shadows, a figure moved.

Flick.

Jay stood rooted to the spot as Flick approached. 'Traitor,' Jay said, off guard at the sight of the girl she had considered a friend.

'You two can't do anything here,' Flick said. Her expression was almost of concern for Jay. 'It's too late.'

'We'll see.' Stitch stood alongside Jay as she pulled her rucksack off her back. 'I trusted you,' she said.

'We *helped* you,' Stitch said.

'It's too late, Jay. I'm sorry.'

Jay ignored Flick and opened the zip of the rucksack. 'You have to find the Given to feed into your machine before this will have any impact.'

Flick sighed in resignation. 'The power we get from the core on this Island does more than transform the Given. We can transform any member of the population.'

Jay remained silent. She looked at Stitch, and he nodded encouragement for her to get on with it.

'We can also use it for the *refinement* of Readers. With the energy of these new sink-rooms, we can increase the strength of power of existing Readers.' Flick looked frustrated as Jay continued to ignore her. 'Don't you see?' Flick said. 'There will soon be great numbers of level *eight* Readers, and of course diminishing numbers of the Given as we work through your population.'

Jay shook her head, no longer willing to discuss Flick's dark plans. She pulled the source stone from her bag and allowed the bag to fall to the ground. She held it in front of her with both hands, expecting Flick to react. Flick simply looked at the floor as if disappointed in Jay.

Atta appeared first as a shadow, barely more than a wisp of smoke. Then his physical form materialised much like it had the first time Jay faced him. Stitch stepped backwards at the sight of him. Jay felt his extraordinary energy once more.

'Thank you,' he said to Jay, his voice gravelly. 'For bringing the stone.'

Jay looked at the stone and stepped closer to the edge of the hole that stretched down into the core.

'I enjoyed our little game on the Islands yesterday,' Atta said.

'When I took you down, you mean?'

Atta laughed. 'That's not the real world, you know that.'

Jay readied herself. 'Your weakness felt real enough to me.' She looked from Atta to Flick. Flick averted her gaze.

Jay gathered her Given power from within, opening to the energy of her surroundings, both the dark and the light - building her strength. She drew closer to Stitch so that their arms touched and their energy flowed together.

'How sweet,' Atta said, smiling.

The anger Jay should have felt for Flick's betrayal was strangely absent. Her only emotion towards her was pity. Flick continued to avoid eye contact, choosing instead to slip behind Atta as he stepped towards Jay and Stitch. His physical form consolidated, he was a man of little more than thirty, athletically built. Jay focused her and Stitch's energy on their shielding, anticipating his first attack and preparing to throw the stone. But something held her back.

'Why did you come here?' Atta said, genuine confusion in his tone and in his mind.

'To finish the job I started on the Islands,' Jay said.

Atta turned to Flick and smiled briefly. 'And you two came alone?'

Atta's power came at Jay and Stitch in waves, as if he was struggling to keep it back.

Jay moved quickly. She threw the source stone as far across the hole as she could so that it plummeted towards the centre. Then, with Stitch, she turned to Atta, and they shielded themselves and the trajectory of the source stone with all the power they could muster. He looked at them, then at the stone, and raised a hand. Jay and Stitch fell back, stumbling and slamming against the floor. They watched helplessly as Atta turned to the hole and halted the stone in mid-air.

The stone landed gently in his outstretched hand. 'You thought it would be that easy? Have you lost your minds?' He took the stone in both hands and released Jay and Stitch from his control. He turned his nose up at the source stone, as if it were a lump of dirt. As he placed it upright, he seemed to flinch as its energy pulsed. 'You can't just throw this in there. It's not a football,' he laughed. 'This facility is the most concentrated source of dark energy on all the eight Islands. You think this little stone would simply drift into the core?'

Jay slumped back to the floor. That was exactly what she had thought. She desperately weighed options, furious with herself for her naivety.

'We need to leave,' said Stitch under his breath.

Digging into her fury, Jay attacked, channelling all her energy and desire to survive into Atta, its lightness circling him and piercing his mind. Stitch reached out and touched Jay's arm, channelling his own power through her. The source stone dropped to the floor with a loud crack. Atta staggered. Jay rocked back on her heels as his resistance came hard, deflecting their attack and powering back with a darkness that penetrated to her very bones. Stitch seemed to glow in the energy and crumpled to the floor. Jay's legs trembled and gave way as she dropped to her knees.

The darkness swirled around her head and into her body – through her nose, mouth and ears. It filled her as Flick looked on and the source stone rested, inert, up against Flick's foot.

She had misjudged Atta, misread the strength of his

power – or completely over-estimated her own ability to control the power of the Given in her own land, even with Stitch. Her head swam, and she felt Atta's sense of victory.

He crouched beside her. 'Not yet,' he said, breathing in her face. 'I still need you.' Jay looked over at Stitch, his body still.

Atta stood, keeping his dark grip on Jay and turning to speak to Flick. Jay couldn't hear the words, but Flick picked up the source stone and turned to leave as Atta returned to Jay's side, tightening his grip. Jay struggled to keep her eyes from closing. The blurred images merged into one. She sensed that if she closed her eyes, then that would be the end.

'Let me in,' Atta said. Jay felt his energy pushing at the edges of her deep subconscious, and she resisted. He seemed to lose patience and stood, grabbing Jay by the collar of her top and dragging her towards the edge of the room, flinging her against the wall then pulling her into an upright sitting position. She slumped to the side. He grabbed her by the hair and forced her upright once more.

He stood before Jay. He raised his head and closed his eyes. Through her blurred vision, the edges of his body seemed fluid, with wisps of dark smoke escaping his form every few seconds. His eyes closed. Jay felt his attack once more, and she was helpless to resist. She screamed as his energy opened her up and she saw what he was trying to do.

Atta's eyes sprang open, and a smile crept across his face as he gained control of Jay. Images flashed through her mind of her friends, of Alf, her dad. 'What are you doing?' she mumbled through pain and weakness as her head lolled. Alf's image came to the front of her mind, his face grey and his expression grave. Jay's eyelids drooped.

'Don't resist,' Atta said.

'Stop...'

'You are my channel to the old man.'

'Alf...' Jay mumbled. A spike of adrenaline forced her eyes open. 'Don't hurt him.'

'He evades me, always. Not anymore. Thanks to you, he will no longer be a threat.'

The image of Alf in her mind was squeezed and distorted, his face a picture of pain and hurt. 'Leave him,' Jay said, pushing back at Atta's power. She refused to be his conduit to attack Alf. Pain shot through her head and into her chest. It felt like her heart had stopped. She couldn't breathe.

Jay slumped to the floor. She felt her friend's presence. Alf was with her. But the strength of his energy slipped away and after a few seconds, he was gone.

Atta took a deep breath, then sighed with a sense of satisfaction. 'Thank you. That's been a long time coming. You feel it?'

If you could feel the absence of something, then, yes, she could feel it.

ALF HAD BEEN a big part of what Atta saw as the defence of Island 8. He had dealt with him, and now he would deal with the last remaining threat. He would finish Jay. Without her and Alf, he would be free to complete what he'd started here on Island 8.

Atta faced Jay. The pain in her head doubled. She could no longer focus on shielding and the pain ramped up in waves. She thought of Stitch.

Then there was nothing.

Everything stopped.

She fell onto her side. The darkness receded from her eyes and she saw Flick standing over her with Stitch. Flick leaned down and shook Jay by the shoulders. 'Get up! You need to go. Now!'

Jay staggered to her feet and pushed Flick away from her. Stitch held Jay's arm. 'We need to go,' he said.

Flick handed Stitch Jay's rucksack and she could see that the source stone was inside. She looked at Flick, whose eyes bore into her, pleading with her to leave before it was too late.

Jay could do little more than be guided by Stitch towards the exit. Flick hurried them up as she looked back over her shoulder. The dark wisps of smoke came once more. They circled, and a warm breeze flowed into the building from the outside as if sucked into a vacuum. Flick turned to face Atta as he re-formed in front of her. 'Leave,' she said to Jay and Stitch. 'Don't look back.'

As they fled, the noise of battle grew behind them. At the entrance, Jay glanced backwards. Flick faced Atta. She would stand no chance of resisting his power. Jay took a step back towards Flick and Atta, but Stitch held her back, and a shake of the ground knocked them off their feet. Warm air flushed through the corridors.

Dust and debris flew through the air. Flick screamed as Jay tried to summon some power to help, to resist Atta, but already the noise abated. The fight was over.

Jay and Stitch backed towards the door.

As the dust settled, Atta stood over the still body of Flick. Stitch grabbed Jay by the arm and dragged her towards the exit.

Dark energy buffeted them, pushing them from the building. Now Jay knew the truth: she was no match for

Atta, even here in her homeland, with Stitch, with her power at its strongest.

As they reached the car, Stitch pulled at the passenger door and shoved Jay inside, she looked back towards the building. It shook and rattled, the top floors buckling. The remains of the windows and doors imploded, sucking in air so that Jay felt the car being dragged towards the building. Stitch stumbled as he tried to prise himself into the driver's seat. It was as if a black hole had opened up inside the building, consuming all matter within its reach.

The vortex grew stronger, and Stitch had to hold on to the side of the car to prevent from being dragged across the car park. He climbed into the front seat and used all his strength to shut the door. The engine started first time and Jay breathed relief.

A figure appeared at the epicentre of the destruction. Stitch slammed the car into gear and spun it around in the car park. Without looking back, he powered towards the exit. They were out of Atta's reach. In the wing mirror, Atta continued to suck everything within range into his tornado of darkness.

29

D ark clouds thickened. Jay asked Stitch to drive to the Hill; she was drawn there, as she often was in times of desperation. Being anywhere else seemed to make no sense, and she needed to recover. The clouds moved in unnatural patterns in the sky and Jay knew that the influence of the Dark was growing.

She wiped the rain from her eyes, and they crossed the boundary into the central ring of trees. The energy of the Given flowed through her on the Hill with a renewed vigour. They both sat on the floor next to the log seats around the fire. Jay stared into the cold, wet ashes as a deep ache of sorrow grew in her chest. Alf. Her dear sweet friend. Had she yet again been responsible for the destruction of one of her friends?

She looked at Stitch. He felt her pain. 'Alf,' Jay said.

'I know,' said Stitch.

She felt nothing of him in the power.

* * *

JAY AND STITCH lay back on the sodden woodland floor and looked skyward. The rain had stopped, but big droplets continued to fall from the trees. A half-moon peeked through the clouds to illuminate the branches. The wet leaves shone, sprinkled with diamonds.

'Alf?' she said aloud, closing her eyes and taking deep breaths of the cool, fresh air. A cool droplet landed on her forehead, the sound exaggerated, echoing through the trees. She allowed herself to be consumed by the power of the land, sinking into the woodland floor and into the network of tree roots, earth fissures and groundwater flows. She submitted to their direction, flowing with the power, searching for Alf.

'Alf?' she said again. 'I'm sorry.'

His image came to Jay. His energy was low. He was weak. Whatever Atta had done, he had succeeded in diminishing Alf, and he'd done it by channelling his dark power through Jay - *she* had provided him access to Alf.

She sank deeper into the power.

Alf appeared as if he was sitting before her, inside the ring of trees at Highdown. He reached out for her hand and she sat up. The woodland floor no longer wet, daylight streaming through the gaps in the branches above their heads. The sky shone blue.

'Alf?' Jay stammered. 'What have I done?'

Alf smiled. 'You've achieved more than anyone else I can think of. In this messed up world, you, my girl, are a shining light, a beacon of hope.'

Jay shook her head and looked up at the sky for inspiration. 'What is this?'

'This is *my* creation. You brought me here, but I created the backdrop, so to speak.' Alf waved his hand to take in the sky and as he did, a rainbow appeared above. 'Look, there's only so much I can do. Everything that Colson said is right.'

Jay looked Alf in the eye and could see his anxiety as clearly as if it were her own. He continued: 'But I have faith in you, my girl.'

'We can do this together. Whatever we need to do, we will beat him.'

'I know,' Alf said with a sad smile. 'I *never* doubted. But now is the time for you to focus.'

'What do we do?'

'That's for you to work out, but you are not alone. You need to remember your roots.' Jay frowned, and Alf leaned closer. 'In here,' he said as he tapped his chest. 'Dig deep, my girl. Trust your instincts, your intuition. I can't do this for you. You are far stronger and more capable than me or anyone else.'

'He's too strong.'

Alf shook his head.

Jay slumped. This test, or whatever it was, was designed for her to fail.

'Remember where all this started?'

Jay thought for a moment. Her powers had come to her at a relatively young age. She was drawn to Alf's bookshop back then. At first it was an inexplicable draw, but after time, as her power became clearer, the draw was clear to Alf, and the community of the Given, although she still didn't understand it back then. 'The bookshop,' said Jay.

'Yes, and your connections. Stitch. And Cassie,' Alf said, taking Jay's hand once more. 'Cassie has lost her way. You need to help her, and she will help *you*.'

'She's so angry with me.'

'She's scared. Of becoming isolated. She's scared for *you*.'

Jay almost laughed at the thought of Cassie being

scared, but Alf's expression was serious. She looked up at him and his energy seemed to fade, his complexion becoming paler as she watched. He glanced up at the sky. 'It's time,' he said.

'For what?'

'For you to get to work. Remember what I said.'

'Which bit?'

Alf smiled, his hand still holding onto Jay's, but his grip weakening. 'Whichever bit you think is important.'

The sun seemed to slip behind a cloud and the area inside the ring of trees on Highdown darkened. They both looked up as clouds thickened. The sun made way for a half-moon before that too became obscured by black clouds. 'Alf?' Jay said. His hand slipped from hers and when she turned to him, he was gone.

The rain came.

Jay stood and lifted her face to the sky, the rain bouncing off and splashing into her open mouth. Stitch stirred and stood with her.

There was a missing part to her world now. Alf had gone. Not just gone from her mind, but gone from this world. He was dead.

His words pinged around inside her head, not yet able to find a home where they made any sense. A hole in her gut expanded to swallow her entire body. Her tears mixed with the rain on her face.

The rain stopped abruptly, and the moon reappeared, casting light over the hill.

What they faced now was something *never* seen before, not even Sasha Colden, *Maram,* the first recorded 8C of their homeland, had faced anything like this, and with Alf gone, there was no-one to help.

PART IV

30

Cassie approached from the inner tree-line, like a ghost in the light of the moon. She pulled a towel from her rucksack and threw it at Stitch before sitting down on the log. Jay and Stitch joined her, Stitch rubbing the towel on his head. 'Thanks,' he said.

Cassie's expression was grave. She looked from Stitch to Jay and was about to speak when Jay said, 'I know.'

'Know what?' asked Cassie.

'Alf's gone,' said Jay. 'Atta used me to get to him.' She explained to Cassie what had happened. As she spoke, it was as if she were outside of herself, watching herself explain the death of Alf. He was family. She couldn't stop thinking about what would happen to his dog, Buster.

Cassie nodded and lowered her gaze. 'We thought he was OK. Then he slipped away.'

'I'm sorry, Cass,' said Jay. 'I've been doing this all wrong.' She looked away into the trees. 'I've made everything worse.'

'It's not your fault,' said Stitch.

'Otis is improving,' said Cassie, standing. 'He'll be OK.'

'Thank God,' said Jay.

'What now?' said Stitch, standing with Cassie and helping Jay up.

'We'll work it out, but we need to stick together,' Cassie said. She drew Jay into a hug and immediately recoiled. 'Ugh, you are soaked.'

'I'm all out of plans,' said Jay. 'This hasn't happened before.'

'Not since 1667,' said Stitch.

Jay used Stitch's towel to dry her hair. '1667,' she said. 'We don't know what happened back then. Alf and Colson were guessing.'

Cassie said, 'If anyone knows what happened, then it's those two old guys. Alf knew all there was to know about the origins of the Given, and what Colson doesn't know about the powers isn't worth knowing.'

'What happened at the prison?' asked Cassie.

'Atta was not what I imagined him to be, not what I'd seen on Island 7. He barely had a physical form. It felt like we were grasping at mist in the air. He was impenetrable. His power was like nothing I've experienced from the Readers.' she said.

'What is he?' asked Cassie. 'If he's not human, then what?'

'He looked human to me,' said Stitch. 'Mostly.'

'How did you get away from him?' asked Cassie.

'Flick,' said Stitch. 'She did something. Distracted him. Shielded us. I don't know.'

'Is she dead?' asked Cassie, as if she already knew the answer. Jay nodded. Cassie snorted. 'She deserves whatever she got.'

They were silent for a moment as Cassie's words bounced between them. Neither Stitch nor Jay responded.

Cassie felt deeply for Otis, and Flick had attacked him in a way that Jay could barely imagine.

'Look,' Cassie said, 'if Atta can be distracted, like you said, then he's human enough for us to get to him.' A characteristic confidence came through in her voice, despite the obvious imbalance of power, and the uncertainty. This was the Cassie who Jay remembered from before, from the Interland. 'Is that the stone?' asked Cassie, pointing at Jay's bag, sodden and scrunched up next to the log. Before waiting for Jay's answer, she grabbed the bag and pulled out the source stone. A breeze seemed to pick up and rifle through the trees as she held it in both hands. 'So how do we get this into the core.'

'We tried that,' said Jay. 'We have to get past *him* first. And however many Readers he's created.'

'Since when have a few Readers scared us off?' said Cassie

'Us?' Jay said, liking the sound of the word.

'You bet,' said Stitch.

* * *

STITCH TRAVELLED with Jay in the old Ford. Cassie travelled alone, using Otis's moped. By the time Jay had parked the car back in the garage at Jay's house and walked to the pub, Cassie was already annoyed. 'Took your time,' she grumbled as Jay and Stitch strode into the pub car park where Cassie had parked the bike.

Jay and Stitch chose not to respond.

'There's a bunch of them already in there,' said Cassie. 'I saw your dad and Colson go in.'

Jay pushed through the pub door towards the basement steps. The landlord caught her eye and nodded for them to head down. The door at the top of the stairs scraped along the concrete floor as Jay pulled it back. She stepped down into a waft of musty basement air tinged with the smell of burned paper from the remains of their library that they'd transported to the basement from the shop. She checked once over her shoulder that Stitch and Cassie were still with her.

Jay dumped her bag on an empty chair. There were three men and two women in the basement, all leaning over the table in the middle of the room. Alf's dog, Buster, ran to her, jumping up and licking her face. 'Oh, Buster, I'm sorry,' said Jay, hugging the dog.

As well as Ben and Colson, Matchstick was there, along with two women Jay had never met. All heads lifted to look at Jay and her friends as they entered. 'What happened?' Ben said to his daughter, appraising her for damage. 'We all felt it.' He motioned towards his colleagues. 'For a moment back then, we thought you were dead. It was only when I felt your power coming back to you we stopped short of heading out to find you. You know Alf is...'

Jay nodded. At her feet sat Buster, looking up into her eyes as if for answers.

'It's not your fault,' said Ben, holding on to Jay's shoulders. The immediate insistence from everyone that Alf's death was not her fault was convincing Jay that her gut was right, and it was no-one else's fault but her own that Atta had found a way through her to get to him.

'I should have...'

'What?' Ben interrupted. 'Alf would be the first to say that you had no way of predicting this.' Ben drew Jay into a tight hug. 'Come. Sit. Tell us what happened.'

Jay described her experience at the prison, sparing no details. She told the gathered resistance gang about Atta's presence, his power, and what was happening at the new sink-room, as well as repeating the story of the blight of Island 7 for the new members around the table.

'Like I told you,' Ben said to the others.

'It's a repeat,' one of the two women said before lowering her eyes to the floor.

She looked deeply sad. Her words stuck in her throat and the other woman had to continue. 'A repeat,' she said. Her beautiful red hair draped over her shoulders, ringlets stretching lower than the level of the table. She reached down to stroke a dog at her feet, smaller than Buster, older.

'This is Hannah,' Ben said to Jay. 'She's come down from the London branch.'

Hannah smiled. 'And this is Benji.' She motioned to the terrier at her feet. 'And Judith.' She nodded to her friend, whose tears now made sense to Jay as she connected the woman to Alf.

Her dad's reference to the resistance groups as different branches would have amused Jay at any other time. Not on this day.

'A repeat of what?' asked Cassie.

Hannah remained silent, as if deep in thought. Ben spoke: 'Tell them what you told us, Hannah.'

She snapped out of her trance and looked around at the expectant faces. Her eyes lingered on Colson as he met her gaze. 'Like Alf, and Colson here,' she said, 'me and Judith have studied the history.'

Judith straightened in her seat, put a hand on Hannah's arm, and took over for her. 'We have some unique literature on the powers in our own personal library.'

'Yes,' said Hannah, her enthusiasm building.

Judith continued: 'Materials we haven't even dared to bring down here before today, before we had the call from

Colson. Given what has happened to Alf...' She paused, unable to complete the sentence.

Hannah took over and Jay thought that these two women were connected like odd twins. 'If what you say is true...' Hannah said.

'Of course it's true,' Stitch snapped.

Jay put a hand on Stitch's arm to calm him. Hannah raised her hands in defence.

Judith leaned forward. 'I know, but we have to be sure. We have to check every detail, tick every box if we are to save our homeland from the same fate as the other six.'

'Six?' said Jay. 'There are seven other Islands.'

Judith and Hannah nodded in unison. 'Yes,' said Judith. 'But there is one other that has successfully resisted. Island 4, we think.' She paused a moment to catch her breath, and Jay thought she looked a little tearful.

'Sorry,' Judith said. 'It's been a long journey to get to this point in our understanding. We always suspected that the events of 1667 occurred at a centre of power, but we couldn't be sure.

'Until now,' Judith and Hannah said in chorus. Hannah's dog Benji struggled to his feet and moved closer to where Buster lay curled at Jay's feet. He sniffed at Buster's nose and curled up next to him.

'So Island 4 is free of the Readers? Like Alf and Colson said?' Jay asked.

'Yes,' said Hannah. 'And free of Atta. In 1667, they severed the Island's connection with the core. The Dark can never penetrate their land, not even if the Readers approach by land. No dark power can prevail on Island 4 without a connection to the core.'

'Can the connection be re-made?' asked Jay.

'Not if the severance has come from the clash of power

between the Dark and the Given. The impact is catastrophic and final.'

'And the other Islands?' said Jay.

'The other six Islands are already dark. We have lost contact with all six...'

'Contact?' said Jay. 'You have contacts in the other Islands?'

'Of course. Within the Given, we share knowledge,' said Judith. Jay tried to read her. She sensed only a wisp of power in Judith or Hannah. Their minds were open books, their thoughts pure, and intentions almost entirely altruistic as far as Jay could read. These two women cared about their environment, their society, and all within it. She even sensed pity and compassion for the plight of the Readers.

'But, one by one,' Judith continued, 'our contacts have been silenced, the last being Island 7.'

'Tiago?' Jay said.

'Yes! He is a good man.' Judith fizzed for a moment, then slumped once more. 'We are afraid for him.'

'I met him. The man I met on Island 7 was their 8C, Tiago.'

'He's alive?' Hannah asked. Jay nodded, bringing synchronised smiles to the faces of Judith and Hannah. 'We thought Island 7 would be the one to succeed in its resistance,' Hannah said. 'Tiago is strong. Almost as strong as you.'

Jay turned away at the thought of Tiago on Island 7, trying to stay hidden whilst the Readers ravaged his homeland. Spikes of guilt and sadness ran through her veins, and she did her best to push them away.

Jay looked at Colson. He stared admiringly at the two women. His expression hardened, and he reached for Jay's hand. 'Hannah and Judith, with their London team, filled us in when we reached out for help, when Atta destroyed the shop.'

Through Colson's touch, Jay could feel Alf's energy. It saddened her. She pulled her hand away and turned back to Judith. 'So what do we do? How do we follow those on Island 4?'

Judith looked at Hannah, as if handing her the baton once more. 'The *source stone*,' said Hannah, looking at Jay's bag on the chair. 'The stone is the key.' Jay handed it over the table to Judith, who shifted some papers on the table to set it down like a dinner party centre-piece. 'With Colson, we have shared our knowledge and pieced it together.'

As Judith inspected the stone, Hannah said, 'There is a stone in each of the eight Islands.'

'Are you sure?' asked Stitch. We've been to Island 7 and there was nothing there.'

'It stands to reason,' said Hannah. 'Each of the sources of power of the Given is a confluence of three rivers, right?' Stitch nodded, and Hannah continued, 'And at each of these places, there is a point, a distinct point, where the three rivers meet. It might be inside the rocks, the caves, or above ground, we don't know. But each of these lands will have something at this point that has been the recipient of the power of the Given for centuries. It is the minerals at this point that form what we call the *source stone*.' She nodded towards the stone in the middle of the table, a little awe in her expression. 'And here is ours. Finally, we see it.'

Cassie stared at the stone, then, speaking for the first time since they'd arrived, said, 'Shouldn't it be glowing or something?'

Colson stood and moved closer to the table, leaning heavily on the edge with both hands so that the light hanging from the ceiling provided a glow to his grey hair.

He looked at the stone and reached out his hand, stopping short as if not daring to touch it. To Jay: 'This is it.'

Jay nodded.

'*This* is how we sever the connection.'

Jay nodded again.

'We just need to figure out how to get it past Atta,' he said.

31

On the short walk home from the pub, Jay's body temperature plummeted. She was still wet from the rain up on Highdown, and now that the adrenaline had truly subsided, the cold had sunk into her bones. Her teeth chattered as she slotted her key in her front door and pushed her way inside.

The house was warm and smelled of cigarettes. In the hallway by the front door, she pulled off her wet top and replaced it with one of Sammy's hoodies that was hanging on the banister. She hung her bag on a coat hook and made her way through to the lounge.

'Oh...' Her mum startled, stubbing out her cigarette and wafting her hand at the smoke as if to cleanse the air. She jumped up from the sofa and took Jay by the arms, looking her in the eye. 'You're OK?' she said, examining Jay for wounds.

Jay nodded.

'Sit down,' Sonia said, guiding Jay to the sofa. 'I'll make you a hot drink.'

She disappeared into the kitchen, leaving Jay alone on

the sofa. She looked out through the patio doors, barely recognising her reflection in the glass. A minute later, Sonia returned with a cup of tea for Jay and the remains of a bottle of red wine for herself.

Jay warmed her hands and sipped the tea. Far too sweet. 'Thanks.'

'Your dad still at the pub?'

Jay nodded. Then she started to tremble and tears fell from her eyes. Her voice shook as she said, 'I don't know what to do.'

Sonia moved from the chair to sit beside her daughter on the sofa. 'Oh, honey. Once you've had some rest, things will seem less complicated. You shouldn't have this all on your shoulders. I know what that can be like.'

Jay looked sideways at her mum.

'OK, fine. Not the same, I know,' said Sonia. 'But I feel for you. I'm your mum. I feel what you feel. Not like powers, but *mum* power, you know?'

Jay smiled. The thought had crossed her mind that the battle she was soon to instigate could be her last. What she hadn't thought about was how her death would affect her mother or the others she might leave behind. Yet the thought was also strangely calming. It carried no fear. If this was her intended end, then so be it, so long as it secured the long-term survival of the Given in her homeland.

'What is it, love?' Sonia asked.

Jay looked at her mum, and for the first time, felt no animosity. It was the first time she could truly say that to herself. Her mum was human, flawed, like everyone else. Like Jay herself. 'Thanks Mum,' Jay replied. 'For listening. I feel better.' She sipped her tea, the warmth at last reaching her core.

The knock on the front door was so gentle that Jay

barely heard it. She looked at her mum. 'Are you expecting someone?'

Sonia shook her head. 'Probably your dad forgot his key, or Sammy.' She stood.

Jay knew that it wasn't the knock of Ben or Sammy. 'I'll get it,' she said, placing her empty mug on the coffee table and heading for the door.

She recognised Angie's parents immediately and looked down to see Angie standing between them, a broad grin on her face.

'She insisted,' Angie's mum said with a smile.

'She can't stay long,' her dad added, an eyebrow raised as if suspicious. 'She's under doctor's orders.'

Jay stepped aside. 'Come in...' she motioned to Angie's dad.

'No,' he said. 'We'll come back for her.' Angie's mum gave him a searching look, and he added, 'If that's alright with you? If you don't mind our daughter imposing on you for a few minutes?'

Angie's head snapped up to look at her dad. 'We agreed. Half an hour.'

'But that's a long time to impose on...'

'Half an hour is more than fine,' Jay said, leaning to take Angie's hand in hers and feeling an immediate connection, like the closing of an electrical circuit, a warming jolt of energy. Angie flung her arms around Jay.

'Angie, give the girl some room,' her dad said.

'I've been worried about you,' Angie said to Jay.

Angie's mum took her husband's arm. 'We'll come back in a while.'

Jay nodded and beckoned Angie into the house, closing the door as her parents retreated down the pathway to the road.

'Who's this?' Sonia exclaimed as Jay and Angie entered the lounge.

'This is my friend, Angie, the one I told you about.'

'Oh my. Are you feeling better? Jay told me what happened at the bookshop.'

'I'm fine, thank you,' Angie said, taking a seat on the sofa between Jay and her mum. She looked smaller than the last time Jay had seen her, but still as smiley as ever despite an underlying pain Jay felt but couldn't quite decipher.

Jay made eyes for her mum to leave them alone to talk. 'Oh... sorry,' Sonia said, jumping up. 'I'll be in the kitchen if you need me. Would you like a drink of anything, Angie?'

Angie smiled and shook her head.

After Sonia had left the room, Jay said, 'It's good to see you up and about, in the flesh. You've been in my head the whole time. I was worried about you.'

'That's why I'm here,' Angie said, her tone more serious now that they were alone. 'It's like we have a connection, right?'

Jay nodded.

'I don't know what it is, but this connection isn't just *your* power, it's more than that. Something just between us.'

'You think...?'

'I know it. I've been with you these last couple of days. I mean really *with* you.'

'I've felt you there,' said Jay.

'I was inside your head when you went to the prison. I saw you fight that thing with Stitch, the dark man.'

'Atta.'

'Flick saved you. She used her power to distract Atta for long enough for you and Stitch to escape. I saw what she did.'

Angie closed her eyes and reached for Jay's hand. Jay felt

the electrical connection once more, but this time, she felt something more. Angie's image swirled around inside her mind like before. She too closed her eyes and Angie came to life in her head, more real than she'd experienced before. Her entire being seemed to be connected, to be at one with Jay's, as if they were joined in mind and body. Some minutes passed before she snapped her eyes open and withdrew her hand. 'What is that?'

'The powers.'

'But you're too young.'

'Not *my* powers. Your powers. Something in your power is drawing me in.'

'How?'

'I have no idea. But the point is, I *know what's wrong.*'

'Know what?'

'That you need to get a grip.'

Jay almost laughed out loud. Angie was without doubt one of the wisest kids she'd ever met, but she'd not been told to wise up by a pre-teen before. 'Let me see your wrist.'

Angie smiled. 'Too young for that.' She pulled back her sleeve and showed Jay her unmarked skin. 'It's *your* power I am tuning in to. I'm like a radio or something.'

'I told you that you were special.' Jay smiled.

Angie looked at the clock on the wall. 'Fifteen minutes left,' she said.

'And I can tell you still have more to say,' Jay said.

'There's something missing. I can feel it, and I have seen it. Missing from your heart.'

'Angie, what do you mean?'

'Tell me why you feel that this is your mission alone. Your mission to protect the whole of this land with no help from all these people who can and want to help you?'

Jay bristled despite herself. 'Stitch was with me. I only

want to keep more people from getting hurt. There's been enough pain in the people I love.'

Angie didn't answer, just smiled her sad, wise smile.

Jay thought of Alf and marvelled again at Angie's maturity.

'You see what you're doing?' Angie continued. 'By keeping others apart from you, you end up putting them at greater risk.'

Jay stood and moved away from Angie, feeling like she was slowly losing her sense of self. Who was this little girl to erode her confidence, and at such a critical point when she needed to be strong?

'I've felt it. Your power is weakening. The longer you deny your wider connections, the further you will get from your true goal. You can't do this on your own. This thing, the darkness, Atta, he is more than a Reader. You know that. I saw it in him, through your eyes. If you go alone to fight him again, then I don't know what will happen. We will lose you for sure. And if we lose *you*, we lose everything.'

Jay scratched her head as she paced the room. 'How?' she said. 'What am I supposed to do?'

'That's your job to figure out. I'm just telling you what I know. If you shut everyone out you risk us all, and you lose out on the greatest power the Given have. Our connection.'

There was a knock at the door - three assertive knocks. 'My dad,' said Angie, and stood to leave.

32

J ay slipped through the Velux and onto the roof of her house. The moon was obscured by clouds on a night as dark as she'd ever seen over the hills. A wind gusted off the sea in angry bursts. She pulled her hood snug around her head and slid herself down the tiles to sit.

Angie's words fizzed around her mind and under her skin. Try as she might, she couldn't resolve the tension she felt with a decision. Losing Alf hung over her like a cloud as dark as the moonless night. Could she really risk any more of those she loved, or was she risking them already by trying to tackle Atta on her own? The decision of what to do next left her paralysed.

Stitch and Cassie crept up the back wall onto the roof and sat one each side of Jay without so much as a "hi". Together, they looked out towards the hills in silence, each caught up in their own thoughts.

'We need to get the stone into the core,' Jay said eventually. They all knew that disrupting the flow of dark energy would not be simple. This would be their last chance.

'How?' said Stitch.

'We'll all work together.'

'But how? And even if we do, what next? Colson said that it could create a massive explosion.'

'I have an idea,' Jay said. 'But we'll need *everyone* for it to work.'

'Who?'

'Everyone. Toyah, Sammy, Colson.'

'Speak of the Devil,' Cassie said as Sammy climbed out through Jay's window, Toyah close behind, and planted himself next to Stitch. Jay and Toyah exchanged a glance, and Jay sensed that she and Sammy had finally worked some things out. She gave a half smile.

'Don't let us interrupt you,' Toyah said as everyone went quiet.

Sammy leaned forward to peer at the others. 'Anyone would think the world was ending.'

They were quiet for a minute.

'What's the plan then?' asked Stitch.

First, a good night's rest. We're going to need it,' said Jay. 'Tomorrow we meet in the pub to go through the plan.'

* * *

AFTER EVERYONE HAD LEFT, Jay closed her eyes and turned her face into the wind, a light sea spray cooling her face. She felt energised with anticipation for what was to come in the morning. She was no longer afraid. She at last understood what needed to be done.

She drifted into the fog of her thoughts. The energy of the environment was alert, nipping at her consciousness and preventing her from drifting off to sleep.

The whispers came, becoming louder with every hiss

and crash of the sea just over the rooftops to the south. She opened to them, breathing in their energy, their urgency. Whispers turned to white noise that came with colours flowing through her mind. She filtered the white noise as she had become adept at doing and the words became clear.

The power and energy of the Given was with her, connecting the hills and energy sites of Highdown, Cissbury and Chanctonbury, amplifying and growing the force with each connection.

As the colours brightened and the energy flowed, a wisp of darkness crossed her mind, like the passage of a train before her eyes. When it returned in the next breath, it dispersed and diffused into the white light like a puff of smoke. She sensed Atta - his confidence, arrogance. He was letting her know he was ready for her, for whatever she could muster.

33

At the prison, the buildings below the ground now outnumbered those above.

Atta drifted through the corridors, making mental notes of the numbers of people in the rooms approaching the main hall, where the sink-room resided above the connection to the core. It used to be that only those with power could be subject to the process of generating Readers. Now that the power of the system had been optimised during Atta's push through the Islands, the process could be applied to any person.

Many of those in the holding cells had turned into willing participants. They sensed what was coming and the advantage in choosing the right side to support. Many, of course, remained resistant, an exercise in futility. The sink-room could create a level six Reader from anyone, even the hesitant. The Island 8 facility was already creating over twenty Readers per day at level 6 and above.

For the Given, much fewer, but much greater potential. Someone with Given power of any level, even a level 1 or level 2, could be transformed into a level 8 Reader. The process was now so efficient that Atta was almost guaranteed a level 8. It was a similar case for the Readers. Any Reader of any strength would emerge as a level 8.

'Sir?' A Reader raised a hand like a schoolchild to get Atta's attention at the entrance to one of the open holding cells, a room containing members of the public open and willing for the transformation process. 'We have some difficult subjects.'

Atta stepped up to the entrance to the room, a simple concrete box of a structure. No windows, no furniture.

'Some are expecting something more from us in return for their cooperation and support.'

As the Reader said this, three men from the room stepped closer to the door to address Atta. 'Sir,' one of them said, a short man with mousey hair thinning to a bald patch on the top of his head. 'We are looking for someone to put a case for something rather more comfortable than we have here.'

'I'm listening,' said Atta, his tone measured, without emotion.

'We are willing participants here. And we think we can offer great potential. We are physically fit, being part of the community rugby 1sts for some time, and I think you can see,' he turned to draw attention to the rest of the room, 'that we are, relatively speaking, likely to offer you more than most.'

'Do you have power?' Atta asked, knowing full well that no-one in the room had power but for him and the Reader who stood next to him.

'Not power in the sense that you mean, but we have skills that, when combined with the power we will pick up in the transformation process, will put us up there in the management potential.'

Atta turned back to the corridor. 'Follow me.'

The man with the thinning hair turned to the others with a victorious grin and the three of them filed past the reader to follow Atta.

At the next junction in the maze of connecting corridors, Atta stopped and opened the vision panel in the door in front of him. He opened the door and gestured inside. The room was a little smaller than the one the men had come from, but it was empty of others, and there was at least some furniture - a single chair in the centre of the room.

The three men entered, and Atta could see the metal floor flex a little under their weight. 'Just one chair?' the taller of the three men said.

'You won't need the chair,' said Atta as he closed the door behind them. In the corridor, he opened a control panel next to the door and slammed his palm into the centre button to begin the process. Then he tapped at the keypad.

The three ex-rugby players squirmed and writhed on the floor. Their screams echoed in the close confines of the metal box. As one man fell into his death throes, gasping for a last breath, his leg kicked out, sending the lone chair skittering across the floor and into the wall.

34

Jay, Ben, and Sammy were last to arrive at the pub. The basement room hummed with fear. Judith and Hannah were sitting at the table, Benji at their feet with Buster, watching as Pinto displayed his early telekinesis skills by moving a pen across the table. Toyah and Matchstick were over by the far wall, flicking through some of the Given literature charred at its edges.

Colson was crouched, talking to a little girl. 'Angie!' Jay said, approaching her. 'Why are you here? I thought your mum and dad had whisked you away?'

'I convinced them that this was a matter of life and death.'

Colson stood to greet Jay. 'You look like you have a plan.'

Jay nodded, then turned to the room. 'Let's do this.'

The room fell silent and everyone drew closer to hear what Jay had to say. Colson was the first to break the silence. 'When do we leave for the prison?' He sat down at the table. Others took seats as Jay remained standing, gathering herself.

She drew a deep breath. 'We know that a straight fight will not work.' She nodded at Angie. 'Something this wise little girl said to me last night has given me an idea. We need to get the stone into the core, no doubt about that, right?'

Colson nodded, and others murmured agreement. Stitch raised his head, his voice low and resigned: 'She's planning to plant the stone herself, physically. To *take* it into the core.'

'That's madness,' said Colson.

'It could be the only way,' said Judith. 'The dark energy in that place would never allow the source stone to fall naturally into the core.'

'What about the energy interface?' said Colson, agitated.

'The what?' asked Stitch.

'The inevitable expansion and chain reaction. Explosive *runaway*?'

Blank faces.

'If the source stone, the very focus of Given energy, comes into contact with the deep core, then chances are we'll be seeing a mini black hole develop here on earth. It's one thing to launch the stone into the hole and get clear, it's quite another to follow it in there.'

The room remained quiet as they processed what Colson had said. He continued, 'Everything within a mile radius will be levelled. Everything could be sucked into the cavern that is created, at least in the initial event.'

'There really isn't much point dwelling on possibilities right now when we have certainties,' Jay said. 'It is certain Atta will soon have enough power to obliterate the Given for good. So I don't see where we have a choice.'

Colson refused to concede. 'If you and the core are connected with the source stone, you will die.'

Jay ignored him, pushing the thought away. 'Something

came to me yesterday, after talking to Angie, and then connecting with the power. I think we need an opening to the power of the Given at each of the three hill forts as we confront the darkness.'

Silence.

'A connected consciousness will allow us to amplify the energy.'

'How?' asked Toyah, frowning.

Colson scratched his head, thinking.

'Jay's right,' said Stitch, shooting her a supportive glance. 'We've used the hill forts before to help channel the power. We know they are a source of energy. But we will *all* need to connect deeply. Not just Jay.'

Colson nodded. 'It makes sense, but how? What are you thinking, Jay?'

Jay glanced across the faces around the room, all looking to her for the answers. 'Toyah, we will need your strength of power to get things moving. With Cassie, you are the highest level among us.'

Toyah nodded, touching the inside of her wrist instinctively where her number seven was clear, deeply defined, reflecting the clarity of her power. 'Just tell me where you need me, and what I need to do.'

'Colson, Dad, up on the hill forts, you will need to connect with the ground, the roots beneath our feet. Everything is connected. The power in the hills will guide you.'

Ben and Colson nodded as they thought it through.

'We'll need someone here too, at the basement.'

'Why?' asked Cassie. 'What's here?'

Hannah took the question. 'This room has become a centre and focus of the energy since the bookshop was destroyed. The Given literature is that source.'

'That makes no sense,' said Cassie.

'She's right,' said Jay. 'Our collective presence, our shared mindset, and even our documents, carry a focus of energy to this place. The physical locations of energy, like the hill forts and the Interland, are just part of the picture. An equal, and possibly *more* important, element is the essence of those with power - what is in their heads and their hearts, and how they choose to channel the power.

'I think if Dad gets to Highdown Hill and Colson to Cissbury Ring, then Sammy and Toyah can head up to Chanctonbury.'

'I'll take Highdown,' came a familiar voice from the foot of the stairs. Jay looked up to see Otis standing with a walking stick, a grin on his face. Pinto went to him, helping him stand.

Cassie stood. 'What are you doing here?'

Pinto answered for Otis, 'He's here to help. Me and Otis can help. He's a level five, and I'm a five in the making. We can help.'

'You two take Highdown then,' said Jay with a smile for Otis. 'If you think you can do it?'

'With this little power-pack,' he nodded at Pinto, 'we can do anything.'

'I'll come with you,' Cassie said.

'I need you and Stitch with me,' Jay said. 'And here in the basement we need Angie.'

Angie visibly slumped. 'I want to be with you,' she said to Jay.

'You will be,' Jay said, tapping the side of her head. 'In here.' Angie humphed. 'I need you here with Judith and Hannah. You can help them guide me. You will be their eyes, through me, into the darkness.'

Angie gave in. 'OK,' she said, looking up at Hannah and Judith, who both smiled.

'We have one chance,' said Jay. She hoped that her inner fear was well contained and shielded from her friends, and that her doubts about their chances were not leaking through.

35

The basement emptied, leaving Angie with Hannah and Judith. She felt small, uncertain of how she would play her part in what was to come next. Jay, Stitch and Cassie were the last to leave, heading for Jay's garage to pick up the car and head off to the prison.

Judith and Hannah busied with the papers on the table, sorting and arranging into piles that seemed to have some kind of order that Angie couldn't fathom. 'What are you doing?' asked Angie.

Hannah paused a moment and took a breath. She was fidgety, looking to the door and back to the papers. 'We need to be prepared. They will need us focused.'

'What for?' Angie was confused. Hannah and Judith seemed to know what was coming, and what they needed to do.

Judith sat down, motioning for Angie to do the same. Hannah continued arranging the papers. 'In the past day or so, we've been talking through all the ways that this could play out. Truth be told, we don't know the answer, but there are things we can do to prepare for the worst, then hope for the best.'

'Jay said she needs me to be your eyes. What did she mean?'

Judith looked over at Hannah. 'We may have limited power, but we have a lot of knowledge about the power, and how the energy of the Given and the Dark behave - how they interact and how the darkness might be a threat to Jay. That's what Colson and Alf think...' Judith corrected herself. '*Thought*. That's what Alf thought.'

'But what about me? Why am I here?' Angie pressed.

'You have power,' said Judith.

'Great power,' Hannah added, shifting a pile of documents into the corner of the table. 'If Jay's intuition is right, and I'd guess it is, then you have a new kind of power. For someone so young, your connection with the Given energy is unprecedented.'

'Except for Jay herself, perhaps?' Judith said.

'Perhaps,' said Hannah with a nod.

'So,' Judith continued, 'with your ability, we think you will illuminate the path as Jay moves in on the core. You can be our eyes and senses into the darkness, so that we can best help Jay understand what she's seeing.'

'You can tell her what to do?' said Angie.

Hannah stopped sorting papers for a moment. 'We hope so. At least, we hope we can make some kind of contribution.'

* * *

OTIS POWERED the little moped up the last section of dirt track to his camp on the edge of the summit at Highdown.

With Pinto on the back, the bike was heavier, and it had been a struggle to keep from flipping over backwards as he negotiated the steepest sections.

'Here,' said Otis, carefully stepping off the bike to protect his heels from pain. Pinto jumped off and positioned himself to help Otis. They staggered together the few feet to Otis's camp, where he sank down onto a log. 'I might need you to do the fire,' he said.

'On it,' said Pinto, turning to look at the remains of their last fire, burned almost to nothing. 'I'll top up the wood stock.'

'We have some time,' said Otis. 'I reckon we have a good half hour before Jay is anywhere near the prison. We should eat.'

Pinto scurried away to collect wood as Otis opened his bivouac and unpacked cans. Pain radiated from both his heels. The hospital had warned him that leaving so soon was not recommended, and that he should rest, keep the weight off his feet for a few more days. If he wasn't careful, an infection was possible, or further tendon damage. The doctor told him that he was lucky. Slightly deeper and his healing process would have been months, not weeks. He didn't feel so lucky. Despite Flick's grievous attack on him, he felt no great malice towards her. He could tell that she was conflicted. She had her reasons, mostly fear, he thought, for following the wishes of Atta.

Behind him, Pinto dumped an armful of wood and arranged it in the fire pit. From his store, made with reclaimed stones from around the perimeter of Highdown, he pulled a loaf of sliced bread, still within its best-before date, and three tins of soup.

'Sit down,' called Pinto as Otis emerged from cover.

Otis dumped the food beside Pinto and slumped back down on the log. 'I feel so useless like this.'

'You will be useless if you don't ease up. Like the nurse said.'

'Yes, boss.'

'And if we are going to be any use to the others, we need to conserve our energy and get focused.'

Within a few minutes, the fire raged, and Pinto suspended a pan from a metal tripod above the flames. He opened the tins with Otis's penknife and poured the contents into the pan, singeing his hair as he did so.

Otis laughed. 'You're supposed to prepare the pan before you light the fire. Or let the fire die down before you hang the pan.'

'No time,' said Pinto.

'Who needs eyebrows anyway, eh?'

Pinto rubbed his eyebrows. Otis laughed again. 'Sit down. You're fine.'

He sat opposite Otis. They exchanged a glance. 'Are you ready?' Otis asked.

Pinto nodded, knowing that Otis wanted to test the strength of their power, to get ready for what was coming later.

Otis took a breath and, with a quick glance at the flames, opened up to the power of the earth. Pinto closed his eyes. Otis let his eyelids droop and channelled his energy into a connection with Pinto. Like they'd done before, and like they would need to do to help Jay, they connected.

* * *

THE WALK up to the summit of Cissbury was steeper than the other two hill forts. Sammy had sensed an easing of

Toyah's frustration over the past couple of days, but she seemed distant on their journey to Cissbury. He tried to focus on the job at hand.

'Wait,' Sammy said, stopping to catch his breath, Toyah a few feet ahead. Three sparrows circled above their heads, coming closer as Sammy watched. His connection with birds was nothing new, but it had grown stronger over recent months. He had tried to cultivate it but it seemed to have a life of its own. He would put all his focus into connecting with the energy of the birds, like he had done back at the Interland, and it seemed random whether it had any effect. Then, when he wasn't trying, the visions would come to him.

'What?' said Toyah, her tone impatient. 'We need to get to the top. Get ourselves organised.'

'There are people up there,' said Sammy.

'How do you know?'

Sammy looked up at the birds. One of the three came close, and he ducked out of its way, sliding to sit on the grass. Toyah watched. As the bird retreated, a familiar curtain of blindness came down over Sammy's eyes and he knew what was coming. The opaque screen before his eyes faded to a transparent blur as he soared with the bird into the sky. His eyes cleared as he rose, travelling with the little sparrow as it skirted the outer ring of trees towards the summit of Cissbury.

'I'm at the summit,' he said to Toyah.

'People there?'

'Some. Our age. Drinking. Smoking.'

'How many?'

'Only a handful.' In Sammy's mind's eye, he circled the ring of trees and peered down on a group of six teenagers around a fire. They would be no threat. There was no power that he could detect. His vision blurred once more and Sammy's sight came back to him. Toyah was watching him with pride.

'Thanks,' Sammy said.

'For what?'

'For having my back. Believing in me.'

'Always,' Toyah said. 'It's easy. OK, let's go.'

At the summit, Toyah strode into the inner circle and told the four girls and two boys to leave without explanation. When one girl squared up to her, Toyah used her power to force the girl to the ground, her hands clutching the sides of her head in pain. She didn't need to ask again.

Sammy lumped another branch onto the fire and sat down on a log. 'How long do we have?' he asked Toyah.

Toyah checked her watch. 'Twenty minutes. We'll hear something from Jay or Stitch when they're close. Keep your senses open for something from your sister.'

Sammy delved into his powers once more, feeling confident after his success with flight. He connected with the energy that flowed freely at the hillfort. Smoke rose in the distance towards the south. He stood and walked to the edge of the treeline for a better look. At Highdown, the smoke rose in a tight plume and mixed into the wind above the trees. 'Otis,' he said under his breath, just loud enough for Toyah to hear. 'Can you connect?' Toyah asked.

'Not yet. You?'

Toyah shook her head.

'I can feel him though,' said Sammy. 'His power is strong, coming over the hills in waves. I've not felt someone's power like this from such a distance.'

'It's the hill forts. The amplification.'

* * *

THE THIRD HILL FORT, Chanctonbury, was the highest of the three, and probably because of this, the least visited by the Given. The energy of the land was spread over a wider area, with less of a focus at the summit. Nevertheless, the flow of Given energy was significant, and its importance in the full connection of Given power to support Jay's quest undeniable.

Ben called Colson's tiny, apple-red Mazda a 'mid-life crisis' car as they jumped in, Ben pulling his seat forward as far as it would go so Matchstick could scrunch up in the back. 'Better?'

'You need to get yourself a proper car,' Matchstick muttered.

Ben smiled to himself. Matchstick had become his closest friend since their time escaping prison and trekking to the Interland. Matchstick was the most powerful of the three of them. At a level 4, he could connect well with the Given energy. His telepathic ability was modest, but he had a little something more in the heat he generated from the energy. His nickname wasn't unrelated to his ability to create fire from his hands when the energy flowed at its maximum. Ben's own level two power seemed to be enhanced when he was in the presence of Matchstick.

Colson turned onto the straight road that would lead them to the peak at Cissbury. There were two locations for them to set up, and Jay had suggested that the highest peak was the one they should find. It was there she was sure that the power flowed at its greatest. Colson's own power was tangible. Ben could feel its strength in the car alongside that of Matchstick, although his felt more muted, subdued. 'What's your level?' Ben asked Colson.

'Four.' He awkwardly pulled back the sleeve of his left arm whilst holding on to the steering wheel.

'Same as me,' said Matchstick from the back, thrusting his wrist between the two front seats.

'Ten between us then,' said Ben.

'More than a match for any Reader,' said Matchstick with a grin.

'There are level 4 Given and then there are level 4 Given,' said Colson.

'What do you mean?' said Matchstick.

'Alf was a level 4 and he was far stronger than me.'

Ben nodded. Matchstick remained quiet. Ben felt a strange pang of guilt for the way he'd always been towards Alf. They never saw things the same way. It was true. Perhaps he suffered jealousy for how well he and Jay got on in recent times. The closer Jay and Alf became, the more distant Jay seemed to become to Ben. Nothing that Alf had done was ever in confrontation with Ben, yet Ben had never seen fit to communicate with him, to accept him into his world. 'We left him out in the cold for too long,' said Ben.

Colson nodded. 'He was a good man, and a major contributor to the knowledge of the Given. In a different life, we would have been good friends. I will miss him.'

From the car park, the walk took longer than they had thought. Almost twenty minutes and they were only just reaching the high point. Matchstick gathered dry wood, held his hands over the tinder, and in seconds a flame took hold.

'How do you do that?' asked Colson.

'To be honest, I'm not entirely sure. The energy just seems to flow through my hands, and when it's flowing well, the heat is intense and I can concentrate it enough to generate a spark or a flame.'

'Useful,' said Colson.

Matchstick shrugged and looked up into the trees. The sky was grey, fast-moving clouds hiding the sun. 'Come on.' He called Ben over to sit down. 'We need to get ready.'

36

'Tell us the plan then,' Cassie said, taking a roundabout at speed. The old Ford handled like a minibus, and Cassie enjoyed the challenge of keeping the wheels on the road around the tight corners. Stitch leaned forward between the front seats to catch Jay's answer.

Jay thought for a moment. She knew exactly what she needed to do, but she had to put it in a way that offered up no opportunity for alternatives from Cassie and Stitch. They wouldn't like it, but it was non-negotiable.

She picked the rucksack from the footwell and took out the source stone. Its energy expanded through the car. Jay felt its connection. 'You feel that?' she asked the others. Cassie didn't respond, but Stitch nodded.

'Can't quite make sense of it.' Jay said. 'I can feel it, but it's not like the power from the hill forts, or the Interland itself. In those places, the energy is clearer, like a communication. This thing is radioactive. A little atomic bomb. I need to get this into the core.'

'You mean *we* need to get it into the core,' Cassie corrected.

Jay avoided her glance. 'I'll have to go in with it, *take* it in there, as deep as I can get.'

'I knew that's what you were planning,' Stitch said. 'So what do *we* do whilst your body is becoming vaporised, scattered to all corners of the planet?'

'I might get out, once it's in there, deep enough that we know it will do its job.'

Cassie was incredulous. 'I'm not taking part in your suicide mission.'

'Remember what Colson said? At least a mile radius when this thing goes in. You two need to be a mile back from the opening to the core. This isn't negotiable.' She turned to look out of the window, hugging the source stone to her.

'No way,' Cassie said. 'We find another way.'

'There must be another way,' said Stitch.

'There is no other way,' Jay spat the words, losing patience. 'This is my call. I'm the one who's seen Atta, seen what he can do. We only get one go at this. The others are ready and positioned to channel the power. I need you to play your part. This needs all of us.'

Cassie shook her head, and they were silent for a minute.

'What do we do?' Stitch asked, his head down, resigned. He looked at Jay. 'Tell us what you need.'

Jay forced a smile. 'You know where we went before, in Northtown?'

'Sebastian's?'

'That's a mile or so out from the centre of the prison, so that's around the spot you need to be. Not at his house, at the river. But no closer than that. You'll be no use if you're in the prison. Use the river and the sea, and help me focus the power from the hill forts. We won't be able to get past Atta if we can't draw the full potential of the Given energy.'

Stitch nodded.

Jay continued, 'We're making connections. Otis with Pinto at Highdown, Colson and Dad at Chanctonbury, and Toyah with Sammy at Cissbury. Their connections will draw the power of the land. I need that power here, and I need the power of the sea that we have coming in on the river through Northtown. That's what I need from you.'

'I can't do that without you,' Stitch said.

'I will be with you. I need to be connected to you. I'll help. We just need to connect with the others. Then I will have the full power of the Given and I'll have a chance with Atta.'

'How do you know it will work?'

Jay looked at Stitch. She shrugged.

'What about Angie and the others at the basement?' Cassie asked.

'They are our intelligence. Angie has something I've not come across in any other Given. She is a power in development for sure, but even now she has an extraordinary ability. She seems to connect with me, see what I see and feel my thoughts from a distance.' Jay looked at Stitch. 'A bit like you can. But she's not even a teenager yet, let alone eighteen.'

'You think she'll be a "C"?' asked Cassie.

Jay shook her head. 'She's the next generation of the Given. Today she's the eyes and ears for Judith and Hannah's knowledge.'

Cassie let out a sigh. 'Let me and Stitch come with you. We can help channel the power from inside the mile radius just as well as we can from Northtown. In fact, if we are closer to you, then we stand a better chance of directing it to where you need it.'

'Too risky,' Jay said. 'Do it like I said.'

'What if we can't connect to you from back in Northtown?'

The question put words to Jay's biggest fear. Under the cloak of Atta's darkness, she might not receive the power from the others, and all the efforts of positioning people at the hill forts, and having Stitch and Cassie channel the energy from Northtown, would be a waste of time. There was no way to know for sure. 'We have to try. It's the only way. His energy is too much to fight on my own. He will simply take the stone, preventing it from ever entering the core. If that happens, then it's over.'

* * *

'THIS IS THE PLACE,' said Jay as she pulled the car up to the side of the road at the main river wall of Northtown. The estuary and the sea were just visible in the distance. Rain pounded the metal roof of the car, drowning Jay's words.

'How do you know?' said Cassie. The windscreen wipers struggled to keep up with the snap downpour and Jay switched them off, then turned off the ignition.

'I can feel it,' said Jay, turning to look at Stitch.

'She's right,' said Stitch. 'This is it. See the sea?' He nodded downstream. 'And feel the power of the river?'

Cassie rubbed condensation from the window and peered out. 'This is where we entered the tunnels last time,' she said.

'Bit further up,' said Jay. 'It's not the tunnels we need, it's the power of the ocean. You need to combine the energies.' She looked at Stitch, trying to read if he really understood what was being asked of him and Cassie. He gave a slight nod and Jay continued. 'Connect it with the power from the hill forts. Only you two can do this. Channel it to me. But do it from *here*, keep your distance. I'll know when you have it.'

Stitch nodded again, his thoughts revealing his fear for Jay. He searched his mind for an escape plan for her, but came up with nothing and looked away, out of the window.

'How do we do it?' Cassie asked.

'Stitch will know. He will just need your power to keep it all under control. Take your lead from Stitch.'

'Whatever you say,' Cassie said. The rain eased and the noise in the car ceased.

Jay opened her door to let out some of the humid air and to take a breath of the fresh, salty breeze. 'Go, now,' she said.

Cassie flung open her door and stepped out into the cool air. She stuck her head through Jay's open door. 'Just make sure you do it right this time,' she said. 'OK?'

Jay nodded.

She turned to Stitch in the back of the car. 'Send a message to the others. Tell them to start.'

He nodded, lingering for a moment. 'Please,' he whispered. 'Get yourself back here in one piece.'

She leaned and placed both hands on the sides of Stitch's face, looking him in the eye. 'We can do this,' she said. 'We have to do this. It's bigger than me, or you, or anyone else.'

'I know.' Stitch lowered his gaze.

'Go!'

Stitch hesitated.

'Go!' Jay repeated and pushed the Ford into gear. Stitch stepped out and Jay pulled away.

37

J ay drove directly to the staff entrance to the prison, her mind clearer and more focused than it had ever been. She screeched to a halt at the gate as two Readers in the security box watched, open-mouthed. From the car, she attacked both Readers simultaneously, reducing them to their knees with little effort. Her power bubbled below the surface, ready at her fingertips. The Readers screamed in pain, their hands to the sides of their heads, then slumped unconscious to the floor. She used her power to push the button to release the gates.

She drove on to the main car park, using the same space she had used the last time, making some point that was lost in her subconscious. She stepped out of the car. Her trainers were scuffed and coming apart at the seams. Her jeans were dirty, one leg riding up over her high-top shoes. She looked at her hands, turning them over to inspect her palms. She had nothing. No weapons. No protection, only the stone. She felt naked suddenly. Scratches, old and new, on the backs of her hands and up her arms, reminded her of what she'd been through already. She turned over her hand to see the "8C" marking on her wrist. *This* is me, she thought. This is my calling, my mission. Her arms by her sides, she clenched her fists and turned towards the main building.

The building structure was barely standing, dilapidated further after the tornado generated by Atta the last time she was there. She walked through what was once a set of double-doors and stood at the top of the steps down to the lower levels. The power of the darkness flowed up from underground like the pulse of air from an underground train. She stepped down, taking the steps slowly as she acclimatised to the energy flow around her. There were no guards, a reminder of Atta's arrogance - his belief that there was no-one on Island 8 to threaten him.

On the first floor down, the building had been expanded and modified. She shrugged her shoulders to feel the reassuring weight of the rucksack on her back. Although she sensed the closeness of the source stone, feeling its weight was reassuring. She wondered if Atta knew already that she was here.

She came to a corridor with rooms off the central route that she'd not seen before. Everything was grey concrete - the floor, wall, ceiling. Only the doors themselves were not concrete, their shiny steel surfaces reflecting the grey of the walls. Her skin prickled with anticipation.

Through the vision panel in the first door, she saw a room crammed full of people. Their fear hung like a grey cloud in the air. They had no power, and they feared for their lives. Using the control panel on the wall, Jay released the lock and pushed the door open. The people inside recoiled, shrinking away from Jay as she entered. She raised her hands to show that she meant no harm. 'What are you...' she began, but needed not finish. She read in their minds the plan that Atta had for them.

Jay's head swam as she tried to take it in. The dark energy could not create Readers from those without power. It wasn't possible. She looked at the faces staring back at her. It was true. He had found a way. 'Go!' Jay said, pointing them back towards the steps to the car park. 'Now!'

They moved. A man edged past her through the door and headed in the wrong direction. 'This way,' Jay said. 'Head for the east exit. You will see it from the car park. The security hut is unmanned. Leave and don't look back.'

He needed no more instruction. He ran to the steps, leading the way for others. A woman stopped as she passed Jay. 'Thank you,' she said, and took the hand of the man next to her, leading him away with the others.

Jay stopped the last man out of the room. 'Hey,' she said. 'Are there more?'

The man nodded and motioned towards the remaining doors along the corridor. 'These are the holding cells for the resistant, like us, those who refused to sign up to their doctrine.'

'There are so many,' Jay said.

'This is just one batch. And we were not the first. Before us, these rooms were full of other people, already turned no doubt.'

The scale of Atta's plans floored Jay. She'd had no idea.

'The next level down, the bigger rooms, are the willing participants,' the man said. 'Those people *want* to become Readers. I don't know if they are deluded or scared, but they have undertaken to be transformed in return for their loyalty.'

Once transformed, Readers could be easily manipulated by whomever has control of the sink-room. Reader power is not innate, it flows from the core via the sink-room. Without the channelling of that energy, Readers can be stripped of their power.

'Then beyond that you have the Given. They are held close to the core. First in line for transformation.'

'Help me open up these rooms?' Jay said to the man. He nodded, and they set to unlock each room off the central corridor from their control panels. There were six, and more than a hundred people. When the last had filed through to the steps, Jay thanked the man and turned towards the steps to the deeper levels.

'You need me to help?'

Jay shook her head and smiled. 'Thanks. You get moving. Make sure those people get clear. They need to be at least a mile out. Don't hang about.'

He nodded. 'Good luck,' he said.

* * *

JAY SENSED the change in the energy's feel on the next level down. The holding rooms were not locked. The atmosphere was one of celebration, like graduation. There were Readers too, patrolling the corridors with guns, keeping the levels of excitement under control as people waited for the call to the sink-room. You people are crazy, she thought.

A Reader carrying a pistol turned in her direction and she ducked behind a column. He seemed to sense something and walked towards her, his gun held at waist level. As he approached, he slowed, treading carefully over the final few paces. She shielded, holding back until the last minute before attacking his mind. Simultaneously, she dragged him around the column and out of sight of the rest of the readers and pulled the gun from his weakened grip. He went down, and she intensified her attack, pushing him physically to the floor before looking back towards the others to check that she'd not been detected. She was safe. The Reader at her feet was out. She kicked the handgun away into a dark corner.

Peering over the edge of the landing, Jay saw that the shaft plummeted into the depths directly below. She could drop the source stone from where she stood without having to head any deeper. It might make it into the core, but the dark energy would be sure to deflect it, and if the source stone were to get into Atta's hands again, there wouldn't be a third chance. She cursed. She would head lower.

The next level down was like the top floor - doors off a central corridor and no sign of Readers. Through the first door vision panel, Jay saw that the room was empty, as was the next room along. The third room contained a single person, sat on the floor, her head in her hands. Jay sensed that this woman had Given power. She pressed the door release, and the woman looked up, her face lighting up as she sensed Jay's Given energy. 'Thank God,' she said, standing.

'Let's go,' Jay said. She saw on the woman's wrist that she was a level 3. 'Are there more Given?'

The woman nodded and moved to the next door in the corridor. She pushed the button in the control panel and ran in, embracing the man stood the other side. 'This is my husband, Ravi. I am Jess.'

'Are there more?'

'There were,' said Jess, moving further down the corridor and looking through the vision panel in each door. 'All empty,' she said, looking at her husband, whose eyes dropped to the floor. 'There were people we knew in these rooms.'

'They will probably be Readers now.'

'But they can be turned back?' Ravi asked Jay.

Jay nodded. 'Only if they can escape the control of the sink-room. Jay felt a wave of dark energy and stumbled, holding on to the handrail to stop from falling.

Jess held her arm. 'Steady,' she said.

'Sorry,' said Jay. 'I need to press on. You head back to the entrance. Be careful on the next floor up, there are Readers, but beyond that it's clear. Head to the exit and...'

'Where are you going?' asked Ravi. He looked at Jay's backpack. 'There's a powerful signal from there.'

Jess looked at Jay with a flicker of recognition. 'You're Jay. The 8C. I've read about you.'

'I need to get down to the lower levels and get this...' she motioned at her backpack, 'into the core. There are others, as we speak, channelling the energy. You need to go. We don't know what will happen when this thing is inserted. This place could be levelled.'

'We're coming,' said Jess. 'You need our help. You don't look well.'

'No,' said Jay, emphatic.

'We're not asking,' said Ravi. 'We were put on this planet for a reason. *This* is the reason.' He looked at his wife and she nodded.

JAY LED the way down the final set of steps. She stepped onto a steel platform that circled the rim of the crater below. The hum from the electromagnets was loud, releasing a pulse of energy with every rotation.

No Atta. No army of Readers. Jay felt a deep unease. Why was it possible for her to just walk right up to the core of their power with such ease?

The circular landing had three entrances. A control panel was fixed to the wall next to the door. Jay knew what she needed to do.

'What now?' asked Ravi.

'Throw it in?' asked Jess.

'You two can leave. Now,' said Jay. 'I can take it from here.'

Jay looked over the edge and tightened her rucksack over her shoulders. She looked up through the centre of the shaft, past the levels of holding cells and to what she could see of the dilapidated building above. She wished she could see the sky for one last time.

'But...' Jess started.

Ravi continued for his wife, 'But you don't know how deep this is. We can't see the bottom. How are you planning to get out?'

Jay remained silent, and the penny finally dropped for Jess and Ravi. 'No...' said Jess. 'Throw it. Then we leave together.'

Ravi saw the determination on Jay's face and took his wife's arm. 'Come on,' he said.

Across the opening of the crater, darkness descended the corridor opposite. Jay's heart sank into her gut as figures appeared at the entrance from the corridor. 'Readers,' Jay said under her breath. Jess and Ravi turned back, one standing on either side of Jay like bodyguards.

'Good,' said Jess. 'We like a good fight. If we can keep them off you, then you do what you have to do.' Jess held Jay's eye for a moment and they silently agreed the plan. She looked skyward once more, wishing to see a shard of white light, Given power coming in to help, but there was nothing.

Atta appeared in the shaft with a burst of warm air from the corridor. He was as Jay remembered, wisps of darkness floating from him as if his very being was not completely physical. He immediately waved away the Readers approaching the steel platform towards Jay. They fell back behind Atta, and Jay sensed them retreating down the corridor. Jess and Ravi exchanged a look of concern.

'So, here you are again,' said Atta. 'You do surprise me.'

Jay tightened her rucksack and glanced down into the hole. She wouldn't be able to do this with Atta's power resisting. She wasn't sure that Jess and Ravi's power would be enough to pave her way into the core. She needed the others, but she had no sense of them, no feeling for any building of the Given energy. *Where are they?* She looked around the cavern as if for inspiration. 'Ready?' she said to Jess and Ravi. 'We're going to have to do this.'

'Ready,' said Jess.

Jay clenched her fists, gathered her full strength and launching an attack at Atta. He reeled, caught by surprise. She sustained the attack, sensing some success in penetrating his mind. Jess and Ravi backed her up, pressing their own power through with Jay's. Atta stepped back, pushed by their energy.

Atta's form became more fluid and for a moment Jay thought that their attack was succeeding in taking him apart. Then a dark smile crossed his face as if he were enjoying the moment and fear flowed through Jay, interrupting the attack.

Atta raised his arms into the air, deflecting the Given energy with the merest of movements. Jess and Ravi hit the wall of the shaft, slipping to the floor in a daze. Jay crouched to help Jess up as Ravi, too, got to his feet. When she looked again to where Atta had stood, he was gone.

The door to the room off the side of the platform was open, a red light blinking in the control panel on the wall.

'Come on, Stitch,' Jay said under her breath, certain now that she stood no chance of succeeding in her plan without the full power of the Given. She looked back to the steps, contemplating their chances of getting out before Atta pursued them.

Ravi nodded towards the holding cell. 'If he's in there. Will it hold him?'

'If we can close the door. But he won't let that happen,' said Jay.

'He's luring us,' said Jess.

'All we have to do is hit the button,' said Ravi, taking a step around the circular walkway towards the door.

'Wait,' said Jay. 'You two go together. I'll come around from the other way. Give me a minute.'

Jay skirted the perimeter of the shaft on the metal platform until she was opposite Jess and Ravi. Jay had a bad feeling about what Atta was doing in the holding cell. This had to be a trap, but there didn't seem another choice.

Ravi made a dash for the control panel. He reached inside for the button to close the door, but as he did so, he crumpled in pain, withdrawing his hand and holding it to his chest as he fell to the floor. Jess went to him, then quickly stood, looking into the room as Jay arrived next to her. Atta was sitting on a chair alone in the middle of the room. He locked eyes with Jay and the grin returned to his face. Jess reached for the button on the control panel and Atta's eyes flicked to look at her. She fell like Ravi, clutching her hand, groaning with the pain.

Jay looked at the control panel. Atta shook his head. Ravi and Jess had crawled clear of the door and propped themselves up against the wall of the shaft. Ravi recovered a little and helped Jess, inspecting her hand.

'Come in,' Atta said. Jay shook her head, looking once

more at the control panel. 'Try it if you like,' he said.

In her peripheral vision, Jay saw Ravi stagger to his feet, extending a hand to Jess. They conversed for a moment, then turned to Jay. Jay read their plan. *Distract Atta*, they told her.

Jay took a step forward into the threshold of the doorway. 'Why do you want me in here?' she said. 'So you can generate a Reader out of me? You'd like that. A Reader from the Given 8C.'

'Why not?' said Atta.

'Maybe I will,' said Jay, as a look of victory dawned on Atta's face.

Ravi and Jess both screamed with determination as they launched themselves at the panel. They hit the button, and the heavy door swung. As Jay stepped out of the path of the closing door, Atta moved. The door thumped closed. Atta banged into it from the inside. He looked at Jay through the vision panel, a familiar smile returning to his lips. He nodded behind her. She turned. The hand rail behind her had fallen, and there was no sign of Ravi or Jess.

She ran to the edge. 'Jess!'

Nothing but darkness.

She turned and looked back at Atta, his grin visible through the vision panel. Without taking her eyes off him, she straightened her rucksack once more and stepped back towards the hole. Atta shook his head, as if advising Jay not to do it. She turned away from him, not willing to risk any further influence of his power. She looked into the hole and hesitated a moment. It reminded of her leap of faith into the hole that landed her in the Interland. She thought of Stitch, Cassie, and of Sammy, and ached to know what had happened, and why their plan had not worked.

Then she jumped.

38

She couldn't jump. She hung as if held back by a harness. The energy from the depths flowed up and out of the hole, preventing her progress. With Atta in control, she could not overcome the resistance.

She stepped to the control panel and from the cell, Atta read her intention and shook his head. 'This facility can't be used against its maker.'

Jay said, 'You can't get out.'

He laughed. 'I can't be contained within these walls. I *am* these walls. You still don't get it. This is why you will never win.'

As Jay watched, the door between them seemed to quiver. Then she felt the heat radiating from it. She stepped back, shielding her face.

Atta continued to talk on the other side of the door, but Jay could no longer make out his words. His anger grew and the thick metal door melted at its edges. Atta's words grew louder. His tone changed, twisting in a flow of dark energy. A language she didn't understand.

The door slipped off its hinges, no longer able to hold its

own weight. Smoke rose from the molten metal and Atta stepped through, looking down on Jay like she was nothing.

Jay pushed at his chest and used the reaction force to throw herself towards the shaft, but Atta's power stopped her. He ripped the rucksack from her back and wrenched it open. With the source stone held aloft in his hands, he continued to speak in indecipherable tongues.

* * *

THE BASEMENT SHOOK like there was a minor earthquake. Angie held on to the side of the table, the motion of the floor making her queasy. 'What was that?' she said, looking at Judith and Hannah for reassurance.

The women looked just as perplexed. 'There was supposed to be a quake back in 1667,' said Judith. 'The last time there was a big confrontation between the Dark and the Given. Can't be a coincidence.'

'This is not the same,' said Hannah.

'It could be the power? From the hill forts,' said Judith.

'We need to try again,' said Angie. She'd been unable to get into Jay's head, despite several attempts. The last time she'd made some progress, and saw Jay fighting with Readers in the lower levels of the prison. 'She's in trouble, we have to try again.'

'Anything from Toyah or Colson?' asked Hannah.

Angie shook her head. There was no power flowing. Angie felt flooded with doubt. Was there any power buried deep inside her? Could she help Jay? She sat down at the head of the table once more and closed her eyes.

Judith and Hannah busied with their papers. They searched for something that Hannah recalled about the clash in 1667 that told of a means to connect the Given when under attack from the Dark. 'Here,' said Judith, pointing Hannah towards a passage of old text.

'Yes,' said Hannah. 'This is what I thought. I remember now. Keep trying to connect, Angie.'

Angie concentrated. 'Jay!' she screamed. 'I have her. She's down. On the floor. She's hurt.'

'Is she alone?' asked Hannah.

'Atta is there.' As Angie took in Jay's surroundings through Jay's own mind, she saw the outline of Atta come closer to Jay. He held the source stone in his hands. Jay struggled to her knees, and he taunted her. 'He's moving in on her again.'

'Can she hear you?' asked Judith.

'Jay?' Angie said, trying to get her attention. Jay seemed to register Angie's voice and opened to the connection. 'She can hear me,' said Angie.

'Tell her not to resist his attack,' Hannah said. Angie looked at her like she was mad, waiting for explanation. 'Only at first. Tell her to flow with his power, like you might do in directing the force of someone's punch. You know?'

'I think so,' said Angie.

'Then she needs to picture it flowing around her, not *into* her. If she can roll with the punches, so to speak, she will direct his strength so that it surrounds but does not penetrate. It will buy her time.'

Angie relayed this strategy to Jay. She pictured the streamlines of darkness flowing towards Jay and then around her, like the flow of a river past a bridge pier. 'It's working,' she said. The smooth boundary layer of darkness in Angie's mind became a harmless stream of energy diverted from its target.

* * *

UP ON HIGHDOWN HILL, Pinto and Otis both stood, the energy flowing through them. Otis felt no pain in his heels as his skin tingled with the power. He looked down at Pinto. He seemed to shake with the strength of the power coming through the ground at the hill fort.

'It hurts,' Pinto called to Otis, his eyes remaining closed. Otis cast his eyes around the ring of trees. Shards of light penetrated from below as if the sun was rising beneath their feet. Pinto became bathed in white light.

'Look,' said Otis.

Pinto opened his eyes. He and Otis watched as their power drew the energy of the land up from below and from the surrounding air. The noise grew louder as more and more shards pierced the woodland floor. Pinto grinned, laughing. Otis was too scared to laugh. He felt as though it needed all his concentration just to keep the energy flowing, that if he lost concentration for a moment, the power would spin away and career off into the atmosphere and be of no use to Jay. He held his nerve, and Pinto calmed down to focus once more.

'What now?' shouted Pinto above the background noise.

Otis didn't know what to do next. But he sensed it didn't matter.

* * *

ATTA CROUCHED NEXT TO JAY, the source stone in his hands. He held it away from her as if tempting her to take it from him.

Her legs wobbled as she tried to stand, deciding instead to lift herself onto her knees.

A flash of white light.

Angie was in her head. Jay almost cried from the flood of

relief. Angie's presence gave her strength. Pictures flowed into Jay's mind as Atta continued to talk. She could no longer hear him. Angie's voice was predominant. She pictured the streamlines of the low of darkness around her body and she recognised Angie communicating resistance tactics. 'Angie,' Jay said aloud into Atta's face.

'Who?' he said as he stood, preparing himself to attack. Jay cleared her mind of everything but Angie's pictures, the streamlines. Atta took a breath. 'We could be so powerful together,' he said.

'No chance,' Jay mumbled back to him.

Atta growled at her rejection and attacked once more, but Jay was ready. She focused not on stopping his power entering her mind, but on its diversion, deflection, and re-direction around her. The strength needed for the re-direction was much lower than for a full defence. The energy flowed and instead of wearing her down; she drew from it, taking a little of the energy into her own reserves to replenish her strength.

'Interesting,' Atta said. 'You have some control over the Dark. From your connection with it.'

'Don't make me sick, I have no connection to your power.' Jay stepped back.

'The combination is powerful,' Atta said, continuing to search inside of Jay. 'You have kept something from that connection. You have a mix of dark and light. Feel it. Breathe it in. It's part of you.'

Jay shook her head, filtering the darkness and gathering her Given power.

'Why would you want to destroy this connection? The core? This is the pathway to your dominance over all the power. You can draw on the darkness and the light of the Given. This hasn't happened for centuries. You can be all powerful. More so than even I could hope for. Embrace it,' Atta said.

* * *

'JUST FOCUS,' said Toyah, irritation in her tone. Sammy had done nothing to help her draw the energy at Cissbury. She sensed he was sulking when he should channel all his efforts to helping his sister. 'If Jay stands any chance of living through this, she needs us.'

Sammy took Toyah's hand. Together they stood inside the ring of trees atop Cissbury. Toyah felt the energy flowing beneath their feet and drew from it. With every passing minute, the power grew, and the ground seemed to warm the soles of her shoes.

'It's coming,' Sammy said.

'Open up,' Toyah said, gripping his hand even tighter.

* * *

AT CHANCTONBURY, Ben, Matchstick and Colson formed a connected circle, their hands clasped tight as they stood around the embers of the fire.

Colson directed. 'Clear your minds,' he said. 'Steady your breathing. In for three, out for five.' The three of them breathed deeply as Colson instructed.

Ben felt little in the way of Given power and was feeling sceptical about the whole thing. 'Perhaps we should just head over there, to the prison. We can help Jay more by fighting with her than we can summoning the spirits up here?'

'Shush,' Colson said. 'It was Jay who defined the plan. We need to see it through. She knows what she is doing.

'Look,' said Matchstick, nodding towards the hill fort in the distance at Highdown. Streams of white light shot up from the crest of the hill and into the sky like searchlights. 'And there,' he motioned to the other hill fort at Cissbury, where a similar array of lights pierced the tops of the trees and shot up into the sky.

'Stay connected!' Colson shouted as both Ben and Matchstick loosened their grip. 'It's time. Focus!'

The lights in the distance continued to ascend high into the atmosphere, joining above their heads. The ground at Chanctonbury shook. Ben's head vibrated like he was in a dentist's chair. His vision blurred and a shard of light shot through the ground from between the three men. Colson audibly squealed with delight. 'This is totally awesome!'

More lights shot up out of the ground and they looked up into the trees just in time to see the Chanctonbury energy connect with that from Highdown and Cissbury.

* * *

ATTA DROPPED his force of power and came nearer to Jay. He pushed her back against the railings and drew his hand up to her throat, still holding the source stone in his other hand, hugging it to himself. Jay sensed he sought a connection with the Given energy as much as he needed to retain the dark power.

'It doesn't matter to me whether you embrace both elements of the power, or if you die right here. Either way, the outcome is the same.' Atta pushed Jay so that she leaned back over the railing. She glanced down into the hole. She could see the intermittent flashing of the rotating electro-magnets and feel the pulsing energy. This was as close as Jay had got to the source of the darkness. The strength of power was clear. It felt different to the Given energy. It had an edge to it, a promise of something transformative.

* * *

STITCH HAD NOWHERE TO GO. All he knew was that he needed to be away from Cassie before she wound him up any tighter. The energy from the hill forts had not come. And there was no contact from any of them. Cassie seemed to think this was Stitch's fault, despite him being the only one of them not to have an actual number on his wrist. The level C had proven useless.

'Hey,' Cassie called, waving him back. He turned, relenting slowly. He took a step and then stopped when Cassie followed up with, 'Don't be such a diva,' at the top of her voice. Stitch turned away from her and walked towards the river.

At the top of the steps down to the riverside, the pavement was suddenly illuminated as if a flare had gone up overhead. He looked skyward, and his jaw dropped.

Streams of light from three locations in the hills thrust into the sky to combine at a point high above them. The white light burned through the low-lying clouds, forcing out all darkness. Stitch continued to stare as Cassie came crashing into him, out of breath. 'This is it. Let's go!'

Stitch followed Cassie to the wooden jetty above the surface of the river. At the end was a circular viewing platform ten feet in diameter, where they stopped and turned to look at the growing ball of white light in the sky. 'They've done it,' said Stitch under his breath. 'All of them. They've done it.'

'Come on,' said Cassie, taking Stitch's hand, then looking up into the sky. 'That's Highdown,' she said, pointing to what looked like the strongest stream of light. 'That's Otis,' she said with pride.

'And Pinto,' said Stitch. He looked to the two streams further north and thought of Sammy and Toyah, and of Jay's dad with Colson and Matchstick.

'Come on!' Cassie repeated, taking Stitch's other hand and dragging his gaze from the sky. 'Concentrate.'

Stitch heard Cassie's words, but he needed to clear his mind and trust in his intuition. Cassie managed the power differently to Stitch, and he'd never been able to figure her out. For Stitch, the power has never been controlled through strength of mind. For him, it is a flow of energy through the body. It takes its course from the essence of the person through which it flows. All he had to do was to be open to it...

Cassie screamed. Stitch knew it was a scream of effort and concentration as the energy from the ocean and the river grew around them. He felt light on his feet, buoyant, as if the level of the river had risen to take them higher. Then it came. The light from the joining of the power of the hill forts shot through the sky and enveloped Cassie and Stitch. The end of the pier lit up like a firework, light scattering over the surface of the river.

Cassie shone in the power of the Given and Stitch opened up like a conduit to her energy. Together, they channelled the flow of energy towards Jay. Light flowed down from Cassie and Stitch like dry ice in a nightclub, flowing over the wooden boards of the pier and down to the surface of the river, where it slowly enveloped everything in its path.

Stitch opened his eyes and saw that the streams of light remained strong, but along the road a crowd gathered. 'Readers,' he said to himself. Then louder, 'Readers!' he shouted to Cassie.

Cassie's eyes snapped open, and she followed Stitch's gaze to see the gathering of Readers, some looking up to the power in the sky, attempting to disrupt it, others making their way towards the pier. 'Keep it flowing,' said Cassie. 'We need to keep the power flowing to Jay for as long as possible.'

'We can relocate,' said Stitch, shouting above the noise generated by the flow of energy.

'No time,' said Cassie.

Stitch looked across at the advancing group of Readers. There must have been over twenty of them filing up the wooden jetty towards them. They had no escape route now, even if they had decided to run.

'Hold it...' Cassie said.

Stitch looked beyond the advancing Readers to see more arriving. They teemed through the side streets, congregating along the river wall. 'We need to relocate,' Stitch said again.

Cassie looked towards the Readers, now just a few feet away and tentatively edging closer, looking a little unsure of how to breach the white light of their power. 'OK,' Cassie said.

Cassie and Stitch broke their connection and opened out their arms. The white light bowled through the Readers, knocking them to the floor, allowing a route along the pier for Cassie and Stitch to escape. As they reached solid ground, the Readers gathered themselves. More Readers appeared from the side streets.

Before they could carve a route to get clear, the Readers closed in around them, their exits cut off. Stitch felt attacks coming in, but he deflected. It wouldn't be long before they'd get it together to attack with multiple Readers at the same time. There would be no chance they could resist a collective attack. A thought flashed before his eyes, and

Stitch hoped that there were no Readers attacking the hill forts.

Cassie nodded at the moped behind Stitch, a Honda C50 with an ignition barrel that was even weaker than the one in Jay's car. He could probably turn it with his fingernail. He reached into his back pocket for his swiss army knife, holding it behind him as he opened one of the blades.

'I'll shield,' Cassie whispered, and immediately stood in front of Stitch.

He felt the attacks intensify, but he was quick. He pushed the bike off its stand and rammed the blade into the ignition, turning it with no resistance. The lights on the round display on the front of the bike lit up, and he flicked the kick-start into position, then thrust his foot down to the warm sound of the engine kicking in first time.

Cassie made a final push of Given energy at the advancing Readers and jumped onto the back of the bike as Stitch picked up speed. Readers reached for her, one of them getting a hold on her top but releasing when Cassie's foot connected with his jaw. She punched and kicked at any Reader who came within range. She almost lost her balance more than once as Stitch twisted and turned the bike through the parting crowd.

Just as Stitch thought they were clear, a stocky Reader got a hold on the handlebars. The bike spun around precariously on the promenade that formed the river wall, then burst through the railing protecting pedestrians from the twenty-foot drop to the shore of the river. Cassie flew off the back of the bike and slid to the edge, toppling but hanging on to the wall, her legs dangling over the shore of the river. The moped slipped from beneath Stitch and slid towards Cassie, narrowly missing her as it toppled over the wall, catching on the railings to stop it from landing in the river.

The Reader who had grabbed the handlebars went over the wall and into the water. Stitch held tight to the bike, his hands gripping the handlebars as he slipped over the edge. The only thing stopping him following the Reader into the water was his vice-like grip on the bike.

He swung with the bike, its front wheel slipping from where it had caught on the railing. One more slip and both Stitch and the bike would end up in the river.

'There!' shouted Cassie, hanging from the river wall and motioning Stitch towards the six foot round opening in the wall. The groundwater outfall that they'd used as a route in to the prison before. Stitch didn't need a second prompt. He swung his legs and got enough movement to catch his feet on the invert of the outfall and slide inside.

'The bike,' Stitch shouted at Cassie, a plan materialising in his head. He grabbed the back wheel of the bike, dangling in front of him. Cassie read his plan and, after a moment of hesitation and a look of incredulity, she edged herself along the wall to where the bike hung snagged on the railing.

Readers appeared at the top of the wall above Cassie. Stitch warned her, but it was too late. A Reader snatched at Cassie, taking her by the arm of her top and pulling her. Another joined him and they both dragged her back towards the top of the wall. Cassie shrieked. Stitch attacked the closest Reader with his powers the best he could, but in the end it was a flying punch from Cassie that wrenched her free of the Readers' grasp.

As Cassie fell, Stitch reached out for her, but it was the bike she got a hold on. She clasped the back wheel and swung into the outfall. Stitch grabbed her and pulled her towards him, but her top was attached to the bike. The force of her fall had dislodged the moped from the top of the wall.

Time seemed to slow as Cassie and Stitch realised the bike was free of the wall at the top and that Cassie was still attached to the other end of it.

They braced themselves. Stitch held on to Cassie and with his other hand grabbed a metal step-iron before the bike jolted to a stop, hanging from Cassie - half in the hole and half teetering over the river. Cassie screamed.

'Pull it in,' Stitch shouted as Cassie gathered herself. Together they pulled the bike into the outfall, offloading the weight from Cassie's arm and they both collapsed back on to the floor. It was only then that Stitch realised that the engine of the moped was still turning over- idling, as if nothing had happened.

The sound of Readers from above spurred Cassie and Stitch into action. Stitch pulled the moped upright and revved its engine. The noise echoed through the tunnel. Cassie registered Stitch's plan and jumped on the back of the bike. They sped away into the tunnel, through the earth towards the prison.

AN IMAGE of Angie came into Jay's mind, and almost immediately, she felt an almighty eruption of Given energy, a powerful enough burst for Atta to release his grip from her throat and reel backwards. The cavern filled with white light. They had done it. Her sense of relief and euphoria exploded to the surface as the energy filled every cell in her body. Now she had the advantage.

Atta stared around the cavern in disbelief. 'I don't understand.'

Jay waited no longer. She drew in the entire power of the Given and attacked. She pushed into Atta's mind and immediately felt his pain. He stumbled for a moment, then straightened, and for a second Jay thought that her attack was being deflected. She opened further to the energy, allowing it to flow through her. It was so intense, the pressure almost hurt. The darkness ignited within her when she opened the channel had already dissipated. There was nothing flowing through Jay but the power of the Given.

Atta recovered once more, the attack appearing to affect him in waves, between which he took the time to shield and regain his strength. But the light continued to stream into the cavern from above, bleaching the walls. Atta weakened. He put a hand to his head and leaned heavily on the railing. He dropped the source stone at his feet and Jay prepared herself for a final push.

Then it stopped.

The light faded and, once again, the cavern was illuminated only by a few electric lamps slung from the walls. Jay looked hopefully into the roof of the cavern and up towards the higher levels. Nothing but darkness. Fear permeated her mind.

Jay made a move for the source stone, but Atta had already righted himself. With a grimace, he straightened and raised a hand, throwing Jay back against the railings like she was nothing. She slipped to the floor. Through half-closed eyes, she saw Atta reach down and take the source stone once more.

* * *

CASSIE AND STITCH entered the main building unopposed. Jay's presence radiated from below them. 'Do it here,' Stitch said to Cassie.

'We're inside the zone, the mile that Jay talked about.'

Stitch shrugged. 'What choice do we have?'

'Can we really do it here? No river carrying the energy of the ocean?'

'We're close enough,' Stitch said, then turned to climb the steps back to the outside. He looked into the sky. The white ball of light hung like an alien craft above the hills and he thought of the others, their resolve in keeping the flow of energy. Of Angie, who he felt was keeping the communication between the groups, keeping them going. He turned to Cassie and took both of her hands in his, then looked up at the sky once more.

As Jay crumpled under the resurgent power of Atta, Readers came to his aid, flowing down the steps like ants around a discarded piece of fruit.

In her weakened state, she couldn't determine if the picture of Angie in her mind was simply wishful thinking. Angie spoke to her. She said that Stitch was close.

'No,' said Jay. 'Not here. Tell him to leave. It's too dangerous.'

Angie spoke again, this time her little voice clear and defined, 'Throw it in.'

'I can't' Jay whispered aloud, under her breath.

Angie's voice: 'Stitch is coming. He will free you. Throw it in.'

Jay slipped further to the floor, the metal grate of the platform cold against her cheek. Her vision blurred. She could just make out the outline of the source stone smothered in Atta's grasp.

There seemed to be no sound but for her own breathing.

White light exploded into the cavern once more, this

time with such a force that it knocked the gathering Readers to the floor. Atta stood, looking up into the shaft, the light blinding him. The energy flowed through Jay once more and she staggered to her feet just as Atta recoiled from the light, shrinking into the wall.

'Throw it in' Angie's voice came.

Then an echo in Stitch's voice, 'Throw it in.'

She threw herself at Atta, pushing him back against the wall. He held tight to the source stone, his smile at last dissolved from his face. The light streamed from above. Readers shrivelled, some appearing to melt into the walls of the cavern with the power of the energy from above.

Atta continued to resist. Jay combined an attack with her Given power with a physical onslaught. She kicked, punched, and pushed him.

He fought back, his elbow catching Jay and momentarily knocking her off balance.

She released him from her physical grip and used her powers once more, opening her heart to the full power of the Given energy.

He reeled from her, stumbling.

She ran at him again, head down, catching him in a kind of rugby tackle. She kicked out, flung her head up, catching him on the chin. Then she stood and punched him, landing a blow to his chin.

He weakened, dropping to one knee but still refusing to release the source stone. She made a grab for it, grappling with Atta like they were challenging for possession of a football. They spun around on the platform. Jay had a firm grip on the source stone, but Atta refused to release. His power was weak, but his body remained locked around the stone.

With a cry of effort, Jay spun Atta around and to the edge

of the gaping hole. He looked her in the eye, and for the first time, Jay saw his fear. She made a final push.

Jay and Atta's hands remained firmly locked around the source stone, as Jay launched them both over the edge - diving, falling, deep into the core.

39

I've got one of those feelings, like your brain can't quite click into gear and you don't really know where you are. Well, you know, but you can't quite recall why, or how. Then you just kind of hope something will tick over, a cog will slip into place, and it will all become clear. And it always does. But it hasn't yet.

No pain.

Nothing to see. Only light.

Orange light. Not white, not dark, orange. Smells too. Like the smell you get when you light a match.

Matchstick.

Dad's friend.

The cog is turning.

I did it. I think? I pulled the stone into the core. I took it there. Now I remember.

Atta was with me, but I don't feel him. He's gone. The energy here is thick, like soup.

Throw it in.

The energy is transparent, clear as day. I can see through to both sides. If I look down, I can see the power of the Given, a physical entity. And above me is the power of the Dark. Both spheres with solid cores and fluid edges.

I am in the middle. A part of both. In the orange treacle which forms the space between the energy of the Given and of the Dark.

Sasha Maram Colden. My grandmother.

Maram. Atta. Maramatta. Attamaram.

* * *

JAY WOKE on the shore of a lake. Before opening her eyes, she heard the gentle trickle of water from the rocks, and could smell minerals in the air. She knew she was at the Interland.

I'm alive, she thought, opening her eyes to bright sunshine and a cloudless blue sky. She sat up, inspecting her hands as if to check that they were real, and that she had a physical presence. *Cassie and Stitch*, she thought, looking around the perimeter of the Interland lake.

A noise drew her attention. She turned to see Cassie walking towards her over the stones, like a vision obscured by the brightness of the sunshine. She dragged herself to her feet to accept her embrace. 'Thank God,' said Cassie.

Jay looked her friend in the eye, and she knew that Cassie and Stitch had been within the blast zone at the prison. 'You came into the zone?'

'We had no choice.'

Jay smiled. 'Thanks.' She looked over Cassie's shoulder. 'Where's Stitch?'

Cassie shrugged. 'I can feel his annoying presence. He's here somewhere.' She smiled.

Jay turned to see Stitch emerging from the shallows on

the other side of the lake. He must have re-materialised in the lake. Water poured from his sodden clothes. Cassie laughed. They watched as Stitch looked into the sky, then over to where they stood. He headed towards them.

Cassie looked up into the sky. 'Did you see it? The power?' Jay shook her head. She knew what Cassie was talking about, and could see in Cassie's thoughts what she'd seen. 'It was something else. Everyone did their bit. I've never felt anything like it.'

Stitch trudged over the stones towards them. Cassie laughed and Jay couldn't help but smile. Stitch didn't yet see the funny side. 'What happened?' he said.

'What do you remember?' Jay asked, directing her question to both Stitch and Cassie.

Cassie motioned to a space they could sit down. Jay and Stitch followed. 'We were channelling the power when everything went white, like before,' said Cassie. 'Except this time there were no Islands, nothing. Just *white*.'

Jay and Stitch sat down as Cassie collected an armful of wood and built a fire.

'Me too,' said Stitch. 'It was weird. But it wasn't scary. I kind of knew it was OK.'

'And me,' said Jay. 'But my colour was orange.'

'Orange?' said Stitch.

Jay nodded.

'What does that mean?' said Stitch.

'No idea,' said Jay.

Cassie finished building the fire and turned to the others with a smile. 'Anyone bring any matches through the inter-dimension?'

Stitch and Jay laughed, and Jay shuffled closer to the fire. 'Watch,' she said, rubbing her hands together and then presenting them to the fire. She did not know how she could generate the heat in her hands, like Matchstick could do. But somehow she knew. Her hands glowed orange, and sparks emanated, sprinkling through the dry wood and catching the kindling.

'Who needs Matchstick?' said Cassie as Stitch stared open-mouthed.

'Since when?' asked Stitch.

'Since I swam in the orange soup,' said Jay.

THEY RESTED BY THE FIRE. It grew dark. It was as if they each needed to process what had happened in their own time and in their own way. They talked about the work that the others must have achieved at each of the hill forts. And they talked about Atta.

'Is he gone for good?' asked Cassie.

Jay shook her head. 'He's gone from here. The connection with the core has been destroyed. That's not coming back.'

'So we are like Island 4?' asked Stitch.

'If what Judith and Hannah said is right, then yes. We are free. But Atta remains free to trample wherever he likes in the other six Islands.'

A look of relief came over Stitch's face. They, at least, were free from the darkness. Jay thought of Tiago on Island 7. With Atta banished from their own homeland, Tiago would be in greater danger than before. The focus of the Readers would be on spreading through the dark lands, taking more for their own purposes. It would surely be a matter of time before they got to Tiago and his family.

Cassie seemed to read Jay. She nudged at her foot with

her own. 'One step at a time,' she said, and leaned back on the stones.

Jay looked at her two friends. Their colours came to her. They were tired, worn down by the past few days of battle. She also saw the light inside them, and the glow of energy that drove them. She felt warmth for them both, and a deep sense of peace.

40

J ay drifted down the steps to the basement as if she were walking on air.

Since they'd returned from the Interland, something had changed. Her energy levels were higher than she'd ever experienced. She could see deeper into the power, into people, and into the energy - its nature, and its fundamental essence.

In the basement, Buster ran to Jay, with little Benji scampering after him. Colson and Hannah lit candles. Judith placed them around the room so that the place resembled a church mass. They'd agreed to meet to talk about what was to happen next, and to remember those who fell in the *Event,* the day at the prison when the earth quaked. Some of them insisted it was an earthquake, much like the one in 1667, but others were not so sure. The aftermath, Colson said, resembled the aftermath of a nuclear event more than an earthquake, and anyway, how could an earthquake be so localised?

Whatever they wanted to call it, to make sense of it, Jay

knew the Event was neither an earthquake nor a nuclear event. It was the head-on collision between the peak of the powers of Dark and Given. It resulted in everything within two miles being razed to the ground.

Angie ran to Jay, wrapping her arms around her. They'd spent much of their time together in the two days since Jay returned with Cassie and Stitch from the Interland.

Ben and Colson busied themselves ferrying plates of food from the hatch in the wall, then sending the mechanical lift back up for more. Otis sat with Pinto and Toyah at one end of the table. Pinto practised his power by passing objects to his sister and to Otis with his telekinesis. Jay waved at him across the room, and he grinned with pride.

'Before we start,' said Judith. 'Can we take a moment to remember?'

Jay took a seat with the others, electing to sit between Stitch and her brother Sammy. Judith continued, 'Jay, would you like to say a few words?'

Jay straightened in her seat. A hush came over the room. 'Two people who you guys never had the chance to meet. Ravi and Jess. I knew them for less than an hour, and in that time they gave their lives to enable my access to the core. They were Given. Their drive was for the greater good. They will have a place in the history of the fight for the cause.' She paused a moment. 'Alf, of course,' she said, her eyes dropping to the floor as she focused on keeping it together. 'I feel a sense of responsibility for Alf.'

'Hey...' started Stitch, but Jay held up a hand for him to let her finish.

'I know he wouldn't want me to blame myself. But the fact will always remain that I facilitated Atta's attack on him. And that was Atta's plan. Alf was the glue that connected all of us. He was the common factor. He affected every person in this room in a way that advanced our cause. He is an enormous loss to the Given. And an even bigger loss to me personally. So, Alfred Harvey, I'm sorry, and I thank you on behalf of all the Given for what you've achieved. And, I vow to re-build what you created, and what we lost in the fire.'

Colson wiped a tear away and cleared his throat. 'Hear hear,' he said, raising his glass. 'A great man, and a friend.' Buster ambled over to Colson and sat at his feet.

They all drank a toast to Alf, and the silence felt heavy on Jay's shoulders.

'Who else would like to say something?' asked Judith, breaking the spell.

Cassie cleared her throat. 'I want to remember Reuben and my grandad. They've both been gone for a long time now, but it still feels like yesterday. Reuben was taken by Readers. He was my mentor as a Runner. And he was my friend. I will remember him. My grandad was my idol. He knew the powers, and he made sure I connected when we were at the Interland. I miss him.'

'And Davey,' said Otis. 'He gave his life for mine.'

Sammy shifted in his seat next to Jay. 'And Marcus,' he said, looking over at Ben.

Ben returned Sammy's gaze and gave him a reassuring nod. 'Marcus was Sammy's biological father,' Ben said. 'And he was a Reader. But in the end, he fought for our cause. We will remember him.' He caught Sammy's eye and Sammy thanked him.

'We also remember those who died in the final battle,' said Stitch. Northtown had largely escaped the effects of the *Event*, but there were casualties inside the facility. Mostly, it was the public who had volunteered for transformation to readers. They were in the open holding cells when the Event reached its peak, and all were lost, some two or three hundred people Jay estimated, along with an unknown number of Readers.

'Thank you,' said Judith. 'Now we pray for a period of peace. Let's eat.'

* * *

AFTER THEY'D EATEN, and the conversations drifted into analysis of the Event, and the fate of the Readers, Jay slipped away and up onto the roof terrace at the back of the pub where she could be alone.

It was late in the afternoon and the sun had already dipped on the horizon, a cool breeze coming off the sea. She looked up to the hills. They seemed unfamiliar to her now, looking from the roof of the pub, a different perspective perhaps than that from the house. She wasn't sure. Whatever it was, it intrigued her. The effects of the Event had been more than simply the physical destruction of the connection with the core. The collision between Dark and Given, with Jay in the middle of it, had affected her connection with the power in ways she was only beginning to understand.

Stitch appeared at the top of the steps to the roof terrace. He had two pints of Guinness in his hands, spilling white froth of the head over his knuckles. Jay took one and thanked him. 'Haven't had one of these for a while,' she said.

'Thought as much.'

They were silent for a minute as they drank and looked out over to the hills in the distance.

Stitch spoke first: 'Talk to me,' he said.

Jay turned to him. 'What about?'

'What's on your mind? You've been ruminating since we got back.'

'What do you expect after...'

'Something more,' Stitch interrupted. 'This is me you're talking to. You think I can't read you?'

'Sorry,' Jay said, turning back to look at the horizon. 'There is something. I just don't know what it is yet. Not sure I can find the words.'

'Give it a try,' said Stitch.

Jay took a deep breath and let out a sigh. 'There's something deeper in my power.'

'How do you mean?'

'It's as if I connected deeper into the source. That *Event*, whatever happened, opened me up to greater strength of power.'

'You mean you can do more? Like when you created fire up at the Interland?'

Jay nodded. 'But more than that. The fire was just a simple concentration of the energy. I'm not sure, but I might have been able to do that before. This is more than that, and it comes from different places.' She looked Stitch in the eye to see if he understood what she was saying, what she felt.

He returned her gaze. 'Different places?' Jay nodded. 'Like more than one source?' Jay nodded again. Stitch turned away to think for a moment, then said, 'Do you mean more than one Given source, like one from here and one from Island 7 or something?' Jay shook her head. 'Oh. You mean the Dark,' Stitch concluded.

'I can't be sure about anything. But it's as if the collision of those forces created some kind of combination power inside me.'

'You connected with the Dark before, up on the rooftop of the house. I was there.'

'This is different. This is inside of me.'

Stitch let out a frustrated sigh. 'What does it mean?'

'Search me,' said Jay. 'Maybe I'm turning into some super-Given or something,' she said with a smile.

Stitch laughed.

41

Within two short weeks of the *Event*, Jay and her dad had persuaded the pub landlord to allow them to transform the basement into a new centre of literature for the Given, and had begun to fit it out. Ben rediscovered his love of carpentry and had shelved most of the basement walls, as well as fitting out a storage room which used to be a wine cellar.

Jay and Angie worked tirelessly to re-catalogue the remaining works that had survived the fire in the bookshop and were already a good way through re-shelving them. With new lighting and other fittings, the basement had turned from dingy meeting place to an open-plan library-come-bookshop. One thing that remained untouched was the little mechanical lift in the hatch that led to the bar upstairs. Above the hatch were two pictures: the Sasha Coldon portrait that once hung in the main cavern in the Interland, and a picture of Alf that Jay had framed.

Jay and her dad were on their own since Angie's parents had persuaded her to take a day off from the basement. Although it was only the first week of Angie's summer holidays, her dad wasn't keen for her to spend its entirety underground. Jay could think of little she'd rather do than avoid human contact and surround herself with books.

The bell rang, telling Jay that someone was coming through the door from the pub. She turned to look and saw Toyah step down onto the basement floor. Buster ran to her.

'Wow,' she said, stroking Buster. 'You really have transformed this place.'

'In memory of Alf.' Jay nodded towards Alf's picture on the wall.

'He'd be proud. Seriously. He'd be staggered at how you've done this.'

'Much thanks to that man over there.' Jay motioned towards her dad, hammering away at the shelves in the corner.

'What's up?' asked Jay.

Toyah nodded to the table in the middle of the room, the only piece of furniture Jay had insisted on retaining - somewhere for people to sit and read. Somewhere people could simply *be*. They sat, and Toyah took a moment to gather her thoughts. 'I've decided,' she said.

Jay smiled. 'Go on.'

'I'm leaving.'

'Wha...' Jay started.

'It's OK. I'm going to college,' she smiled. 'I've talked to Pinto, and he's good with it. And you're here for him?'

'Of course,' said Jay, thinking how much she'd miss Toyah. 'He's like a brother to me too, you know. Have you spoken to Sammy about it?'

Toyah nodded. 'Wasn't easy, but he understands. We'll be in touch.'

'What are you studying?'

'You'll laugh.'

'Hey,' said Jay. 'Come on.'

'Combined honours degree. Physics, with a focus on earth physics, and Powers.' She smiled. 'You'll be a visiting lecturer on the Powers.'

Jay laughed, and Toyah gave her a friendly shove. 'You said you wouldn't laugh.'

'Sorry,' said Jay, continuing to laugh. 'I'm just pleased for you. I'm happy. This is the best news. You need to do something for you. Pinto will be fine. He's strong. He has a good home, and he has us.'

'Thanks, Jay. Thanks for everything.'

AT THE GATE to Pinto's school, Jay stood under the cover of the trees, the rain easing now, and most of what was landing on Jay's head came from the accumulation on the leaves. She stepped out into the sun, watching as the kids filed out towards the front gate on their last day of the summer term. Their spirits were high.

She saw Pinto. He walked with a girl next to him and they laughed together. Jay remembered the little girl with power, the only other person in Pinto's year with any level of Given power developing. Jay smiled, watching them together, their genuine laughter.

As they moved up the main pathway to the exit, Jay watched as the girl elbowed Pinto and motioned towards a group of boys sitting on the grass under a tree on the front lawn of the school. Pinto responded by shaking his head and linking his arm with the girl to persuade her away.

She wouldn't be diverted. She dragged her arm away from Pinto and moved under the cover of the trees, where she could observe the boys from a distance. Jay laughed aloud as she tried to guess what the girl was planning. Pinto joined her, dragging his feet.

There were four of them under the tree, older than Pinto. Jay guessed they were likely nearer sixteen years old. One of the boys was rolling a cigarette, or something more illicit, a last-day-of-school rebellion, rolling a joint on the front lawn. Two of the other boys smoked cigarettes as they waited for the joint. Jay looked back at Pinto and his friend, debating her plan in the shadows.

Pinto seemed to agree with something and they both turned to face the group sat on the floor. Jay saw it then. The sprinkler system spread through the grass area of the lawn. It was attached to a valve and standpipe near to where the boys sat. Jay watched the valve handle as it slowly turned under the power of Pinto and his friend. She laughed as the water emerged at pressure from the sprinklers, soaking the four boys. They sprang up, their drug paraphernalia scattering as they ran from the full force of the spray.

Pinto and the girl doubled over with laughter as they made their escape. Pinto turned to see one of the boys running back in to the middle of the spray to salvage his weed. Jay decided she'd add to the game and manipulated the boy's balance so that he slipped onto his back, sliding through the water as Pinto and his friend looked on, doubling over once more.

Jay dissolved away from the school, satisfied that Pinto had it covered.

* * *

BACK AT THE BASEMENT, Jay and Angie shelved the last pile of books received from the London branch. Judith and Hannah had sent through their stock which they hadn't room to display, as well as the stock that would sit better alongside the material that Jay and Alf had retrieved from the Interland, and that which had survived the fire.

Jay looked around the basement. The new sign that Ben had made identified the shop as *Alf's Books*. She was surprised at how much of the wall space was covered by the salvaged material. There was a wealth of information for them to build upon. 'We'll get there, Alf,' she said. 'Thanks to you, we will get there.'

Stitch came up from the lower, connected store room and brushed some dust and cobwebs out of his hair. Jay laughed at him, his hapless, awkward demeanour. 'What?' he said as he approached. 'It's full of spiders in there.'

'There's a duster out the back.'

'Maybe later,' he smiled. 'Anyway, are you done?'

'Almost. Angie's on the last pile of books.' She nodded to where Angie was sitting cross-legged on the floor, brushing the dust from the covers of the books before placing them on the shelves.

'So I'll see you tonight?' Stitch asked.

'A date?'

Stitch stammered and looked away. 'Yeah... I mean, all of us. Cassie too, if you like. We can just hang.'

'I'm kidding,' Jay said, enjoying winding up Stitch. They'd grown close again over the time since the *Event*. It was like before - before they even understood the power. It was fresh, and Jay felt something more developing. She was still petrified of losing what they had, the friendship and the bonds they'd established as best friends for years. But there was something coming that she felt powerless to stop.

'Great. Nice,' said Stitch, turning to head for the steps up to the pub.

'Hey,' Jay said, taking his arm and pulling him back to

her. She hugged him, and he froze a moment before relaxing into it and holding her tight. She took his face in her hands as she'd done in the car. His blue eyes sparkled in the lights in the basement.

Angie called from across the room, 'Jay!'

'I'll see you later,' Jay said to Stitch.

'You bet,' he said with a smile, turning to leave.

'What's up, little one?' Jay said as she got to where Angie was about to place the last book on the shelf, with Buster curled up on the floor a few feet away.

'Last one.' Angie held up a hardback book, brushing her hand over the faded-blue front cover with a picture of the human body, lines of white light swirling around the head. 'The Physiology of Power,' Angie read, then placed the book on the bottom shelf. 'Done.'

Jay smiled. 'I have one last book I need you to find a home,' she said, turning and heading back to her desk in the corner. Angie followed, watching as Jay rifled through the drawer of her desk.

She pulled out the Sasha Colden biography and handed it to Angie.

Angie looked from the book to Jay and back again. 'I can't... this is yours.' She held the book like it was made of gold, cradling it.

'I think you're ready,' Jay said. 'And you need to get reading if you're going to help me with Island 7.'

Angie looked at Jay, and her eyes sparkled. She turned her attention back to the book and carefully flipped open the front cover.

End of Book #3

THANK YOU!

I hope you enjoyed *The Dark*, book #3 in the Interland series. If you can spare a minute to leave a short review or just a rating on your preferred store, then I'd be very grateful - Thanks!

Leave a review or rating here for The Dark.

I originally thought that this would be a trilogy, but the Interland Series doesn't seem to want to end here, and book #4 is already taking shape in my head... so who knows eh...?

If you've not joined my Reader Club, where you can keep up to date on forthcoming publications, news and freebies to go with the INTERLAND series - including a free eBook prequel called *The Reader*, an insight to the background of the Readers - then please join by visiting my website - www.garyclarkauthor.co.uk

ABOUT THE AUTHOR

Gary graduated from the University of Surrey in the UK with a degree in Engineering, embarking on a career that has taken him all over the world from the Far East to the Americas. He is a graduate of the Faber Academy and Curtis Brown creative writing programmes. Now a father of three, he has settled with his family close to where he grew up on the edge of the South Downs in Sussex, where he indulges his love of books, and passion for writing.

I'd love to hear from you so feel free to contact me on the email address here - let me know what you thought of the book.

Author email: gary@garyclarkauthor.co.uk
Or visit my website: www.garyclarkauthor.co.uk

Interland Series books can be found here:
THE GIVEN (Interland Series Book #1)
INTERLAND (Interland Series Book #2)
THE DARK (Interland Series Book #3)

ACKNOWLEDGMENTS

With three books in the series published this year, it's been quite a ride, and I must say a big thanks to those who have helped me along the way - especially to Dionne, my editor who has worked with me on all three books. You are brilliant. I learn so much working with you. My proof reader, Katherine, who sees all the things that are invisible to everyone else, you are a magician. Thanks too to my wonderful early reader ARC and BETA team for helping me shape and polish the final drafts - you guys are the best (and Sam M, Michelle S, Sarah M - you are awesome!)

Thank you both to Tim at my local indie bookshop (One Tree Books) and to Lou at Amery School library for providing some of your valuable shelf space to my little books!

Thanks to Ian C for badgering me to *get on with book #3*, it's always nice to know I'll have at least one reader (even though I know you only usually read picture books...) and to Andrea, Hannah, Dave, Geoff & Leah for your continuing and much appreciated supportive words.

Thanks to my family - you guys keep me going. Ella & Evan - so proud of you, and Jude, I couldn't do any of this without your unwavering faith, insight, and brilliance.

This book is dedicated to Ash (and the beautiful little Charlie & Archie) - you guys are amazing x

First published 2021 GCL Books.

www.garyclarkauthor.co.uk

Paperback ISBN 978-1-8384-0102-3

Made in the USA
Middletown, DE
10 January 2023